SARAH ALDERSON

Hunting Lila

SIMON AND SCHUSTER

For my family

First published in Great Britain in 2011 by Simon
and Schuster UK Ltd, a CBS company.

Copyright © 2011 Sarah Alderson

Simon & Schuster UK Ltd
1st Floor, 222 Gray's Inn Road, London WC1X 8HB

A CIP catalogue record for this book is available from the British Library.

978-0-85707-195-8

1 3 5 7 9 10 8 6 4 2

Printed in the UK by CPI Cox & Wyman, Reading RG1 8EX.

www.simonandschuster.co.uk
www.sarahalderson.com

1

Only when the tip of the knife started to shave against the white of his eye like a scalpel about to pierce a boil, did I realise that I was the one holding it.

Or, rather, *controlling* it.

The three of us stared mesmerised as the knife hung there in the jagged space between us. The boy, whose arms were locked around me, and against whose eye the blade was now pressing, let go of me, his arms dropping like a puppet's whose strings had been cut.

And then I felt it. The weight of the knife in my mind. And the blade clattered to the pavement.

I couldn't take my eyes off it, just lying there, like a prop someone had arranged in front of me.

The scramble of metal hitting brick made me raise my head. Both boys were back on their bikes, kicking at the pedals, trying to get a grip on the narrow pavement. They collided as they tore off down the street but kept their balance, bikes weaving down the centre of the road, before disappearing around the nearest corner.

I was on my knees. The thrum of traffic from the main road ten metres or so away cut into me, interrupting the sound of someone nearby choking on barbed wire. I spun my head left to right to see where the noise was coming from, then realised it was coming from me. I bit down on my lip to stop it, then stood up slowly.

A jolt of pain in my right leg snapped me back into the present. I looked around uncertainly, trying to place myself. It took a while before I realised I was standing on the corner of my street. My tights were ripped and laddered where the front wheel and handle-bars of one of the bikes had smashed into me. A tinny noise escaped from the headphones dangling around my neck, and my right hand was still clutching tightly at the school bag they had tried to snatch.

Maria wasn't there when I got home and neither was my dad. He wouldn't be back for another week or so. The house was as echoey and cold as an empty fridge. I put the chain on the door and leant against it, taking a deep breath. Then I hobbled to the downstairs bathroom, lifted the toilet lid and threw up until there was nothing left but stringy green bile. My hands were shaking so hard they were blurring against the white of the porcelain. I sat back against the wall, hugging my knees to my chest, trying to steady my breathing.

I couldn't use it again – whatever kind of freaky mind power *it* was – that much was clear. But I had had no intention of using it in the first place – it had just happened, unconscious as breathing. Except breathing had never led to nearly blinding a person, I didn't think. I was out of control. Dangerously out of control. With just a flicker of thought, without moving an inch, I could have squeezed that blade through the white of that boy's eye as easily as slicing through a soft-boiled egg. A wave of bile swung up my throat again. I ground my teeth and swallowed it down.

Up until this moment this *psychic weird moving things without actually touching them ability* had been a secret. Something I'd wrapped up and bound tightly to me like a deformed extra limb

– a sixth finger; a third arm. Not something I particularly felt like showing off. Yet now two complete strangers knew about it, one of whom I'd almost blinded.

I sat there in the humming dark, waiting for the knock on the door from the police or the men in white coats. Maybe I would just go with them. Clearly I was too dangerous to be walking the streets of south London. Possibly I was unhinged. Definitely I wasn't normal.

I waited and waited, shivering on the floor, but the knock didn't come.

Eventually, I unclasped my hands from around my legs and stood up, resolved. I had to regain control. I wouldn't use it again, ever. As in, *never*.

I wouldn't use it to open doors, to turn on lights or pop the toaster – and I *certainly* wouldn't ever use it again to defend myself against teenage muggers. If I could possibly help it.

I was going to go cold turkey. It was either that, or a future in orange overalls.

I splashed some water on my face and into my mouth and looked up to see myself in the mirror, pale and shadowed as a corpse. Except a ten-day-old corpse would probably look better. My hair was a tangled blonde mess and my lips so white they merged with my skin. I looked down at my legs and, leaning on the sink, carefully peeled off my ripped tights. A bruise about the size of my palm had turned the right side of my thigh an inter-esting shade of black. It looked gruesome and mottled against the paleness of my skin. I touched it lightly and flinched. I could feel the hardness of congealed blood under the surface. I tested my weight on it – and screamed. I looked back at my reflection, shud-dering back a sudden onslaught of tears. I wanted my mum. I

3

wanted Jack. I wanted him to come and rescue me just like he had when I was five and had broken my leg. I wanted my brother, simple as that. OK, truth be told, I really wanted Alex. I wanted my brother's best friend every bit as much as I wanted to see my brother, and then some.

Heathrow's Terminal Five was an immense vault of whiteness. It was close to midnight. I stared at the frozen departures board, willing it to come to life so that I could get on the plane right now and not in six hours' time, because by then my dad might have found out that I'd stolen his credit card and the odds were that he'd try to ground both me *and* the plane.

I stared at the plane details on the board. I couldn't make them move. Not that I was supposed to be trying. I was supposed to be going cold turkey.

I sank into a seat, feeling something like despair shroud me. Or maybe it was outright panic. I was going to have to come up with a believable story for both Jack and my dad. The email I'd sent Jack was not going to cut it. I'd written him just one line saying:

Surprise! I'm coming to LA. My flight gets in at around midday. Lila x.

No explanation.

But what believable explanation could I give?

I almost stabbed someone in the eye with this weird mind power I have. Is it OK if I come stay with you?

That would go down about as well as me telling him that I'd been in love with his best friend my entire life.

I took a deep breath. I was in so much trouble. So I did what I always did in times of stress, I unpacked every Alex memory from

4

where I'd filed them in the most accessible part of my brain and started to slot them together like puzzle pieces.

The day I broke my leg – that was the day I'd fallen in love with him. He may have only been nine, I may have only been five, but it was definitely that day. I had steered the sledge into the tree, or Jack had pushed me into it. But the bone poking like a pencil through my skin was still one of my best memories ever because alongside it was the memory of Alex's face as he'd wrapped me up in his red parka. He'd lifted me back onto the sledge and towed me, with Jack's help I guess, half a mile to the nearest adult. That was definitely the day.

After that, my next memory was of all three of us in the garden of our old house in Washington DC. It was cold. I knew that because I could see the ice crystals on the ground, and the thwacking sound of the shovel hitting frozen earth still echoed loud and clear in my head. I must have been about seven because the hamster had been a present from my parents for being brave about my leg two years before. The hamster had lived 'a long, happy and carefree life', Jack had intoned from his position at the head of the grave. I remembered also the tissued ball that Alex, standing next to me, solemnly lowered into the hole they'd dug out with the neighbour's trowel. I remembered the feeling of hot tears running rivulets down my cold cheeks and the hotter hand he'd placed in mine. He hadn't said anything, just held my hand until I stopped crying.

Without any warning, my mind jumped to another memory, this one from five years ago, a darker echo of the previous one. I was twelve years and three days old in this one. I knew that for a fact because it was seven days after my mother had died and we were at her funeral. Alex had held my hand then, too. For practical reasons really, since my dad, who should have been doing the job, was not keeping it together very well, and was at that moment on his knees by the hollow grave, sobbing. A tangle of well-meaning arms surrounded him. Jack was a blur at the edge, before he backed out of the press of people and took off. Alex, I realised only now, must have chosen to let him go and stay with me instead.

I could recall with perfect clarity the mud-slung soles of my dad's shoes as he knelt by my mum's grave, but that was all. I couldn't remember the people, the words, the hymns, the flowers. I could remember nothing but those shoes and Alex standing next to me, anchoring me with his grip.

At the reception after the funeral, Alex didn't let go of me once. He didn't follow after Jack. I don't know why. To anyone watching, it was Jack and not me who needed looking after. But Alex hadn't tried to find him. He'd stayed with me. He'd sat me down on an out-of-the-way sofa and stayed with me, responding politely when blurry faces hovered overhead whispering vacant words. It was Alex who had eventually led me through the murmuring crowd to the stairs and up to my room. He'd let me lie down, had pulled the duvet over me and had sat on the edge of the bed, his hand resting on my back until I'd fallen asleep.

Then, literally days after, Dad had taken me with him to London. There had been no choice, not even a warning, just *the cab is coming*. I hadn't packed my bags or said goodbye to my school friends. Locked in my silent bubble of grief, I had been incapable of arguing. My dad may as well have told me we were going to the supermarket, for all the impact it had on me. Jack, on the other hand, went ballistic. The fury with which he responded to my dad's news was shattering. It sapped every single last emotion from me, like I was the source of his energy and the battery had died. My dad hadn't had the energy to fight him, either. His battery kind of died permanently along with my mum.

So Jack got to move in with Alex's family and stay in Washington, while I had to move to London, my dad's hometown. At first I'd felt nothing about this, not even on the flight over with Jack's empty seat gaping like a black hole between us. But in the months after, as I emerged from the numb coma I'd slipped into, I'd resonated with anger. A perfect, biting, furious anger towards my dad for taking me away from everything I knew, from my home. Anger towards Jack, for deserting me. And for being the one who got to stay with Alex.

But, like most things in life, unless you really work at it, anger's a hard thing to hold on to, and after a few months that anger had become less perfect, less biting, until it was eventually dissolved completely by the ache of missing Jack. I'd started to email him and to speak to him again and found I couldn't resent him. Because, if I'd had the choice to stay with Alex, I would have done the same. In a heartbeat.

2

I came through customs warily, stumbling a little from the lack of sleep and the tired throb of my leg. I scanned the blur of faces massing at the sliding arrival doors. I wasn't sure if Jack would be there. And if he was, whether it would only be to hand me a return ticket and frogmarch me straight to the check-in counter.

'Lila!'

A familiar voice made me turn my head. Jack was leaning through the crowd, grinning at me. I felt such intense relief that I wanted to collapse right there and then and let him pick up the pieces of me. When I reached the barrier and fell into his arms, a sob came out of nowhere. I forced it down, pressing my face hard into Jack's shoulder. He pulled me away, grabbing my bag from me. I ducked under the barrier and he put his free arm round my waist, tugging me gently through the throng of people.

When we were free of the crowd and walking across the terminal he looked at me quizzically. 'So, good flight?'

I couldn't help but smile at him, ridiculously grateful and relieved that he wasn't leading me to the check-in counter and that he hadn't asked me the question I was dreading – the reason I was there.

'Yeah, it was OK,' I said.

He was different to look at. It was hard to put my finger on why, but there was something about him now that definitely hadn't been there before. Jack had always been confident: good looks and popularity tend to have that effect on people. Now, though, as he manoeuvred us through the busy terminal, I was aware that this aura was somehow enhanced, like he'd been bitten by a spider and had come over all superhero. Whereas before he'd been fully aware of his charm and had worked it to maximum girl-attracting effect, now his confidence seemed utterly unself-conscious. He was completely indifferent to the effect he was having on people. A woman dragging a wheelie suitcase turned to look at him over her shoulder as we passed and a couple of giggling girls a little younger than me nudged each other. He drew people to him but left them in a kind of wake, bobbing hopelessly after him.

Jack was wearing jeans and a white crew-neck T-shirt. His sunglasses hung down from the collar. When we stepped outside into the glaring sunlight he put them on and flashed a smile at me. Yeah, he could have stepped out of a Police sunglasses advert, I thought with a familiar pang of envy. I, on the other hand, felt pale and creased in this land of tanned, polished people. I wanted to get home and shower. *Home*, I thought, with a shock – I was already thinking of this as home. And this was just the LAX arrivals hall.

Jack kept up a steady stream of conversation on the way south to Oceanside. My sudden arrival sat between us, a great white elephant in the car. I ignored it studiously and focused instead on absorbing everything about him. And the car. I knew nothing about cars, but this one was seriously impressive. How much were they paying Marines these days? It had a leather interior, a low roof, a killer sound system and a disembodied voice which welcomed us when we got in. Jack drove the car smoothly, pushing the limit without an ounce of hesitation as he wove in and out of traffic on the freeway. I relaxed back into the seat and let him talk. His eyes flicked from the road ahead, to the rear-view mirror, then back to me. He was telling me about his house – it was near to the beach, which sounded good, way better than living slap-bang in mugging central, south London.

His words started to wash over me as I focused my attention on him, observing his profile. He looked so much older than the teenage boy he'd been when I'd last seen him, he was tanned and his dark hair was growing out of a crew cut. Three years was a long time I supposed, we'd both changed a lot. I wondered how I looked to him.

As if reading my mind, he cast his eyes in my direction, then looked back at the road. 'You look different, Lila.'

'Yeah, I look wasted,' I said, 'I don't think I've slept in thirty hours or more.'

He brooded for a moment. I hoped he wasn't going to ask me why. I could see he was thinking about it.

Instead, he said, 'I almost didn't recognise you when you walked through the arrivals hall.'

I didn't reply. In the three years since we'd last seen each other I'd grown quite a bit taller but was still a good six inches off his six feet. My hair was still long, though perhaps duller than the honey blonde he remembered. No sunshine to streak it in England. We had the exact same eyes, both dark green, both framed with thick black lashes, though his were even longer and thicker than mine. There was, of course, one major change, but it wasn't something physical and as he couldn't read my mind, I was certain he wasn't talking about that. I shifted in my seat, trying to avoid thinking about it.

As he reached to change gears, something caught my eye and I leaned across to touch his arm beneath the sleeve of his T-shirt. He saw my raised eyebrows and reached to tug the sleeve up, exposing his bicep and a tattoo in black ink of two crossed swords. The words *Semper Fi* were etched above it.

'Mum would be so mad!'

'Yeah? Well, she's not around to see it, is she?' He flicked the sleeve down and stared at the road ahead.

I turned to look out of the window too. I shouldn't have mentioned Mum. Five years didn't seem to have softened the effect of hearing her name. I could see the muscles stretched taut around his jaw. He was as easy to read as I was, every emotion slapped across his face like a neon sign. I couldn't believe I'd managed to upset him within half an hour of seeing him again. I really needed to not do that if I had any hope of convincing him to let me stay for the foreseeable future.

'What does it mean?' I asked, to distract him.

Jack's jaw untensed. 'It's the Marine Corps motto. *Always Faithful.* The crossed swords are the Unit's emblem. It's something we all got done when we finished recon and special ops training.'

His unit – he'd spoken only sparingly on the phone to me about his unit. I didn't know much about it at all; it had taken me months even to figure out that recon meant reconnaissance. Though I still hadn't figured out what exactly they were reconnais-sancing. What I *did* know was that the training had been two long years, for much of which he hadn't been contactable. That had been difficult.

11

A thought occurred to me. 'Does Alex have one too?'

'Yep, of course.'

Of course. I could have guessed. I stopped myself from asking him, *If Alex drank poison, would you do it too?* It was what my mum used to say all the time but I didn't think the reminder would go down too well.

'He'll be over later by the way. He can't wait to see you.'

My heart lurched. I was sure it punched out of my chest like you see in cartoons. I looked over at my brother, biting the inside of my cheek to rein in my unstoppable grin. I didn't want him to see how ecstatic that bit of news had just made me.

Half an hour later we were still cocooned in the air-conditioned cool of the car. I was staring out at the blue ocean to my right, wrapped up in imaginings involving Alex in uniform, when Jack interrupted my reverie with a nod to his left. We were passing a turn-off. A large sign announced the entrance to the Marine Corps Base at Camp Pendleton. Several army trucks were turning in ahead of us.

I squinted up the road as we passed it by. 'So that's where you work?'

'It is indeed.'

'Is it big? It looks big.'

'Two hundred square miles. We've been driving alongside it for the last thirty minutes.'

I thought about that for a bit. 'Don't you live on base?'

'No, our unit doesn't. We need to be near to San Diego and the border.'

The border? With Mexico, I assumed, not Orange County. I wondered why that was important. The only thing I could think of was drugs, or maybe illegal immigrants, but I didn't ask as I knew Jack wouldn't give me a straight answer. He always changed the subject when I asked what his unit actually did. I knew they hadn't been deployed overseas, thank God, but it seemed a little weird that they'd gone through all that training just to sit around in sunny California, kicking back in civilian clothes and driving fast cars. And, anyway, didn't the police or border control deal with drugs and immigration?

A few miles further down the road and we came to Oceanside. It was a small, sun-bleached town facing the Pacific, the kind of place you see in the movies, with palm trees swaying languorously in the breeze. We drove through some back streets, away from the ocean, and pulled up outside a small two-storeyed detached house. It had a square of front yard, with scrappy grass and a wooden veranda running along the front. The house was painted grey. There was an integral garage which we drove up to, Jack hitting a button in the car that made the garage door swing open for us.

When we entered the house through the internal door, I stopped short. I had imagined something semi-squalid, like his bedroom used to be, and instead I was confronted with a photo shoot from *Ideal Home*. I caught my breath in the hallway when I saw the little wooden letter table by the door. It looked strange sitting there. The last time I'd seen it had been five years ago, back in our house in Washington. I looked around the house more carefully, spotting one or two other items from our childhood. A whitewashed bookcase in the living room, a framed print of a Klee painting in the hall, an antique coat rack by the front door. No wonder it had appeared so homey on first glance. It was like putting on a familiar old coat in the winter. Even though she'd never stepped foot inside this house, my mum's touch was all over it.

The kitchen, which Jack led me into now, was slightly old-fashioned, with a big ceramic sink, crackly lino floor and a flimsy veneer table and chairs. I glanced around for anything familiar in here. The only thing I recognised was a postcard of Big Ben tacked to the fridge door, one I'd sent Jack a year or two back. I wondered what I'd written on the back, probably some barefaced lie about how happy I was.

I wandered over to it. It was posted amongst a litter of other scraps of paper and one or two photos. I flinched when I saw one was of me, taken the last time I was over in Washington, three years ago. I felt sorry for my fourteen-year-old self when I looked at it. I had a stricken expression, like I was hiding a terrible secret. The irony was, back then I hadn't even known what terrible secrets were – I'd just been a scared fourteen-year-old, confused by the rift opening up between her dad and her brother, and not sure whether she'd see her brother or his best friend ever again. I resisted the urge to tear the photo off the fridge and rip it up.

I almost didn't want to look at the other photo, which I'd clocked out of the corner of my eye. To do so was like tearing off an itching scab: a momentary thrill of satisfaction, followed rapidly by pain and clotting. It was a dog-eared picture of a stunning blonde woman, caught mid-laugh, one of her arms wrapped tightly around a boy who was looking up at her, his head shadowed beneath her chin, blue sky behind them. The boy was Jack and the woman was my mother. The top of another, blonder, head appeared in the bottom left of the picture, but it was impossible to tell that it was me. I turned away, wanting to shield Jack from the picture, then remembered that he had put it there and was confronted by it every time he went to fetch the milk. I guessed that was progress.

'It's a nice place, Jack. Really nice.'

'Yeah,' he nodded, 'it's good to come home to.'

I agreed silently, then, experimenting with my indifferent voice, asked, 'So where does Alex live? I'm surprised you two aren't room-mates.' My indifferent voice needed work.

Jack laughed. 'Contrary to popular opinion, sis, Alex and I are not joined at the hip. Alex lives five minutes away. He has a very cool bachelor pad on the oceanfront.'

My heart rebounded back into my chest. Bachelor pad? Of course. It was absurd that Alex *wouldn't* be dating girls. He was beautiful, and yes, I was blinded by bias, but it was still an indisputable fact. By anyone. Together, he and Jack had cornered the market in good looks and charisma. When I was about ten I'd had to watch in silent agony as Alex dated a few girls – all older than me, all able to fill a bra – and it had almost killed me to watch. But in the fantasy world I'd created in my mind since leaving, Alex lived in a woman-free vacuum. It was the only way I'd kept myself sane. Now the words 'bachelor' and 'pad' were being bandied around and my mind was erasing that carefully crafted fantasy and redrawing it with images of hot tubs and women in bikinis.

Breathe, I reminded myself. *This is Alex. Not Jack.* Alex, who always played the cool, collected one to Jack's extrovert. He'd never been one to chase the girls, he was the one who always apologised to them when Jack forgot their names. He would hang back, watching silently with one blond eyebrow raised whenever Jack went in for the kill. And even if he *did* have a bachelor pad, it didn't mean he was entertaining streams of women every night, or even any night.

Yeah, keep clutching at those straws, Lila.

'You hungry? Thirsty?' Jack asked.

I certainly wasn't hungry now. My stomach was in knots. I shook my head.

Jack led me through into the hallway, where he stopped in front of a small white box on the wall by the front door.

'This is the alarm,' he said, flicking open the box. Inside was a space-age-looking row of blinking lights and a touchpad with both letters and numbers on it.

'The code is 121205,' he said. 'You need to set the alarm when you're in the house, not just when you go out. If something sets it off when you're inside, the whole place will lock down. You won't be able to get out. Just hang tight and wait for me or the police.'

I stared at him in silence for a few seconds. I hadn't taken in the instructions, just the code. It was the date of my mother's death. Jack ignored my expression and snapped the box shut. I understood the paranoia. Dad had installed an alarm on the house in London too. But having an alarm hadn't helped Mum.

Jack picked up my bag which he'd dumped at the bottom of the stairs and waved me forwards, up them. I went first, pausing on the landing, not sure which door to take.

Jack edged past me to the door at the end of the short corridor. He opened it and let me go first into what was going to be my bedroom for the next however many days he let me stay. It was nice and simple. A single bed, a dresser with a spiky cactus in a red pot on top and a blue comfy chair wedged in the corner – another relic from our previous lives. The window looked out over the back garden. I could definitely make this room my home forever.

'It's great. Thanks,' I said, turning towards him. It was kind of awkward, him not knowing why I was there. Me not telling, him not asking.

He put my bag on the chair and said, 'Do you want to have a sleep? You could probably use it. I've got a few things to do this afternoon. You sleep. When you wake up, we'll have dinner and talk.'

Yeah, there, he'd said it, *Talk*. Guess I knew it was coming. I had a few more hours to think up something to tell him. I glanced at the clock on the bedside table. It was coming up for 3.30 p.m. Sleep was seeming like a very good idea indeed, especially when I looked again at the bed.

'OK, sounds like a plan,' I agreed.

I looked at him then walked over to where he was standing by the door. I stopped a few inches away from him and let my head fall against his chest. He brought his arms around me as I mumbled into his T-shirt, 'Thanks.'

'Hey, no problem,' he said softly. I felt his lips press against the top of my head and then he left.

I sat down on the edge of the bed and kicked off my shoes, then fell backwards onto the cool sheets. It felt so inviting but my skin was tacky and glazed from travel and I needed a shower more than I needed to sleep. I groaned and sat back up, glancing around for my bag. It hovered off the chair, unzipped itself and moved towards me. With a shock I realised what I was doing and let it fall to the floor with a thud.

'Lila? You OK?' Jack yelled from downstairs.

'Er, yeah, fine, just dropped my bag,' I called back.

I knelt on the floor, breathing loudly. I had to get this under control. No more using my ability, for anything. That was the rule. I absolutely had to stick to it if I wanted to avoid any more eyeball incidents. Or worse. I had to concentrate. I'd pretty much managed it at school and when I was around people. It was just being tired that made it harder to control. Tiredness and having a knife held to my throat.

I reached into my bag, feeling for my wash things and a clean T-shirt. It felt weird. I was using muscles I hadn't used in a while. I was going to have to get used to that.

3

I sat on the edge of the bed, feeling dazed from jet lag but buzzing like a high voltage power line had been connected to me while I was asleep. I had been woken up by voices from downstairs; one was Jack – I could hear him laughing and joking around. The other was softer, deeper, and I would recognise it anywhere, even in my sleep. It had broken through my dreams and nudged me into consciousness. Alex.

The room was gloomy, it was dusk outside. I twisted around to look at the clock. It was 7.30 p.m. but it felt like I'd only been asleep for ten minutes. The jet lag was messing with my body, but not half as much as that voice downstairs was. My heart was racing, I could feel my cheeks starting to burn. I glanced at the light switch and narrowed my eyes – the light flickered on, then straightaway off. I got up, frowning at myself, and flicked the switch by hand.

A part of me, a big part of me, wanted to bound out of the room and down the stairs right that second. The need to see him was suddenly overwhelming. It felt like I'd been stuck at the bottom of the ocean for the last three years, surviving on one mouthful of air, and now I could see the surface, or an oxygen tank, only a few feet away. But bed hair and a wrinkled T-shirt was not a good look and vanity got the better of me. A few more minutes wouldn't kill, whereas Alex looking at me and thinking I looked like the inside of a used sick bag would.

What to wear, though? I'd not been thinking all that straight when I'd packed and consequently discovered a random assortment of clothing in the drawers. I seemed to have covered all bases though, I noted, apart from skiing. I pulled out an electric blue silk dress. I wasn't sure what scenario would arise where I was going to need that but hey, you never knew. There was also a school shirt, which I scrunched up and fired at the bin. I didn't need any reminders of where I should be right now. In the end I pulled on some jeans and replaced the T-shirt I'd worn in bed with a purple vest.

I turned to look in the mirror above the dresser. My hair was all over the place, I'd gone to bed with it wet and was now doing a good impression of a blonde Alice Cooper. I smoothed it flat, hacking a brush through the ends to get the tangles out. I leaned closer to the mirror. I didn't normally bother with make-up, but tonight I really needed to make an impression. A little bit of mascara, maybe some lip balm. I didn't need any blusher, that was for sure. I cast my eyes around the dresser, searching for my make-up bag. It was nowhere in sight. I let out a groan. Great. Just great. On the one day I needed to look amazing, to look older, my make-up bag was five thousand miles away.

I reappraised my reflection in something of a panic. Yesterday I'd looked like a dead thing, now I looked very, very alive. Almost too alive – like I was on something. Which, I supposed, I sort of was. There was nothing I could do about that, unfortunately. I brushed my hair behind my ears and bit my lips to make them redder, hoping to take the focus away from my burning cheeks.

I took a deep breath, then another. I could do this.

I made it to the top of the stairs and gripped the banister with all my might. How was it I could make inanimate objects do my bidding but couldn't get my own legs to obey? I took the first step and the voices in the kitchen cut off in mid-sentence. I felt like an actor about to walk out on stage in front of the world, without knowing the words or even having read the script. I could hear the sound of chairs scraping back so I picked up my pace, wanting to make it to the bottom before they could. I took the next steps two at a time. I caught sight of the top of Alex's head and inhaled fast, my heart rate skyrocketing. I missed my footing on the next step and went tumbling forwards. In the split second before I hit the wall all I could think was that this wasn't exactly the reunion I'd fantasised about in my head every hour of every day for the last three years.

My eyes closed involuntarily to avoid the collision and I braced myself. I hit something good and hard but it wasn't a wall. I opened one eye slowly, peeking to see. Alex was holding me by the top of my arms where he'd caught me. I'd crashed right into his chest. My hands were splayed against him. He rocked back on his heels, not letting go of me. I was thinking I had to move my hands but, much like my legs earlier, they wouldn't obey. Here he was, literally at my fingertips; I had dreamed about that – though there had been fewer clothes in my dream – for a long time now. I could feel the muscles of his chest and, yep, they lived up to the fantasy. My head barely came up to the height of his shoulders. I just wanted to rest it there and not move but Jack was getting into my peripheral vision and I didn't want him to see the look of dazed delight that was surely on my face. I straightened up, pulling away abruptly. Alex let go of me. I drew in a breath. He was even more beautiful than I had remembered. His tanned face and ice-blue eyes made my stomach lurch violently. I grabbed the banister with one hand to stop myself from falling again. That would be bad.

'Lila. It's good to see you.' Alex chuckled.

I smiled back ruefully.

'Hey, you too,' I garbled, as the power of coherent speech momentarily deserted me.

'Do I get a proper hug?' he said, and he opened his arms wide.

I stepped into them. It felt familiar, warm and, truth be told, unexpectedly painful too. Not physically, but his closeness, the headrush of familiar scent and touch, brought back so many memories from before, it was like someone had turned a television right by my head from silent to full volume.

'Been a long time – you're looking well,' Alex said, as we walked through into the kitchen.

He pulled out a chair for me and I sat while he rested, long and lean, against the kitchen counter. Jack turned back to the stove where something was cooking.

'So, what's the deal then?' Alex said. 'Why the escape to southern California? London not rocking enough for a teenage girl, so you've got to check out the entertainment factor of a military town?'

Maybe Jack had put him up to it. I doubted it though. Alex never did anything he didn't want to.

'Kind of, something like that,' I muttered. I didn't want to answer any questions right now. I just wanted to enjoy the moment. To which end I shrugged off the teenage comment. I was back with the two people in the world who I loved most. I felt complete. And happier than I'd been in a good long time.

'So, when's Sara getting here?' Alex said to Jack.

Well, that didn't last long. I felt the smile melt off my face, my ribcage start to crack. Who was Sara?

'She's working. She said she'd see us tomorrow,' Jack answered over his shoulder.

'That's a shame. She's looking forward to meeting you, Lila. You're going to love her,' Alex said in my direction.

That did it. My heart skidded to a stop. Alex had a girlfriend and he'd used her name and the word 'love' in the same sentence.

'The woman who tamed Jack,' Alex continued. 'I have to hand it to her, she's done something no other woman has been able to.'

I shook my head and felt my heart start to beat once more. 'I don't get it. What are you saying?' I turned to Jack. 'You – *you* have a girlfriend?'

Jack, to my knowledge – which clearly had great big supernova-sized holes in it – was about as likely a candidate for boyfriendhood as I was for getting the attendance award this year at school. Flings, flirtations, one-night dalliances, but Jack usually ran screaming from commitment. Or maybe not. Maybe in the last three years I really had stopped knowing him.

'Yep, little sis, I do have a girlfriend,' he said.

My jaw fell open. I stood up and hopped onto the counter next to the stove so I could look directly at Jack. 'I want details.'

'Her name is Sara. Get the mustard.' He turned, holding a sizzling pan towards the table.

'Sara who? I don't know where you keep the mustard. Don't change the subject.'

Alex moved to my side of the stove and stretched over me to open the cupboard behind my head. I had to duck slightly to avoid the door. As I leaned out of the way, I brushed up against his outstretched arm. My thoughts suddenly detoured as my heart accelerated. The cupboard banged behind me and Alex turned to hand the mustard to Jack. In the second his head was in profile to me, I burnt every single detail of him into my mind like it was photo paper and he was the sun.

He was so close I would only have had to move my face an inch or two forwards to press my lips against his neck. I resisted the urge to trace the shadow of stubble along his jawline to the hollow of his chin. His dark blond hair had been recently crew-cut – I could tell by the thin white line that traced his hairline at the nape of his neck, which stood out against his tan. There was a crease by his eyes that looked suspiciously like the beginnings of a laughter line. I felt a pang of jealousy that someone else was making him laugh, getting to hear him laugh. I was entirely pathetic, I realised that.

Alex turned back towards me as though he sensed me examining him and I looked away, glancing over his shoulder at the steaks Jack had put on the table. I suddenly felt a warmth against the bare skin of my waist, where my top had ridden up over my jeans. Then I was lifted clean off the counter and placed gently on the floor. I tilted my head up. He'd definitely grown too, he was an inch or two taller than Jack now. Alex moved his hands from my waist and gave me a quick smile.

'Dinner?' he said, inclining his head towards the table. He pulled out my chair and I pretty much fell into it. He pushed it in and took the chair diagonally opposite.

I gathered myself and focused on Jack. 'So, come on, start talking. Who's Sara? Where'd you meet her?'

Jack sat down opposite me. 'She works with us, with our unit.' His eyes flicked to Alex.

'She's great,' Alex said.

I didn't like Alex calling any girl, even my brother's girlfriend, great. A hideous thought surfaced like a shark. Just because Sara wasn't his girlfriend didn't mean he didn't have one. But if he had, would Jack have said he lived in a bachelor pad? I didn't know which version I'd rather was true. It was like playing Russian roulette with a full chamber.

'But I thought women weren't allowed into the Recon Marines?' I knew this as I had googled it to check.

'They aren't. She's not a Marine. She's a neuroscientist.'

That stopped me in my tracks. 'A neuroscientist? Why would you need a neuroscientist in your unit?'

I caught the sideways look Alex was giving Jack. As though he too was interested to see what Jack would say. This was bizarre.

'Um, well, it's sort of standard practice,' Jack fumbled.

It was? What kind of weird stuff was the army doing these days? I narrowed my eyes at him.

'So, you're dating someone who studies brains? Is this an experiment for her or something?'

'Ha ha.'

'How old is she?' I was sure that neuroscientists didn't just leave university after three years. Jack must have an older woman.

'Twenty-six.' He caught my eye. A warning to stop right there.

I bit back my original response. 'So, how long have you two been dating? Where does she live?' I asked.

'Eight months. She lives on the base.'

'I thought you said your unit lived off base?' Hah – I'd caught him out.

He continued smoothly, 'We do. She doesn't. It's better for her being on base.'

'Why?' I asked.

25

'Can you pass the mustard?' Alex interrupted, reaching over and giving Jack a hard stare.

Then he turned to me. 'So, talking of living arrangements . . .'

I stared at him now. I always knew when these two were being shifty. Like the time I'd walked into Jack's bedroom and found them acting in exactly the same way. Trying to distract me. They'd been trying to hide a copy of *Playboy*.

Alex's words still hung in the air. They were both staring at me with questions, actually one question, in their eyes. It was a dual-pronged attack. I cut a piece of steak to buy some more time. The steak knife had a serrated edge. I put it down on my plate and stared at it. I suddenly didn't feel like eating.

'Lila, are you going to tell us why you're here?'

I looked at Jack and the words wouldn't come. I didn't know how to tell him. The secret had been inside me for so long it wouldn't come out. I didn't know how to find the words to even describe it. And besides I was going cold turkey. There was no point in telling them. I could make up a thousand excuses but the real truth of it was I couldn't bear the thought of Alex looking at me like I was a freak. It was bad enough that he looked at me as Jack's sister.

I took a breath. 'It's revision time,' I tried. 'I just thought on a whim that it would be a good time to come and check out colleges.'

'Colleges?' Jack was frowning.

'Yeah, you know, the places that you go to get a further education? Or, alternatively, the places you drop out of when you decide to join up.'

'Very funny. You're on form tonight, Lila. Why are you looking at colleges over here?'

He didn't seem happy. I looked at Alex, who had stopped chewing and was now eyeing me carefully. I couldn't tell what he was thinking. Damn, he could be so contained sometimes.

'I thought college over here would be better. San Diego University has a good reputation. Or there's USC . . .' I petered out.

'Lila . . . I'm not sure California's such a good idea.'

His words shot through me, making my insides curl.

'I . . . but . . . I can't stay in England.'

'Look, it isn't that I don't want you here. It's just . . .' He fumbled around for the words. 'There are safer places.'

Yeah, safe like south London, I thought. It crossed my mind that I should just tell him about being mugged. Maybe then he'd see the logic of his argument was seriously flawed. But that would just open a huge can of worms. And, anyway, there was no logic to his argument. Oceanside was hardly a hotbed of crime. A great big army base up the road had to act like a flashing siren to most criminals except the truly stupid ones. But then why did he have the crazy alarm on the house? Maybe Oceanside was some crime capital and I just didn't know about it. But still.

Suddenly Jack's eyes narrowed. He put his knife and fork down. 'Is this about a boy?'

'What?' Where did that come from? My mind seized up at the totally unexpected twist. 'A boy? What? No!'

Did he know about Alex? Was I that obvious? Were they both onto me? For years I'd been plotting my escape back here for college and my reasoning had been nothing to do with the diversity of study options and all to do with a boy. Though he wasn't technically a boy now.

'Then why the suddenness? That couldn't have waited? You're not going to college for over a year.'

Yes, he had me on that one.

'You left in the middle of the night. You didn't even call. Just sent an email. What were you planning on doing if I hadn't got it?'

'Um, catching a bus?'

'Lila.' Jack was irritated now. 'You can't just skip off halfway around the world without telling anyone first.'

'I emailed you,' I said, 'and I left a note for Maria.'

'Forget the email, leaving a note for the housekeeper doesn't count. You knew she'd call Dad and that he'd call me. He wasn't – well, let's just say he wasn't that happy.' Jack paused.

I knew he hadn't spoken to Dad in a long time and could just imagine the tension between them buzzing down the line like interference.

'I told him you'd be fine with me – but you need to call him tomorrow first thing.'

'Jack, do we have to talk about this now?' The evening was going rapidly downhill. Alex was looking serious and I was feeling fed up. I'd always known I'd have to talk to Dad at some point but with the phone I always had the option of hanging up. With Jack and Alex, there was no such easy way out. And it was clear they were both trained in interrogation. They had probably topped the class.

'Lila, what if I hadn't been here? What would you have done then?'

I looked over at Alex. His expression hadn't changed, was still unreadable. He didn't look like he was about to jump in and rescue me.

'I, guess, I . . . I don't know. I didn't think about that.'

But I would have been fine, I wanted to yell. I can look after myself. Have been looking after myself pretty well, actually, all things considered. I looked down at my plate. Tears were pricking behind my eyes. I couldn't believe we'd moved from banter to parental lecture, and from my brother of all people, in the space of ten seconds.

'Well, maybe you should have thought first.'

I shot him a look. What was he saying? That I shouldn't have come? That he didn't want me here? I heard my knife and fork clatter on the plate and the chair scrape the lino as I pushed back from the table. I didn't want to sit here anymore, being interrogated. I needed air. I stumbled to the back door, yanked it open and stepped outside, letting the screen slam behind me. I could hear Alex saying something to Jack and the sound of a chair moving.

I tried to pull myself together before one of them came out after me. I looked around. I was on the back veranda. I went to lean against the waist-high ledge, looking out at the silhouettes of two palm trees waving against the mauve sky. The door behind me opened gently but I didn't hear anyone move. I turned my head slightly to look. It was Alex. He was standing only a foot or so behind me.

'Lila.' He spoke softly, almost a whisper. 'Are you OK?'

'Yeah, I'm just fine,' I said.

He put his hand on my shoulder and I closed my eyes as my body unwound like a sigh.

'Hey,' he said, twisting me gently around so he could look at me. His eyes burnt blue, even in the dark. His hand dropped from my shoulder and I felt my body tense up again. 'It's only because he cares about you,' he said.

'He doesn't want me here.' I looked at him for reassurance that I was imagining it, but it wasn't forthcoming.

'It's not that, Lila. He's just worried about you. You arrived out of the blue, with only some flimsy excuse about college.'

'It wasn't an excuse . . .' But even to my own ears, that sounded feeble.

Alex cocked his head to the side and gave me a half-smile. 'Lila, how long have I known you? You don't think I see through you in a second?'

I hoped I wasn't that transparent or I was in trouble.

'Look,' he said. 'You don't need to talk about it if you don't want to. You're with us and you can stay as long as you need to. I'll get Jack off your back for now, but you should talk to him, he's your brother.'

As long as I need to, he'd said. Hmmm, I didn't think he realised that that might mean forever.

Alex was right, though, I did need to talk to Jack. I had to try to get him to realise I wasn't a kid anymore. That if I chose to go to college here, he couldn't actually stop me. I'd bite the bullet and even finish another year of school in London if I had to, but I was coming back here the day my last exam was over. The thing was, I wanted them both to want me here too, otherwise I might as well stay in England.

I heard the door swing open again as Jack came out to join us. He moved swiftly past Alex, patting him lightly on the back as he passed, as though he was saying *Thanks, I'll take it from here*. Alex took the hint and turned around and went back into the kitchen. I had an overwhelming desire to follow him but Jack came up next to me. I leaned into his shoulder and sighed as his arm came around my back.

'Sorry, sis. I just – I got your email and I was worried. That's all. It just seemed like something must have happened – to make you leave like that. It's not like you to run away.'

30

'I wasn't running away. I was running to, there's a difference.'

'It's still running, Lila.'

'Nothing's happened, Jack. You don't need to worry about me.'

'Of course I worry about you. I worry about you every day. You're my little sis.'

'I'm not little anymore, Jack.'

'You're always going to be my little sis.'

I knew I couldn't argue with that.

'I'm really glad you're here, Lila.' He kissed the side of my head. 'I've missed you. You can stay as long as you want, a week, two weeks, whatever. Let's talk about it in the morning.'

A week or two? My heart burnt at the thought. That wasn't nearly going to be long enough.

4

It was just gone two in the morning and I was sitting bolt upright in bed, the bed sheet balled in my fists. My heart was pumping like I'd just done a cross-country sprint – I could hear the blood drumming in my ears. I took a while to focus on my surroundings, letting my eyes adjust to the darkness. My heart rate slowed as I recognised where I was and the adrenaline began to leach away. I swung my legs over the side of the bed and sat there for a few moments, staring into the fuzzy dark.

Vivid dreams were something I was used to. After my mum died I'd had the same nightmare for months, of her running panicked through our house, her dress hosed down with red. In those dreams, I was always the one chasing her, watching her ricochet off furniture and stumble blindly before tripping on the bottom stair. Then she'd look back at me over her shoulder and start screaming and screaming in my face until her screams woke me up.

But tonight I'd gone one better. The usual nightmare was back, this time in high definition. I could smell her blood. It was like rust and late cherries. I could see the wooden whorls in the grain of the banister spinning like tops. As per the norm, the dream played out with my mum tripping on the stair, looking back over her shoulder and screaming at me. But instead of waking up as I always did, my viewpoint switched so I wasn't in front of her anymore, I was above her, watching her die from a distance. But then I'd seen myself, in school uniform, with ripped tights and a pale, wide-eyed face, holding the same knife I'd nearly taken the mugger's eye out with. The blood was trickling down its serrated edge and I felt it dripping warm and sticky over my hand. Then I woke up.

I ran my fingers through my hair, pulling out the hairband that had come loose. I had to get some water. Had to shake the image in my head and, while I was at it, stop obsessing over what I had or hadn't almost done to that boy back in London.

I tiptoed into the hallway. Jack's light was out. I didn't want to wake him, I knew he had to get up early for work tomorrow, so I crept down the stairs as silently as I could, which wasn't all that silently as the stairs creaked badly. I paused halfway down to listen – no noise from his room. It clearly didn't take too much to outwit a Special Forces operative.

My bare feet squeaked on the lino in the kitchen, I wandered to the fridge and stood there for about five minutes staring at the photo of my mum laughing, trying to burn the image over the top of the dream one. Maybe that was why Jack had it there too, in an effort to erase the other, much worse pictures that the imagination could produce. Eventually, I pulled open the fridge door and let the cool condensed air wash over me, luxuriating in the goosebumps pricking my skin.

'You're not hungry, are you?'

I let out a yelp then covered my mouth with my hand to suppress a scream.

'What the heck? You scared the hell out me,' I whispered, hanging on to the fridge door for support as my heart restarted. It couldn't take much more of these adrenaline spikes.

Alex was standing an inch behind me. He'd snuck up on me from God knows where. I revised my estimation of Marine recon training. I turned slowly, giving him a look, and staggered to the table.

'Sorry,' he said, looking at me with concern as he flicked on the overhead light.

'S'OK,' I muttered, blinking in the sudden glare. 'I just wasn't expecting to see you, is all. Thought you'd gone back to your place.'

'Yeah, we, um . . .' He hesitated and I looked up. 'We had a little situation at work, Jack had to go and take care of it, so I came over to sleep on the sofa, in case you woke up and didn't know where he'd gone.'

I smiled and shook my head at him. 'Usually a note works just fine.'

He was wearing the same blue jeans that he'd had on earlier, but had taken off his shirt and was now wearing only a white T-shirt. It was physically painful to tear my eyes away from his shoulders and arms, like ripping a Band-Aid from my eyelids. The same black inked tattoo that I'd seen on Jack covered the curve of his upper arm and I wanted to press my fingers against it and indent it into my hand.

When I managed to force my mind back onto a less X-rated track, I realised he was glancing downwards and his face wore a questioning expression. With a start, I remembered I was wearing only a T-shirt that came halfway down my thighs, just covering the bruise that I'd gotten from the bike and knife incident. But it wasn't my bare legs he was looking at, or the bruise.

'Hey, I recognise that T-shirt!'

34

Oh God. Inside my head I doubled over, cringing. I could feel the heat rising in my cheeks as, casually, with as much insouciance as I was capable of, I pulled the front of the T-shirt away from my body as though I too was wondering what on earth I was wearing. As if I didn't know. As if I hadn't undressed myself just a few hours ago and pulled that very T-shirt on as I did almost every night. Unthinkingly, or at least not thinking that the person who used to own that T-shirt would come across me wearing it in the middle of the night.

I tried for wide-eyed innocence: 'What, this thing?'

He was frowning at the almost faded Washington State logo across my chest. I wished it had faded off completely. 'Yeah, that was mine, I'm sure of it,' he said.

'Oh, really?' My voice had picked up an octave. I lowered it. 'I thought it was one of Jack's old ones. I found it lying around one day and kind of adopted it.'

I risked a glance at him.

Alex looked puzzled.

'It's good for sleeping in,' I continued.

'Yeah, I can see that.' He was smiling now.

I jumped up. The subject needed changing before I died. 'So, you fancy some tea?'

'Yeah, OK, thanks.'

I filled the kettle, feeling his eyes burning into my back.

'Has it really been so bad?'

I turned around, frowning. 'What do you mean?'

'London. Living there with your dad. I can see you're not happy. I can hear it in your emails too. Tell me what's been going on.'

The kettle almost fell from my grip. 'Nothing much. It's just not home, you know?'

35

Alex didn't say anything but he didn't take his eyes off me either.

How to explain? Telling him the reason I was so unhappy was because I was away from him wasn't an option unless I never wanted to see him again. Urgh. This was so difficult. Especially with him focusing on me so hard it was like he was trying to see all the way through me. It made it difficult to keep a train of thought going. I looked down at the floor.

'In Washington, I always felt a part of everything. In the middle of a family. I had you and Jack.' I risked a glance back up at him. He smiled at me briefly and then lapsed back into a half-scowl.

'In London I didn't know anyone apart from Dad and he wasn't around much. And I couldn't talk for a long time, I felt so numb.' My voice cracked. 'By the time that passed, I just – I just felt so separate, so different to everyone else, like I didn't fit in.' I paused. There was so much I couldn't tell him. Like how when I said I was different to everyone else, I wasn't talking about having an American accent and a dead mother. I was talking about suddenly and inexplicably being able to move things just by looking at them. I think that qualified me for the 'different' category. Hell, it put me right to the front of it.

There was an awkward silence. I turned away and switched on the kettle and reached up for the tea bags from the cupboard overhead.

'There's so much I don't know about you,' he said.

I bit my lip. He had no idea just how much.

'What the hell?'

I spun my head to see what Alex was swearing about. He was staring at my right leg and wincing. I tried with my free hand to yank the T-shirt down to cover the ugly black bruise that spread like an oil slick along my thigh.

36

Alex crouched down, his fingertips grazing mine as he brushed my hand away. He began to trace the line of the bruise towards my knee, like a doctor checking for a break. He was quick and methodical about it and I wondered for a second whether this was some in-built response Marines were trained for whenever they saw injuries. If so I'd have to injure myself more often. I drew in a sharp breath, not because it hurt, but because his fingers were causing little shocks to dance up my legs.

He pulled his hand back. 'Sorry.'

Actually, I was the sorry one. I could have stood there all night and a little bit longer. I yanked the T-shirt down and twisted around so Alex couldn't see the bruise anymore, embarrassed now to look him in the face in case he saw in my eyes the lies I was about to tell him.

But Alex only moved silently to the fridge, opened it and pulled something out of the freezer tray. Then he turned back, reaching for a towel hanging on the side. He wrapped the ice pack up tight and then, with his hand on my shoulder, edged me backwards into a chair. He knelt down and pressed the towel against my leg. I yelped at the sudden cold but he ignored me, taking my hand and placing it on top of the pack so I could hold it in place.

He looked up at me now. 'What happened to you?'

'It's no big deal,' I answered.

He stood up slowly. 'So, why won't you tell me?' A small frown line appeared between his eyes. 'What happened? Is this anything to do with why you're here?'

I realised then that I couldn't laugh it off. He knew me too well to know when I was lying. And maybe a little part of me, the part weakened by the touch of his fingers on my leg, wanted to tell him.

'OK, I'll tell you – but you have to promise not to say a word to Jack or I'm not spilling a thing.'

'I don't like keeping secrets from Jack.'

'What are you guys – married or something? Promise, or I'm not telling.' He didn't say anything so I made to get up out of the chair.

He took a half-step forward as if to stop me. 'OK, OK, I won't tell him.'

'Good.' I paused. 'I was mugged. Two kids on bikes. They slammed into me. It's not important.'

He stared at me, his eyes narrowing. 'So why didn't you just tell us?' he asked quietly.

I swallowed. 'Because I know exactly how Jack would have reacted. You know if he finds out he'll want to get on the next plane over and go find them. You know what he's like.' I took a breath. 'Look, you two can't go around protecting me my whole life. I can take care of myself. You have special Marine stuff to do – you know, important *Mission-Impossible*-saving-the-world type stuff. I don't think babysitting little sisters qualifies in that category and, besides, if you were babysitting me you wouldn't get to blow stuff up.'

I looked at Alex and noticed his jaw was set and his lips pressed together in a hard line. Not necessarily a good sign.

I tried again, as he still hadn't said anything. 'You don't need to worry about me. Like I said, I can take care of myself. I dealt with it. They didn't even get my iPod.'

His eyes widened. 'What? HOW did you deal with it?'

My cheeks filled up like a pufferfish and I let the air out in a rush. 'Um, I guess I'm just pretty damn ninja.'

I waited for the next question. Alex seemed to be absorbing this last bit of information. Perhaps he was imagining me doing some crazy roundhouse moves. I braced myself for another round of quick-fire questions, wondering why I'd opened my mouth in the first place.

Eventually, he broke the silence. 'We don't blow stuff up.'

'You don't?'

'No.'

I was grateful for the change of subject.

'What do you do, then? I thought you were some special unit – don't special units have a remit to blow things up?'

I didn't want him to answer. I didn't really want to know what Jack and Alex did as a day job. My only reference for the shady world of special operations was gleaned from *24* and Bond movies. The thought of either of them getting hurt caused me actual physical pain, a stabbing feeling between my ribs that stopped me breathing, to be exact – so long ago I'd created a Disney version of what a special operations unit was. It involved animals that talked and burst into tune at any given moment and old ladies needing help to cross the road.

'You'd be surprised by our remit,' Alex said. A sardonic smile twitched at the corner of his mouth then vanished, to be replaced again by a frown. 'You should get back to bed,' he suddenly said. 'You must be exhausted.'

I sighed. He was right. I could feel the leaden weight of exhaustion starting to pull me down. I wanted to kiss him goodnight but he stayed where he was, leaning against the counter, arms folded against his chest, and I didn't have the guts to walk over to him.

'Yeah, I should.' I paused, then added, 'Night, Alex.'

'I'll be here on the couch if you need anything. Sleep well.'

I turned towards the hallway and my bed, wondering how he'd take it if I told him the only thing I needed was him – and whether, if he knew that, he'd take back the offer.

5

I was up late the next morning, it was gone eleven. Hot yellow light was billowing in through the window. I threw the cover off and stretched, feeling completely awake and deliciously languid. As I did so, my hand came into contact with a folded piece of paper on the pillow next to my head. I squinted at the familiar writing.

Lila
You requested a note next time. I've had to go. I didn't want to wake you, you seemed so peaceful. Jack should be home by the time you read this. I'll see you later.
Alex

He'd actually come into my room. I contemplated that as I surveyed my sprawl across the bed. The sheets were strewn half across the floor. My – rather his – T-shirt had ridden up over my hip on one side exposing a triangle of back and giving a pretty good view of my underwear. I hoped I hadn't been kicking or yelling in my sleep but I didn't remember any more nightmares. I read the note for a third time. He had said I looked peaceful, so hopefully that meant silent. And beatific. Or maybe not. I didn't want to look saintly to him – I wanted to look sexy. The two didn't seem compatible as adjectives. Oh God, I had to switch my head off.

I decided to take a run in an effort to turn down the chatter in my brain. I got up, took a few minutes in the bathroom then threw on a pair of shorts that covered my bruise nicely and a T-shirt. I did the laces up on my running shoes and headed down the stairs, gathering my hair into a ponytail as I went.

'Jack?' I yelled.

My voice echoed back at me. The house was empty, the silence hummed. I guessed he was still at work – he sure worked some crazy hours.

I stepped out into the midday Californian heat, shutting the door behind me, and took off in the direction of the ocean.

My mind stilled itself, drifting into a consciousness that registered only the rhythmic smack of my feet hitting the concrete, the dry rustle of the palm fronds along the street and the distant sounds of lazy traffic. I kept on until the Alex chatter had reduced to background noise and then I looped back to the house.

As I rounded the corner of the street, I pushed into a sprint for the final fifty metres, desperate to reach the shade of the porch and get out of the bleaching sun, which was drilling like a laser through the top of my skull. A dark shape caught my eye on the veranda by the front door. As I came closer I saw it was a girl, crouching awkwardly as she peered through the letter box. She was wearing a short black-and-white dress, her bare legs flashing like pearls in the shadows. What was she doing?

I scanned the street quickly, my feet still driving me forward but my pulse now elevated beyond the high of my run. All around was a perfectly normal suburban scene: children playing in a back-yard, the cicada hiss of water sprinklers. It was ridiculous of me to panic. She was just a girl. I couldn't let two kids with a knife terrorise my thoughts for the rest of my life.

The slap of my feet on the pavement alerted her and she whipped around to face me, poised and alert as a cat with its back arched. When she saw me though, her pose relaxed, her shoulders dropped and a slow smile crept onto her face. I came to a stop at the bottom of the veranda steps.

'Can I help you?' I panted, squinting up at her.

My first impression was of someone who looked like she'd jumped straight out of a manga cartoon. She was drawn with fast, jagged lines, from the sharp slash of her cheekbones to the zigzag shapes of her dress. She was teetering on three-inch platform heels that gave the impression she was balanced on stilts. Her hair was cut sharply into a jet-black bob that followed the angle of her jaw and sheathed her face on either side. She had straight black eyebrows and dark gold eyes fringed by spidery lashes. I wondered if it was Sara but she certainly didn't look like a neuroscientist, that was for sure, more like a Japanese superhero – she was stunning, to the point of not seeming real – and she was eyeing me as though I was a little bird she was deciding whether or not to pounce on.

As I waited for a response of some description, she tilted her head to one side like she could hear a noise from somewhere behind the house and her eyes narrowed. She looked me up and down.

'You live here?' she asked in a voice like glitter.

'Yeah,' I nodded, wiping the sweat away from my brow with the back of my arm. 'Can I help you?'

She danced down the steps, springing towards me so fast I was forced to take a step back.

43

She smiled wide, baring her little white teeth at me. 'I think maybe you can. I was looking for Jack,' she said brightly.

Now it clicked. For all Jack's words about monogamy, clearly he'd been up to something with this girl. Leopards and spots, after all.

I was disappointed and it came through in my voice. 'I'm his sister.'

She seemed delighted to hear it, glad that I wasn't a rival, I guess. I knew the routine and waited. This was the point where girls would switch into suck-up mode and start to ask me what his favourite bands were and what star sign he was.

'Nice to meet you, Jack's sister. I'm Suki.' She held out her hand.

'Hi, I'm Lila,' I said, reaching out my hand to shake hers reflexively. I was stumped still as to who exactly she was and what she had been doing peering through our letter box. That was stalker behaviour. 'So, um, should I tell him you called round?'

She didn't reply and neither did she let go of my hand. Her grip tightened minutely as she stared at me with a weird transfixed look on her face. I was seriously going to bring this up with Jack. Where was he hanging out to pick up girls like this?

Then suddenly she was back in the moment, shaking her head and laughing her dainty little laugh. 'No, don't you worry about that. I doubt he remembers me anyhow.'

She gave me another big smile and skipped off down the road, pausing once to look back at me over her shoulder with an expression of childish glee which lit up her face.

'Weird,' I muttered to myself.

I trudged up the steps to let myself in. The door was still double-locked, so I knew Jack wasn't home. With a sinking stomach I remembered I'd forgotten to set the alarm. Still, Jack didn't need to know. I let myself in, toed off my running shoes and ran up the stairs into the bathroom where I turned on the shower with just a glance in its direction and then whipped back the shower curtain with a second glance before remembering once again that I was supposed to be going cold turkey with this power thing.

As I was drying my hair, I heard the rattle of keys in the front door. Pulling my towel around me, I stepped into the hallway to peer down the stairs.

It was just Jack.

'Hi,' he said as he appeared in the hallway. He looked tired.

'Hi.' I waved back.

'Why's the alarm off?'

I pulled a face. 'Um, because I forgot to set it?'

'Did you go out?' he asked.

'Yeah, I went for a run.'

He glowered at me. 'Don't go out without telling me first, OK? And don't ever forget to set the alarm.'

I stared at him. Why didn't he just stick a tracking device on me and chain me up while he was at it?

'I'll get you a pass to the gym on the base, you can run there.'

He turned to walk into the kitchen and I watched him go, wondering whether he'd ever let up on the overprotective big brother routine. Then I went back into the bathroom and got dressed.

When I joined him downstairs he was busy frying some bacon and eggs.

'So, what happened to you last night? Where'd you disappear to?' I asked, sitting at the table.

'Oh, just a work thing.' He had his back to me as he flipped the bacon with a spatula.

'What kind of work thing? Why did you have to leave in the middle of the night? Or am I not allowed to know? Is it all top secret?'

'Yep, it's so top secret that if I told you, I'd have to kill you. And seeing how you're my sister, that might not be too good for our relationship.'

'Ha ha. Wow, very James Bond.' I paused for a moment. 'Hopefully without the scantily clad women.' I didn't want to imagine any Bond girl moments involving Alex.

'So, who are the bad guys then?'

I was sparking with curiosity, though a big part of me still didn't want to know. Was it drug busting? Gang wars? Vice? I was pretty sure from the way Jack was trying to avoid the question, it wasn't petty crime.

He rested the spatula on the side and turned to face me, recognising I wasn't ready to let this drop. 'No one you need to worry about.' He gave me a look and then turned back to spoon the eggs onto the plates.

'I'm not worried. Why would I need to worry? Didn't you catch them last night?' I raised my eyebrows innocently.

'We caught one of them.' He didn't sound happy, like he'd won the bronze not the gold. He was always so competitive.

One of them – that seemed to suggest there were a finite number. Maybe it was a gang, then. Jack came and sat down opposite me. I looked at his face and tried again to picture him and Alex catching bad guys. The thought of Alex in uniform induced an automatic smile but then I thought about guns and the fighting that had to be involved in stopping bad guys and I had to struggle from having a full-blown panic attack.

'So you had a chat with Alex last night?'

I almost choked on my eggs. My mind stumbled over itself trying to think what Alex might have told him. When had they even spoken?

'Er, yeah, yes. I was thirsty, came down for something to drink. We chatted. You didn't need to get him to come over.'

'I didn't ask him, he offered.'

'Oh.' That surprised me.

'What did you talk about?'

'Oh, you know, nothing really.' I shovelled some eggs in my mouth so I didn't have to talk. He was still looking at me. I swallowed. 'You know – school, London, that sort of thing.'

'Speaking of which – you need to call Dad.'

I grimaced at him. Jack ignored me and pushed his plate aside, got up and left the room. A second later he was back with a phone in his hand.

I took it reluctantly.

He gave me a brief smile. 'Good luck.'

I dialled the number he handed me. The country code was +39. Italy, I thought. Dad was still away, then. Some things never changed. I did the maths – it would be about midnight. Hopefully he'd be sleeping and be too groggy to argue with me much. The phone gave a long beep, pause, another long beep, pause. I wondered how many beeps I should wait for before I could legitimately hang up and still claim I'd tried.

But then there was a click and a 'Hello?'

He didn't sound groggy, the total opposite in fact. I could picture him pacing the room as he spoke.

47

'Hi, Dad.' This was awkward. Jack was watching me so I walked into the hallway. I heard a sigh on the other end of the phone.

'So, Lila, are you going to tell me why you are in California, when you should be in London?'

It wasn't as though I hadn't expected him to ask the question but I still hadn't prepared an answer.

'I – I just needed to see Jack, Dad.'

Nothing.

'I miss him.'

My dad sighed again. 'I know, Lila. But couldn't you just have called him?'

He had a point. 'Yes, probably, but I didn't really think. I wanted to see him.'

'Lila. You need to come home.' Here it came.

'Dad, I like it here.' I could hear the panic in my voice. Oh, what the hell, at least there were several thousand miles between us, might as well lay it all on the line. 'I want to stay.'

'It's the middle of the school term.'

I stepped further away from the open front door so my words wouldn't carry inside. 'It's revision-time. I'm fine missing a couple of weeks. And, actually, I've been thinking—'

'Lila, I want you home.'

'Dad, you're not even there. What am I coming home to?'

He was silent for a long time. I could hear his breathing and the static on the line humming.

'I'm sorry, Lila. It's just work is—'

'I get it, Dad. You don't need to apologise.' I needed him to see that whatever painkiller or distraction his work offered him was what being here with Jack – and with Alex – offered me. 'Can you understand that sometimes it's hard for me, too? Being away from Jack and being on my own so much?'

He was still silent.

'I want to stay, Dad. I want to stay with Jack.' *And with Alex.* 'I don't want to come home.'

As soon as I said the words I realised that I was prepared to fight hard to make it happen. My dad would have to extradite me if he wanted me back home. It was my life and I was sick to death of being told where I was going to live and what was best for me. Of course there was the little detail of money and the fact that until I turned eighteen in October, which was five months away, I was still legally a child, but I'd deal with that later.

'Lila, we're not having this conversation. You're coming home. I'll fly back tonight and meet you off the plane. I don't want you over there.'

'Why?' I was more determined now than angry.

He hesitated. Maybe he was realising for the first time that I was defying him and there was little he could do about it other than flying to San Diego to confront me. But I knew he'd never come back here – the memories of my mother worked better than an electric fence and barbed wire at keeping him out. He'd told me he was never coming back and while Jack regularly accused me of being melodramatic, the same couldn't be said about my dad, so I believed him.

'Lila, there are things you don't understand. Reasons I don't want you there. Even with Jack.'

'Oh my God, please don't tell me you're worried about my safety too?' I almost yelled. It was so frustrating this compulsion he and Jack had of wrapping me up in cotton wool and treating me like I was a china doll. 'How am I any less safe here than living in Brixton?'

'Let me speak to your brother.'

'Why?'

'Because I have to ask him something.'

I took a deep breath. Talking to Jack was not going to help my campaign much. 'OK, I'll put him on.'

I covered the mouthpiece and walked back into the living room where Jack was still sitting. His hands were motionless on the keys of his laptop and I could tell he had been listening.

'He wants to talk to you,' I said.

Jack frowned at me then closed the laptop with a snap. He swivelled in his chair and held out his hand for the phone. I handed it to him, begging him with my eyes. I didn't have much hope. It seemed that Jack and my dad agreed on only one thing and that was on me going home.

I hovered by his chair, trying to hear what my dad was saying, but Jack got up and stood by the bookshelf, turning his back on me.

'No – I told you that already – she is.' He was behaving like a hostile witness. 'She can – OK. Yes, that's fine.'

A pause.

'You know I will. It won't be the end of it, though, you do realise that? You should ask her yourself. I'll put her back on, hang on.'

I took the phone, my hand trembling a little. 'Hey, Dad.'

He got straight to the point. 'What did Jack mean when he said that this wouldn't be the end of it?'

'I told you. I want to stay. I don't want to go back to London. I've been thinking I could transfer over here to finish high school – then go on to college.'

'You are kidding me, right? You can't go to school over there!'

50

I started to protest but he cut me off. 'You can stay for two weeks now' – I started to interrupt but he just talked louder – 'and we'll talk things through when you get back.'

I mulled it over. It wasn't a great compromise. But I didn't have much choice.

'OK. You promise we'll discuss it, though? It's not just a ruse to get me home?'

'No. I promise you we'll discuss it.'

'Thanks, Dad,' I whispered.

Jack was frowning at me, his green eyes darkening.

'I love you.'

'I love you too.'

I hung up and put the receiver back on its base.

'What did he say?' Jack was sitting on the sofa, his arms on his knees, his hands clasped.

'He said I could stay two weeks. And that we'd discuss college.' As I said the words they rattled inside me. Two weeks was no time at all. And then there was another whole year before I could come back. If Dad even let me. He might just want to discuss with me the reasons why he wasn't going to let me step foot in the States ever again.

'Well, then,' Jack said, getting up slowly from the sofa. 'I guess we'd better make some plans for the next couple of weeks. Make sure you have some fun.'

I thought about offering some suggestions, but they all involved Alex and scenarios with just the two of us and I didn't think Jack would be interested in hearing those.

6

'Who's Suki, Jack?'

'What?'

It was a few hours later and I was chopping tomatoes at the kitchen counter. I had a fetching apron on over my dress and had pulled my hair up into a loose ponytail to keep the strands out of my face. Jack had been upstairs getting dressed. When he came back into the kitchen I asked him the question that had been running around my head ever since he'd mentioned Sara was coming over this evening.

'Suki. Who is she?'

'What?' Jack's brows knitted together in confusion.

'Let me refresh your memory: Japanese, beautiful, slightly strange.'

The confusion cleared on Jack's face, only to be replaced by a look that wiped the laughter from my lips.

'Where did you meet her?' he demanded abruptly.

'She was here earlier. When I got back from my run. I caught her peering through the letter box. She was looking for you.'

He took me by the shoulders. 'Why didn't you tell me this earlier?' His voice had a hard edge to it.

'Um, you weren't in the best of moods?'

'Lila, this is important. What did she look like?'

'I just told you. Maybe you should take snapshots of the girls you get together with, Jack, save you the embarrassing memory failure.'

His fingers dug into my shoulder. 'Lila. Answer the question. What did she look like?'

'I told you – Japanese, like a model or something, and she was dressed in very weird clothes for round here.'

'How tall? About this high?' He indicated a height an inch or so shorter than me.

I thought about it, trying to factor in her high heels. 'Yes, I suppose so.'

'Was her hair cut like this?' He held his hand at an angle to his face.

I nodded. So he did know her then.

'Did you talk to her?'

'Yes.'

'What did she say?'

'She asked if I lived here and when she found out I was your sister she looked pretty relieved. That's how I guessed she was someone you had . . . well, you know.'

He didn't seem to hear the last part. 'You told her you were my sister?' He turned away from me, pulling his phone out of his back pocket.

'Who is she?' I was really confused now.

'It's not important.'

I arched an eyebrow. 'So is this something I shouldn't mention to Sara?'

He paused, about to hit a speed-dial button, and turned back to face me. 'Lila, this is not what you think.'

I sensed that he was telling the truth, so stopped myself giving him my usual sceptical look.

'Stay here,' he said, walking into the hallway.

I looked around the kitchen – the sauce on the hob was simmering and the salad lay half chopped on the cutting board. 'I wasn't planning on going anywhere.'

About ten minutes later, Jack walked back in. He came over to where I was laying the table and put his arm around my shoulder.

'Alex will be over in a bit. He's joining us.'

I tried to act nonchalant, even though the butterflies in my stomach had started to riot. 'I'll set another place, then. So did you just call him? About Suki? What's going on?' I asked, as I laid out the extra place.

'It's nothing to worry about. She's just someone we're interested in talking to.'

'Talking to? I watch *CSI*, Jack, I know what that means. What did she do?' Curiosity layered my words. What on earth could a girl not much older than me, in killer heels, have done to interest a Marine unit like Jack's? A thought struck me – maybe it was vice after all.

'Nothing. We just want to talk to her about some information she might have.'

'What information?' I was like a terrier hanging on to his trouser leg but still he shook me off.

'You know I can't tell you.'

'Yeah, I know, "or you'd have to kill me". Really, that's getting so old. You're going to have to think of a better line.' I pressed my lips together. He obviously wasn't going to give anything away. Now my imagination was running wild. Who was she that he was this anxious about her being near the house – and near me? She hadn't looked dangerous – slightly kooky, maybe, but the most

54

dangerous thing about her had been her hair: one flick of that bob would probably have sliced me in two.

The doorbell rang and I jumped.

Jack went to answer it while I waited in the kitchen. I had a sudden thought that it might be Suki, trying her luck again, but just then Alex's voice reached me from the hallway. I pulled my hairband out, tore the apron off over my head, shook out my hair and took several deep breaths. I could hear the two of them murmuring in the hallway, so I tiptoed behind the door to hear better.

'. . . not sure, we need to find out, though, and we can't leave—'

Alex stopped talking suddenly and turned his head in my direction.

'Hi, Lila,' he called.

I stepped out from behind the door, feeling my cheeks blazing. 'Hi.'

Alex was smiling at me but I could see the tension in his eyes. He came into the kitchen.

Jack gestured at his phone. 'I'm just going to call Sara and see where she is.'

As always when I was alone with Alex I felt the atmosphere charge slightly, my body start to fizzle with static. Out of the corner of my eye I watched him move to the fridge and open the door. He had his back to me, scanning the contents, so I turned my head to watch him. He was wearing jeans again, though a darker pair than he'd had on yesterday. They were a good fit. A really good fit. And his grey T-shirt revealed the line of muscle running across his shoulders. Ow. I realised I was biting my bottom lip.

He turned and I looked away, flustered, spattering myself with hot water.

'So, good day?'

I turned back to face him. He was now sitting at the table with a Coke in his hand. It hadn't been a great day but it was definitely getting better.

It was hard to stay coherent when I looked in his eyes so I turned back to the pasta to give it a stir. 'Jack made me call Dad. He probably told you.'

'Yes, he did mention it.'

'They cut a deal over me. I can stay for two weeks.' I risked a peek at him to see if I could gauge his reaction. His face was unreadable. 'I'm not done fighting, Alex. I am coming back.' I said this to the pasta, which was blurring in the pan I was stirring it so fast.

Alex gave a soft laugh. 'You never did give up on anything you wanted.'

If only he knew the truth of that one. I put the wooden spoon down on the side and let the pasta spin to a stop in the pan. Checking that Jack was still out of earshot, I turned to Alex. 'Why is Jack still so angry with Dad?'

He frowned at this slightly, his sky-blue eyes turning cloudy, then let out a big sigh. 'I know it's difficult for you being stuck between them. I've tried to talk to him about it, but you know Jack – he's even more stubborn than you.' He was giving me a half-smile, so I smiled grudgingly back.

'But what's it about?'

'That's not something I can tell you, Lila.'

'Oh for God's sake.' I kept my voice low but the frustration crept in. 'Why won't either of you tell me anything?'

Alex didn't say anything. He stood up, though, and came towards me. For one minuscule moment I thought that he was

56

going to put his arms around me, but he just stretched past me to pick up the wooden spoon I'd left on the side and moved to the hob to give the pasta sauce a stir. It had gone off the boil. I stood waiting for him to finish, waiting for him to answer me.

He turned the gas off and turned to face me again.

'Lila, there are a lot of things we just can't tell you. I know that must be frustrating but you have to trust us.'

I let that sink in for a second. 'You're both asking me to trust you all the time. But neither of you will trust me.'

'Not now,' he said.

I scowled at him but he just shook his head ever so slightly, giving me a warning look. My scowl turned to a frown, but before I could ask why, he had stepped past me.

'Hey, Sara,' he said smoothly.

I turned around.

My first thought was that I could totally see why my brother had fallen for her. Sara was gorgeous, but not in an obvious way. She had waves of dark brown hair falling down below her shoulders and lustrous olive skin. Her eyes were chestnut-coloured and set wide in her face. She smiled at me, and I liked her immediately.

'It's so lovely to meet you,' she said, stepping forward and giving me a hug. 'I've heard so much about you.'

'Oh dear,' I said, looking at Jack, who was standing beside her.

She laughed, reaching for his hand. 'No, no – all good, believe me.'

I wondered how much Jack had shared with her and glanced at Alex. He had gone back to the stove to salvage the remains of the dinner I'd abandoned.

'I think I have you to thank for domesticating Jack,' I said. I really meant taming.

'Ahhh well, it was my pleasure,' Sara said with a smile in Jack's direction. 'But, really, Jack didn't need much help. I had a bit of a hand in the decorating, is all. He was following a pretty minimalist approach to furniture, shall we say, when I first met him. Alex still is – have you seen his place yet?'

'No. Not yet.'

Alex still hadn't said anything and I wondered what he was thinking. Would I ever get a chance to see this minimalist 'bachelor pad' of his? The image in my head changed from silk sheets and mirrored ceilings to a single futon and white walls. Definitely preferable.

Alex put the loaded plates on the table and we took our seats. He pulled out the chair to my right, his leg stretched out so close to me that my own leg jumped like a cricket and smacked into the tabletop, rattling the plates and glasses. I looked down, horrified, and pressed my hand on my thigh to stop it from happening again.

'So, how long are you staying?' Sara asked, as we started to eat.

I looked at Jack. Had he told her? I was sure he would have. But he was paying me no heed, continuing to look at Sara like I'd seen him look at fast cars in his previous incarnation as my teenage brother. Whatever Sara's secret power was, I wanted it so I could use it on Alex.

'Two weeks,' I said. 'For now.'

'Great! Plenty of time to get to know each other, then.'

I didn't miss the look Alex shot across the table at Jack, but I chose to ignore it and to focus instead on Sara. But it was difficult focusing on anything, even my brother's beautiful girlfriend, with

Alex so close. I could sense every subtle shift in his body. My eyes caught the ripple of tendons as his forearm tensed and I knew he was thinking about something. Worrying about something.

'So, what's the plan for your birthday?' Sara said, looking over at him.

'There is no plan.' Alex's head was bent over his plate but he was looking up through his brown lashes at Sara with a faint half-smile on his face. His eyes were flickering with something like amusement.

'Alex, don't try to avoid it, we're doing something to celebrate whether you like it or not,' she said, laughing.

'When is it again?' Jack asked.

'Saturday,' I replied, a little too quickly.

'Why don't we go to Belushi's – get the guys along? Show Lila some Oceanside nightlife,' Sara suggested.

'Some Marine nightlife? I'm sure she'll love that,' Jack said.

'No – I would. I'd like to meet the rest of your unit.'

'Yeah, and I think they'd love to meet you too, Lila.' Sara gave a little laugh.

Jack's head shot up. Sara laughed louder and pinched him before he could say anything.

'So, it's settled then. I'll put the word out.'

Alex threw his hands up in defeat. 'I guess it is. See how she's organising our social lives as well as our domestic ones, Lila?'

'You just need a good woman, Alex,' Sara countered.

He looked down at the table then back up, his blue eyes hooded. 'I probably do,' he said.

Relief rushed through me. No girlfriend! Alex needed a good woman. He'd admitted it himself. I wondered how I might fit the bill. I was neither a woman nor very good.

At some point the conversation died down. The plates were stacked in a pile to the side and our chairs were pushed back from the table. Alex was toying with his glass, talking across the table to Jack about someone from the Unit – their boss, it sounded like. They seemed to like him.

I was talking to Sara about her job. She had been doing her PhD at Berkeley and had been recruited straight out of college into the Unit.

'What was that like?' I asked. 'How did you know you wanted to work with a Marine unit?'

'I didn't. Nothing could have been further from what I intended.'

'So what made you say yes?' I lowered my voice, hoping that I'd get some more substantial information from Sara than I'd got from Jack and Alex.

'I couldn't not say yes when I found out what the job was. It was just too important. And then I met Jack. And now I'm staying until it's over.'

'It's over? Until what's over?'

Sara flushed suddenly and I could tell she'd let on more than she'd meant to.

Jack suddenly stood up. 'Coffee?'

Sara looked up at him. 'Yes, that would be great, thanks.' She glanced back at the table and then stood up herself, throwing her napkin onto her plate. 'Here, let me clear up.'

'I've got it, don't worry,' I said, uncrossing my legs and making a move to clear the dirty dishes.

'No, you and Alex did all the cooking. You two stay put.'

I sat back down, automatically smoothing out my skirt over my leg.

'How's it feeling?'

I looked up. Alex nodded at my leg.

'Still sore. But better. Thanks for the ice yesterday.'

'You probably shouldn't have gone running on it today.' Jack had told him every little detail, then.

'I needed to run.' I didn't tell him why. 'And it was fine,' I added quickly.

'Next time let me come with you, or run at the base.'

I looked at him with raised eyebrows. 'You'd have to walk to keep up with me.'

'I think I could manage. You can set the pace. Why not come out tomorrow to the base? We can go for a run out there – and I can show you the gym.'

I weighed up the pros of being alone with him against the cons of being with him whilst looking like a sweaty mess. My vanity lost out.

'Maybe I could test your ninja skills out while we're at it.'

I gave him a sideways look, trying to work out if he was joking. 'Er, yeah, sure. I wouldn't want to hurt you, though.'

'I'll take the risk.' His eyes were sparkling – I noticed that in the light they had amber flecks in them, and it stunned me that I'd never noticed before.

'Coffee is served.' Sara reached over to place a cafetière and coffee cups on the table. 'I really have to go after this,' she said as she poured it out.

'I'll drive your car back then catch a cab home,' Jack said to Sara. He glanced over at Alex. 'Do you mind staying with Lila?'

'Of course not,' Alex said.

I wanted to protest that I wasn't a child, that I stayed in a bigger, emptier, lonelier house than this one by myself almost every night back in London, that if anyone ever tried anything I'd uncon-sciously be able to protect myself no matter how much I didn't actually mean to and that I really, really wanted to know why they were insisting on this level of babysitting. But I didn't say a word because I knew it meant alone time with Alex.

I really liked Sara but at this point in time I couldn't wait to see the back of her. I hadn't had any coffee but I was jumping like livebait, waiting for them to leave. I could feel my heartbeat accel-erating as I got up to hug her goodbye.

'I'll see you soon.' She squeezed me tighter and whispered in my ear, 'It's really so nice to meet you. You're every bit as gorgeous as they told me.'

They told me . . . I felt the smile splitting my face. They had told her. Did that mean Alex?

'Back in half an hour or so,' said Jack, heading for the door.

'Take your time.' Alex took the words straight out of my mouth.

7

They left and the kitchen was quiet but for Alex clearing the coffee cups and running the taps. I wondered how to begin.

I cleared my throat. 'Sara's lovely.'

'Yeah, she is. Jack's lucky.'

Suddenly I was struck with the thought that maybe I'd been blind. Maybe Alex had feelings for Sara too. No, that couldn't be right. I forced myself to stay calm. What the hell, I was bouncing on adrenaline, why not just be blunt?

'What about you? Why no girlfriend?'

There, it was out there. It was a legitimate question, I figured. I couldn't look at him though when he answered, so I moved to the fridge door and started playing with the magnets, moving one to cover my fourteen-year-old face.

'We're not officially allowed to date.'

My hand froze. That wasn't the answer I'd expected.

'You're what?' I said, turning to him.

He laughed at my reaction. 'We're not officially allowed to date,' he repeated.

'Why?' I asked. Then immediately, 'And how is Jack allowed to, then?'

'It's better, easier, if we don't get close to people. We have to move a lot and – well – it's just difficult when there are people you care about close to what we're close to.'

I shook my head, not understanding. 'But Sara?'

'She works on base. She's one of us and she knows the risks. It's allowable.'

There was a pause while I took this in.

'And you?'

I looked up, 'Me?'

'Yes. No boyfriend?'

He had done it again, always distracting me. 'Um, no. No, I told you. It's not like that in London. Plus I go to an all-girls' school.'

Plus I'm in love with you, I added silently. There had been no boyfriends. There had been kisses, yes, but no boyfriends. A boy who lived around the corner had once asked me to the cinema and I'd said yes, thinking it might distract me from daydreaming about a boy on the other side of the world who didn't have a clue I liked him. But I'd just spent the entire movie fantasising I was with Alex and that it was his arm sneaking around the back of my seat. Which is why, when the guy leaned in to kiss me, I closed my eyes and kissed him back. Then I opened my eyes and came to my senses. He wasn't Alex. Alex would kiss better.

The second kiss had been even worse. My dad had dragged me to a Christmas party at the hospital and a drunk med student had jumped me. It was lucky we'd been surrounded by doctors and nurses because he'd needed three stitches in his eyebrow. Not that I'd flung his glass into his face on purpose. The glass kind of flung itself. It wasn't the reaction either of us had expected.

So, no boyfriends.

Alex dropped the subject. He had just been trying to throw me off the scent and it annoyed me.

'So, tell me, why is Jack not talking to my dad? Why does he hate him so much?'

Alex walked over to where I was standing by the fridge. He moved the magnet from where I'd stuck it over the picture of me and then moved his gaze to the other photo. How on earth had he even seen me do that? I moved my head unwillingly to look at the picture of my mum too.

'That's why, Lila,' he said, then turned his now grey-blue eyes on me.

I could feel my jaw clench. 'That's so absurd. My dad didn't kill my mum, Alex.'

He looked at me for a moment, a fine frown line between his eyes appearing. 'Come on, let's sit down and talk,' he said eventually.

We walked through to the living room, where Alex crossed to the window and drew the curtains, scanning the front yard as he did so. They were both so paranoid. He moved to turn on the light.

I sat on the sofa with my feet curled under me, waiting for Alex to explain. He walked over to the bookcase in the corner and stood in front of a large portrait shot of my mum. When I'd seen it earlier I'd wondered for a moment where Jack had got the picture of me from. She and I were so similar it was amazing. I had never noticed before, because my dad didn't keep many photos of my mum in the house. I had my dad's chin and straight nose, but from this photograph, it was obvious I was my mother's daughter; we had the exact same colour hair and eyes but it was clear that I also had her oval-shaped face and high cheekbones. I had always thought of my mother as beautiful, and the shock of realising I had inherited some of her features genuinely startled me.

'You know, you look just like her,' Alex said, reading my thoughts again.

I got up off the sofa and came to stand next to him. 'I haven't ever really seen it before, but now I do.'

I could feel the heat of Alex's body radiating against my side. I only came up to his shoulder and it was so tempting to lean against him.

'Jack's angry with your dad for not fighting for her. As he sees it, the fight doesn't stop until the people who did it, who killed her, are caught.'

I was speechless for a few seconds and then gathered myself, stammering, 'But that's ridiculous. The police tried. They didn't catch them. What could my dad do?'

Alex was standing only inches away from me. I could feel his breath on my hair. Then he turned and sat down on the sofa, his arms resting across his knees.

'Nothing, Lila. Your father couldn't really do anything. Jack knows that deep down but until he finds the people who killed her he'll keep blaming your dad. He's his scapegoat.'

I didn't say anything as I absorbed this information. Then something dawned on me. 'You said until he finds the people – what do you mean? He's looking for them?'

Panic started to invade me, making my breathing hike. I staggered forward and knelt on the floor in front of Alex. He slowly lifted his eyes from the ground to meet mine.

'Tell me, Alex,' I pleaded. 'What do you mean? Are you looking for them?' If it was true, Jack wasn't doing it by himself. That much I knew.

He stared into my eyes for a few seconds, weighing his answer. But I could see it before he spoke. 'Yes. We're looking for them.'

My voice shook. 'And have you found them?'

I wasn't sure I wanted to hear the answer. It was like walking a tightrope and knowing that whichever way I fell, to the left or the right, the result would still be the same. I'd be paralysed.

'Yes.'

My heart lurched into my mouth. It seemed impossible. Five years had gone by and everyone had given up on getting answers. It felt like there were only three people alive – four if I counted Alex – who even cared any more whether my mother's killers could be found.

'How? How do you know who did it?'

'We got intelligence,' Alex answered simply.

'I don't understand. What intelligence? From where?'

'The Unit. We find things out through the Unit.'

'What things? What does your unit have to do with my mother or her murder? I don't get it.'

'The Unit has nothing to do with it.' Alex paused again, weighing his words carefully. 'Jack and I just managed to access some intelligence through the Unit that helped us to find them.'

'And now you've found them . . . what are you going to do?' It felt like all the blood in my body froze then started to churn.

'We're going to catch them.'

'Why didn't Jack tell me any of this?'

'He doesn't want to bring you into it.' Alex's voice was low and calm, I had the feeling that he was trying to reel me in.

'Why are you OK with telling me then?'

Alex bit his bottom lip, thinking, then after a second or two he said, 'Because I don't like to see you hurt and I think you need to know.'

We stared at each other wordlessly, his gaze holding mine, his focus tight, trying to anticipate my next question.

It was one I hadn't ever thought I'd get an answer to. 'Who are they? Who killed my mum?'

He didn't answer me. Just continued to stare into my eyes. I could feel them tearing up as I fought the memory of my nightmare.

'Isn't it enough to know that we're going to catch them?' he said eventually.

'No,' I threw back at him. 'Not if it means either of you getting hurt in the process.' I looked down at the carpet, fighting back tears.

Alex's hand was suddenly under my chin, lifting it up until I was looking him in the eye once more. He cupped my face in both of his hands, holding me firmly so I couldn't turn away. My breathing stopped.

'We won't get hurt. I promise you.'

I wanted to believe him but a parent being murdered when you're a child makes promises like that redundant.

'You'd better not,' is all I said. The fear in me gently washed away, like a wave pulling back from the shore. I knew it was only temporary, but I could hold it at bay for now.

'Can you try to forgive Jack, now that you understand?'

Alex's hands were still holding my face. I nodded.

The noise of a car pulling up outside interrupted the silence that had opened up between us. Alex was out of the chair in a second, stepping over me to the window.

'It's Jack,' Alex said, looking through the chink he'd made in the curtains. I wondered who else he thought it might have been.

Half a minute later, Jack came through the door.

'Hi,' he said with a broad smile.

'Hi,' we both answered at the same time.

Jack took one look at me, his smile fading, then asked, 'You all right?'

'I'm fine.' I glanced at Alex who was looking at me strangely. 'It's just, I ... I ...' I had just found out he was hunting our mother's killers on some crazy vengeance mission. I was a billion miles away from being fine.

'We were just talking about old times,' Alex cut in.

I tried to pull myself together. 'Yeah, about the time I broke my leg.' It was the first thing that popped into my mind.

'Oh yeah, I remember that.'

Alex flashed me a look that I found hard to read. I wasn't sure if he was wondering whether I was losing it or whether he was wondering why on earth I'd picked that particular memory. But he looked back at Jack and, without skipping a beat, said, 'I gave Lila my coat – do you remember? You complained about it as you thought I'd get hypothermia and you'd have to drag me back on the sledge too.'

'Sounds about right.' Jack grinned

I watched helplessly as Alex reached for his jacket, hanging off the banister.

No, don't go, don't go! I wanted to yell.

'I'll see you tomorrow,' he said. 'Jack, I've told Lila I'll take her for a run tomorrow on the base, hope that's OK with you.'

'Sure, sounds like a good idea.'

We were crowded into the narrow hall. Alex suddenly wrapped his arms around me, pulling me into his chest. I breathed in deeply.

He kissed the top of my head. 'Night, Lila.'

Then he was gone and Jack was setting the alarm by the front door. It beeped a few times and then he went to the back door to make sure it was locked. I stood watching him from the hallway, questions running like water through my mind and threatening to spill over my lips. I couldn't believe he was keeping this all from me. I turned and walked up the stairs before I opened my mouth and it all flooded out.

'Goodnight,' Jack said.

'Yeah, goodnight,' I replied.

8

As soon as my bedroom door shut, I fell onto the bed and curled up on my side, hugging a pillow to my chest. It had been a mistake to ask Alex who they were. Names didn't matter, what they looked like didn't matter. Why they did it – that was the only question that had ever mattered to me. I needed to know why, for what possible reason, anyone could murder a woman in cold blood, in her house, in broad daylight.

And my brother and Alex must know why, because they'd managed to find the people responsible. With information gleaned through their work. It made no sense to me. How could they find out information five years after the event that the police hadn't been able to? How had they even known where to start looking? What the hell did their unit do?

I uncurled myself from the foetal position I was lying in and sat up. This was bad. Really bad. We weren't talking about teenage muggers. We were talking about murderers. I couldn't let them do this. I had to talk Alex and Jack out of it.

'Lila, what's taking so long?'

'Nothing. I'm here.'

I ran down the stairs. Jack was hovering at the bottom, an impatient look on his face. I was running late because I'd only fallen asleep as dawn was breaking. It was ten in the morning now and though I'd had about four hours of sleep, it felt like only five minutes, all of it restless and filled with ugly dreams.

'Let's go,' I said, smiling at him and walking through the door into the garage.

The car, I noticed for the first time, was an Audi. It was sleek and black and glossy and I wondered how he'd paid for it. I stroked along its side. I wasn't that into cars but this one I could covet.

'Nice car,' I said, as I slid into the passenger seat. We were heading to the base. Jack was popping in to do some work – what I wasn't sure – and I was meeting Alex. We were going for a run and I planned to use the time to convince him to walk away, back off, stop looking for my mum's killers. I'd beg and plead if I had to. I'd be more convincing than last night. I wouldn't let his hands or his eyes or his voice distract me. We'd be running. I'd focus on the road.

'It's a company car,' Jack said, turning the key in the ignition.

I refocused on Jack. Cars. We were talking about cars.

'The military pays for seventy-thousand-dollar cars now? Taxpayers must love that.'

'One hundred twenty with the modifications and yes, the taxpayers would be fine if they knew why we needed them.'

'What modifications?' There were no spoilers. No go-faster stripes. Not even any flashing lights.

'It goes a bit faster than the speed dial admits and it has a few hidden features.'

I guessed he wasn't talking about heated seats. I'd have a play with some of the buttons when I was next in it alone.

Jack pressed a button on his key chain. The garage door eased up over our heads, letting in a wash of bright sunlight. The windows were tinted but I still pulled the visor down to shield my eyes. A laminated card fell onto my lap. I turned it over and saw it was a picture of Jack. He looked a little younger, more tired around the eyes, and thinner than he was now. *United States Marine Corps* was indented across the top and then, in finer print underneath, *Stirling Enterprises: Special Operations*.

The thing that caught my eye though was the word before his name: Lieutenant. I was peering at the rest of the information when Jack snatched it from my hand and tucked it into his side pocket as he accelerated out of the driveway. The street was empty but for a few parked cars reflecting the sun like a row of mirrors.

'Lieutenant Jack Loveday?' I said. 'That's good, right? That means you're in charge?'

'Depends on how you look at it. And no, I'm not in charge – there's a whole load of ranks above LT. But I am a team leader.'

'What's Alex, then?'

I wanted to know whether either of them outranked the other. That would be really awkward.

Jack paused. 'He's the same,' he said. 'He runs another team, though. He's Alpha team and I'm in charge of Beta.'

'OK, so it's a little bit more organised than the A-Team, then?'

He laughed at my amateur description. 'Yes, a little. There are three teams in our unit. Each has eight men at any given time.'

'That's small, isn't it? I mean, twenty-four men isn't many.' I was a bloodhound, sniffing for clues.

'Twenty-four men is a lot.'

I nodded as if I understood. 'But it's not that many for dealing with drug traffickers.'

He let out a hoot that I assumed was mirth. 'What on earth made you think we were dealing with drug dealers?'

I crossed that one off my list grudgingly. It had been my best guess. 'Well, you said you needed to be near the border. And then you have this really cool car, which maybe you could use for undercover work.'

He was still laughing at me.

'What's so funny? I could really picture this car belonging to a drug dealer. I've been living in south London, you know. I have first-hand knowledge of the type of cars drug dealers like to drive.'

'First-hand?' A smile was pulling up the corner of his mouth.

'You know what I mean. I put two and two together.'

'And came up with three. Lila, we don't do anything to do with drugs. That's what the FBI and the DEA and the police are for.'

'Oh.' I pondered that as he steered us onto the freeway. 'Well, you won't tell me anything so I have to infer from the clues you give me. Next time I'll guess vice.'

'And you won't just drop it?'

'Maybe. After you tell me I might.'

He shook his head and floored the accelerator. I looked behind, expecting to see tyre marks on the road. Instead I saw a black SUV hugging our bumper. Its windows were tinted and I couldn't see the driver, though I could make out a blurry square shape behind the wheel. Jack veered suddenly into the fast lane but the car stayed on us as though we were towing it.

'Er, I don't mean to be paranoid,' I said, 'but there's a car right up on our bumper.'

'Yes, I know,' Jack said calmly, veering back into the middle lane. I checked over my shoulder, but the SUV was still on our tail. 'It's OK, it's one of ours.'

'What?'

'It's one of ours, it's been tracking us from the house. I had it stationed outside since you told me about Suki paying us a visit.'

'Why are you in and out of the traffic then like you're trying to shake it?'

'I'm just messing with them. Keeping them on their toes.'

'Hang on a second. I don't get it. Why is the car following us? Why isn't it staying at the house if you're trying to catch her?'

'They've been relieved by another car. These guys are following us back to the base.'

I turned to face forward, feeling an icy blast hit me from the air-conditioning vent. I flattened the shutters and concentrated on the fact that we had an armed escort. I wasn't sure whether that made me feel better or worse.

When we took the turn into the base, Jack held up his card to be checked.

'Don't worry,' he said, 'they've already run a background check on you, so you're fine to come inside.'

Oh crap. How much of a background check? I wondered what they had found.

Still, it couldn't have been too bad, because only a few seconds later two Marines carrying enormous guns waved us through the checkpoint.

Minutes later, Jack pulled up outside a modern-looking two-storey building. It was all dark glass and steel, completely incongruous with the other low brick buildings we'd passed. There were no doors, I noticed, just what looked like three giant glass cylinders. As I peered closer, a man in blue uniform appeared suddenly in one of them, looking just like a GI Joe toy in a cellophane box. The window of glass slid open and he stepped out into the sunshine.

Jack was already out of the car, walking around to my side. He opened my door and I stumbled out, my eyes still on the sci-fi building and its test tube doors.

'It's high security,' Jack said, as he saw me staring.

'Yeah, I figured. I've not seen that at Walmart.'

A spitting roar broke the air and we both turned to see a red motorbike pulling to the kerb behind Jack's car. The rider raised a hand in greeting then pulled off his helmet. My mouth dropped open. It was Alex. And he was grinning from ear to ear.

Alex rode a bike? Since when? And, more importantly, when could I have a go on it?

As I stood there, swooning, he threw his leg over the body of the bike, unzipped his jacket and took a bag from out the back pannier, locking the helmet and jacket up in its place. This was the third time I'd seen him in as many days but still I remained staggered and slightly light-headed every time I saw him. The sinewy solidness of his shape made my heart beat like I'd drunk ten espressos washed down with a vat of cola.

He loped over to where we were standing.

'Ready?' he asked me.

'Yes. I just need somewhere to put my bag and then I'm set,' I answered, not able to prise my eyes from his lips.

'OK, give it to me. I need to go change. I'll leave it in the locker room.'

He took my bag and breezed through the sliding glass tube. I watched him disappear into the gloom.

I wandered over to the motorbike and read the word *Triumph* on the side. 'How long has he had it?' I asked Jack.

'No. Over my dead body.' Jack's expression was hard.

'What? I didn't even ask that. I asked how long he's had it!'

'You are not riding this bike. Or any bike, for that matter.'

'Why not?'

'Because, Lila, need I remind you of the number of times you've tried to copy us and have almost died as a result?'

He was talking about the time I almost drowned swimming the three-hundred-and-fifty-metre diameter of the lake in pursuit of them. I rolled my eyes. 'I was nine and I could easily have managed to swim that distance, I just hadn't expected it to be quite so cold.'

'I wasn't even thinking of that. I was thinking of the tree you tried to climb in Grandpa's backyard. And, hmmm, what about the sledging incident we all so fondly remember?' He continued his lecture, giving a big sigh. 'At some point in your life, Lila, you're going to have to realise that you can't keep up.' He was staring at me like a lawyer who's just presented a winning argument.

It needled me just as much now as it had when I was nine. 'And at some point in your life, Jack, you're going to realise that I'm not a child anymore. I might be five years younger than you but that stopped being an issue a while back. Anything you guys can do, I can do too.'

I moved on quickly. 'Anyway, I wasn't even suggesting that I rode the bike on my own. He could give me a ride.'

'Whatever. It's not happening in this lifetime. I told Dad I'd keep you safe and the Alex you know is not the Alex who drives that bike. He's not known to respect the speed limit.'

Now I definitely wanted to go on it. The thought of having a legitimate excuse for wrapping my arms around Alex meant I couldn't have cared less about the danger, even if it meant almost certain death.

'Shouldn't you be warming up?' He was almost as good as Alex at distracting me.

I sighed and started stretching out my hamstrings. 'What are you doing while I'm being put through my paces by Lieutenant Wakeman?'

He smiled at the description of Alex. 'While Lieutenant Wakeman is drilling you, I shall be going through some paperwork and following up on some leads.'

'Suki-shaped leads?'

He tilted his head at me in wan amusement. 'Possibly.'

Alex emerged from the building at that point and I lost my train of thought. He was in running gear this time. Marl grey shorts and a white T-shirt that proved my earlier theory about his body. He was perfect. He knelt to tighten his shoelaces and the sharp pain in my shoulder alerted me to the fact I was still holding my stretch. I let go and started to rock back and forward on my toes, flexing my calf muscles.

'Ready?' he said, looking up at me through his gold-tinged lashes. His eyes were dancing blue.

I took in a big gulp of air and nodded at him.

'Let's go, then.'

Jack waved us off and walked into the building.

9

Alex let me set the pace, which was lucky as my sprint could barely equal his casual jog. I fought the temptation to look at him, keeping my eyes fixed on the far less appealing stretch of shimmering tarmac ahead.

He led me through a couple of back roads lined with identikit houses until we came to a footpath that led along the western perimeter of the base. We didn't talk much. I was mulling over the questions I had for him, wondering where to begin. Once the footpath opened out Alex slowed his pace to run beside me. The ground was uneven and once or twice I careered into him and he had to reach out a hand to steady me.

'Watch your footing,' he said. 'I don't want you breaking your leg out here, I don't have a sledge to pull you back.'

'Hah hah,' I answered, while picturing myself falling over and twisting an ankle just so Alex could carry me back. There was quite a lot I'd suffer to be that close to him.

I dragged my mind back to the task at hand and asked my question. 'Why did they do it?'

Alex kept running, staring straight ahead. I waited. He very slightly lengthened his stride to pull ahead of me. I quickened my pace to keep up.

'If you know who they are, Alex, surely you know why they did it.'

Again, nothing, just the sound of our feet hitting the ground like thunder. I cast a glance towards him. His face was stony. He was pulling ahead again. I reached out and grabbed his arm. I wanted him to slow down. But he actually stopped completely instead. I pulled up sharp, still holding him. He shifted his body to face me and I let go.

'Do you know?' I said.

'Yes.'

'Then tell me,' I demanded.

We were standing facing each other on a narrow track, there were low shrubs in the cracking earth and a few trees here and there but we were out of sight of any buildings or people.

'Lila, what I tell you has to stay between you and me. You have to promise. I'm betraying Jack by telling you. He wouldn't forgive me easily. But I think you deserve to know some of the details. I can't tell you everything, so don't push for more than I'm willing to give up.'

I lifted my chin and watched him carefully, trying to read his expression.

'Come on, let's go over here.' He turned and walked a few metres to a boulder lying just off the path. 'Sit.'

I jogged after him then lowered myself to lean against the rock. He stood over me and I had to tip my neck right back to see him.

'You asked me yesterday who killed your mother. I can't tell you that. But I can tell you why.'

I sucked in a breath. Alex paused, concern flickering across his face. I nodded at him to go on. He hesitated a fraction of a second, then said, 'Your mother was killed because of what she knew.'

I stared at him. We were both motionless. 'I don't understand – what did she know?'

80

Alex took a breath. 'You know what your mother did for a job?'

'Yes, of course.' Why was he asking me this? 'She worked as an adviser.'

'For who?'

'For some old senator.'

'Actually, she did more than just that.'

'Sorry?'

'Yes, she was a political adviser. But she was also investigating something on behalf of homeland security.'

'What – why? Why would she be doing that? My mum didn't know anything about security. She was an adviser on political issues – she worked on environmental stuff.'

'I can't give you details. The information's highly classified.'

I ground my teeth. 'Just tell me what you can, then.'

Alex frowned at me, his eyes pleading for leniency.

'She discovered something about a group of people –' I could see he was struggling to censor the information. 'She discovered something that could have had enormous ramifications for the government. Not just for government but for the public too, for everybody.'

Now it was my turn to frown at him. 'You sound like the script of a bad B movie.'

Alex bit his bottom lip. 'I realise how this must sound.'

I raised my eyebrows at him a little more.

'Lila, just listen and then make judgements.'

I tried to lose the sceptical face.

'Your mum discovered something. And it was enough to cause the people she was about to. . . expose, shall we say . . . to kill her.'

It took a minute for the words to sink in. I played with them, trying to move them around like an anagram in my head, my mind riffing on the same checklist as before – drugs, corruption, organised crime – but making no sense. What could she possibly have discovered? It all sounded so absurd.

'What did she discover?' I asked.

'I can't tell you.'

If I heard him say that one more time I thought I might start unconsciously throwing things – not that there was anything much to throw out here, unless I tried uprooting a tree. Then the rational part of my brain suddenly burst into action, and my heart reacted by stuttering wildly.

'But, Alex, if Mum discovered something and was killed because of it . . .' I almost couldn't finish the sentence, '. . . what about you and Jack? If you know it too – what about you?'

He gave me a half-smile that faded into nothing. 'You don't need to worry about us, Lila.'

I stared at him, wondering whether he realised how crazy he sounded.

'Have you told the police? Shouldn't you be telling someone? The FBI, maybe? So they can do something?' I wasn't leaning on the boulder anymore, I was standing looking up at him, shouting. 'If you know who killed her and you know why – why aren't you involving them? Why aren't you leaving it to the professionals?'

Alex was looking at me and his half-smile returned again. I didn't get it.

'Lila, what do you think we are?'

I was confused.

'Jack and I are professionals. We're more highly trained than the police and the feds. We have better equipment and more intelligence than any other government body. We're using all that to help us find your mum's killers.'

82

Now I had stepped into the realm of disbelief. But just as I was about to open my mouth to say something sarcastic, a shadow fell across his face and I saw him differently, as a stranger might. Not as the Alex from my childhood but as Lieutenant Wakeman. It was like those pictures of dots that you stare at until the hidden image leaps out at you. He was actually intimidating to me all of a sudden – like he'd just grown another six inches.

'Is that why you joined up in the first place?' It was all falling into place.

'Yes.'

Suddenly Jack's decision to drop out of university became clear.

'But I still don't understand what your job has to do with any of this.'

He looked uncomfortable, like I'd caught him out. 'We're using intelligence, like I told you.'

'Yes, so you keep saying, but I still don't understand why.' My temper was pricking at the edges of my voice.

Alex looked away, staring off towards the ocean.

I tried a different tack. 'That girl, Suki, who is she?'

'She's someone we want to talk to.' His face was still unreadable.

'Why? Is she anything to do with them?' My mind was frantic. Who knew Suki was such a fountain of knowledge? She hadn't looked like she even knew her times tables.

Alex shook his head, 'No. She just might be able to help us with our enquiries.'

I knew that was a line detectives used when they thought someone was guilty as sin but didn't have enough evidence to prove it. Yet.

'Could you be any more cryptic?'

'Yes.' He was being serious.

'What can I say to make you change your minds about this vengeance mission you're on? Tell me and I'll say it.'

He looked at me a little sadly. 'I'm sorry, Lila. We're not going to stop. It's about more than just your mum now. That was the reason we joined up. We hoped it would lead us to finding her murderers. And it almost has. We're very close.' He looked at me, his eyes burning, the amber in them flaming. 'But, Lila, it's more than that now. We're fighting something bigger than them, and we'll keep fighting even when we've caught them.'

I stayed silent. The processing filter part of my brain was on overload. Nothing more could go in. What were they fighting? And why? It was all becoming so unreal I wondered for half a second if perhaps I was still kneeling on a south London street in some catatonic state and was imagining all of this.

'Come on, I've told you all I'm going to tell you. Let's get back.' Alex reached out a hand and the gentle pressure of his palm in mine was a reality check. Energy leaping around like that could only be in a real world, not an imaginary one.

'But . . .' I tried to pull two coherent words together but my vocabulary was melting at the sight of a strip of lean, tanned torso that Alex was displaying as he stretched his arms up over his head. Another pang of fear, mingled with desire, tornadoed my insides.

'No, Lila. I brought you on this run because I knew you were going to ask me questions and I wanted you to ask them away from Jack. But I've told you everything I can on the subject and you've just got to trust me now.'

Of course I trusted him. I trusted him with my life. But there was so much going on that he wasn't telling me about. Bad stuff, I was pretty sure. And I had completely and utterly failed to change his mind about getting involved. This so wasn't working out as I'd planned.

Neither of us spoke, and Alex set off again, staring calmly ahead. We hit the tarmac and ran down the centre of the road. I was barely aware of the route we were taking or the traffic passing us by. I was too busy obsessing over the fact that my brother and Alex were throwing themselves into danger like it was a game. Like the consequences weren't deadly. When in fact they were.

I stumbled and fell, crying out as I hit the tarmac, palms forward to break my fall. I stayed where I was, breathing hard, grit breaking the skin of my hands. The sticky black tar granules of the road filled my vision. Alex's hands on my shoulders brought me to, and he pulled me easily up off my knees then turned my hands over. I realised he was talking to me and I shook my head, staring blankly at his moving lips.

'Are you OK? Let me see.' He brushed the dirt away gently, revealing some scrapes on the heels of my hands. I winced at the sting, like sticking my hands in nettles. He held on tight to my wrists so I couldn't pull away.

'You OK?' he said again.

'Yes.' I couldn't look at him.

'You sure?' he asked, not letting go of my wrists. The pressure was firm but I liked it, wanted him to hold me even tighter. It made me feel connected to him, anchored again.

I looked up at him. The expression on his face was so concerned that I knew he wasn't asking me about my hands.

'I don't want you to do this,' I suddenly blurted out.

'I know,' he said. I waited for the bit where he said, *OK, we won't, then, we'll let the cops deal with it.* But it didn't come. A bird tweeted to fill the silence where his words should have been.

'Lila,' Alex's voice was soft, 'I told you yesterday, nothing bad is going to happen to us.'

'Promise me.'

His eyes clouded and a muscle in his jaw contracted. 'I promise you. Now come on, we need to clean you up.'

I brushed down my knees, which were sticky with scrapes, and sighed. My body was getting such a bashing at the moment. I eased into a jogging pace, the skin of my knees screaming in protest as it stretched and contracted until it just became one constant sting. It was only a few hundred metres back to the sci-fi building.

A group of men were out the front. From this distance, I couldn't really tell them apart. They were all over six feet tall, with broad shoulders, and solid, tree-trunk legs. They were dressed identically, in black combat trousers, and T-shirts that clung tightly to well-developed six packs. I gave Alex a fleeting look – with his short crew cut and similar physique he should have blended with the crowd, but there was something about him that made him stand out. He was less square, more lean and graceful, and, to my totally unbiased eye, there was just no competition.

The group broke apart as we came near, and turned to face us. I slowed up, suddenly self-conscious of being the only girl, and looking such a wringing, filthy mess. Alex looked back over his shoulder, seeming to sense my reticence, then slowed his pace too and said, 'Don't worry, they're just some guys from the Unit, I'll introduce you.'

I looked at him warily and prepared myself. After a few more metres, we pulled up. I was panting and stood a little behind Alex, in his shadow, trying to brush the dirt off my shorts and wipe my hair out of my face. Then Alex turned, and I was suddenly in the centre of a circle being given the once-over. I felt myself cringe.

'Well, I see you got all the looks in the Loveday family. Poor Jack. No wonder he's been hiding you away on the other side of the world.' The others started to laugh and I glanced at Alex. He was laughing too.

Another man, with arms so big and meaty that they hung out over his sides like he was wearing a lifesaver jacket, reached out a slab of a hand. 'Nice to meet you. I'm Nick, I'm in your brother's team.'

I shook his hand, feeling my stinging palm squashed within his paw. The other guys followed suit, bombarding me with a phalanx of arms and hands to shake.

'Hi, nice to meet you,' I said to each one, noticing how most were a lot older than Alex, at least in their late twenties or early thirties. I wondered how that worked when he was in charge of them.

There was only one who was younger – he looked about my age. I thought he'd said his name was Jonas. Now he took a step forward, chucking me a dazzling grin. 'You coming to Alex's party?'

He had quick brown eyes and an easy grin. He was the least beefy of them all and slightly less intimidating.

'Yes, I'll be there,' I said, looking again at Alex.

He was now standing a few paces back from the group, observing things. He had a faint smile playing at the corner of his mouth but his eyes had set into blue ice.

Jonas grinned at me like a jack-in-the-box. 'Great. We'll see you there.' Another man from his unit got him in a headlock and dragged him away.

I felt my face redden. I really wanted Alex to rescue me from this – I felt like I was on display at Ripley's Museum of Believe It or Not. He must have seen the expression on my face became he stepped forward into the group again. This time I felt the change in the mood, the men's playfulness dropping a few notches as they quietened and moved closer, as though Alex was drawing them in. He hadn't even said anything.

'Right, I've got to get this girl cleaned up,' he said now.

There were no innuendos from any of the men, though I was acutely alert to them. Alex put his arm around my shoulder and started to turn away towards the doors.

'See you around, boys,' he said, steering me towards the building.

Just at that moment the cylinder doors whooshed open and a woman, as whippet thin and airbrushed as a model on a runway, strode out into the sunlight. The men behind me fell silent, a hush of awe descending over them. I felt myself shrink inwards as she came towards us.

Then I heard Alex say, 'Hi, Rachel,' and something in me snapped in two. I think it was the last vestiges of hope that he might one day look at me as anything more than Jack's sister.

A wide and dazzling smile split the woman's perfectly symmetrical face. She had high cheekbones and almond-shaped eyes that were almost as blue as Alex's. She sashayed over to him, like a heat-seeking missile programmed with a new target. I almost expected her to swing one of her endless legs over his hip and wrap herself around him like ivy. She was wearing a grey two-piece skirt suit, which clung to her body, nipping in at her tiny waist. As she came close to Alex I saw she was almost as tall as him, though at least three and half inches of this was made up of steel-tipped stiletto heels.

I felt my heart cave in. She was so impossibly beautiful that Alex had completely forgotten I existed.

'Why, hello, Alex,' Rachel said, flicking her straight blonde hair over her shoulder. Her voice was husky, with a hint of the South.

I suddenly became very aware of how I looked. My clothes were like sticking plasters against my skin and I longed to rip them off and get into something clean, if only so I didn't feel so much like a sewer rat standing next to an arctic fox.

'What are you doing here?' she drawled, her long vowels tripping over themselves to keep up. Her lips were glazed like morello cherries.

'Just been for a run,' he said.

Remembering I was there, Alex turned suddenly to look for me, seeming surprised that I was standing so close behind him. He moved out the way and Rachel's gaze fell on me like a searchlight beam.

'This is Lila,' he said, 'Jack's little sister.'

Little? It felt like he had given me a paper cut down the length of my body.

Rachel's gaze flicked over me, from my filthy trainers to my sweat-streaked, sun-baked face. For a brief moment she looked like she had just broken a tooth, but then she threw me a huge pearly-white smile and held out one manicured hand. 'How lovely to meet you. Jack's told me so much about you.'

I really wanted to say that he hadn't told me anything about her, but I bit it back and politely shook her hand.

'Rachel works with the Unit,' Alex explained, smiling. 'She's our boss.'

I did a double take. She was the boss? She got to order Alex around? The reasons for hating her were piling up.

Rachel discarded me with a subtle turn of her shoulder and focused her gaze back on Alex, fixing him with her enormous cornflower-blue eyes. I looked back and forth between them, half a foot shorter than them both, feeling like a child being ignored by its parents.

I must have sighed, or maybe he heard the noise of my heart blowing up, because suddenly Alex glanced at me. 'I've got to get Lila inside,' he said and made to move off. 'I'll see you later, Rachel.'

Later? Another paper cut. This time it left an open wound.

'Bye, Alex,' she said. 'I'll call you. Enjoy your babysitting.'

It took a second before the comment sank in and when it did I drew in a sharp breath. My cheeks started to flare. I refused to turn back to look at her but I risked a glance up at Alex and caught the tail end of a frown. His mouth was set in a line. He threw me a glance too, no doubt to check whether I had picked up on the comment. When he saw me looking he shook his head dismissively as if to say *Just ignore it*.

Then two things happened almost simultaneously. A screaming, thunderous, splitting noise ripped through the sky. It seemed to flatten everything to the ground with its vibrations. And then, with bewildered shock, I realised that it wasn't the noise flattening me, it was Alex's weight pressing me hard into the ground. I was on my knees and Alex was bent over me, pinning me to the floor, his arms braced against my head and his chest angled against my side. I couldn't work out why at first, my only thought that he had been hurt, but just as I started to panic and push against him, Alex uncoiled and stood up, pulling me harshly up with him.

The noise was still piercing my eardrums, making my brain feel

90

like it was being spliced in two, and everything seemed to have slowed down. I could see the men from the Unit running in different directions. It was like watching them through strobe lights. Some had their guns in their hands and some were reaching to unholster theirs. It took me several seconds to put two and two together. The noise, the panic, the guns – someone was attacking them. *Us*, I realised with shock.

I was being jerked forcefully away from the noise, which was coming from the building. Alex's grip was a steel tourniquet around my arm and he was holding me flush to his side. He was half running and I was stumbling and tripping into him as he yanked me towards his bike, the pain in my head making it all but impossible to put one foot in front of the other.

I felt myself lifted up into the air and then somehow I was on the back of the bike. My legs automatically gripped the leather seat to stop myself from sliding off, but then Alex was in front of me, his back a wall against my face. He kicked up the stand and fired it up. As I felt the thrum of the engine underneath us, Alex reached back with his arm and grabbed my hand, pulling it around him and pressing it hard against his waist.

'Hold on,' he said.

10

It wasn't quite what I'd had in mind when I expressed a desire to get a ride on Alex's bike. I was too terrified to take anything in, least of all his proximity. I closed my eyes and let the roar of the bike overtake the sound of the siren, which quickly faded into the distance. The wind was whipping my hair round my face but I couldn't unlock my hands from around Alex's body to push it back. The pain in my head receded with the decibel level, until it was just a faint vibration against my skull.

After what seemed like only a few minutes I felt the bike slow. It turned a few corners and then came to a gentle, rolling stop. I prised my eyes open. We were in front of Jack's house already. I felt Alex's warm hand on top of mine and realised that I had him in a vice-like grip. My fingers were clasped so tightly together it took the gentle pressure of his thumb to unhook them. He slowly shifted around so he could see me.

'Are you OK?'

'I think so.'

He climbed off the bike. I wasn't sure how to get down, so tightly was I glued to the seat. Alex lifted me off as though I was an infant, which I now realised was exactly how he saw me. Rachel's words still smarted in my ears.

'What just happened?' I asked.

'I'm not sure. It was an alarm. But I have no idea what triggered it.'

'So why the great escape?'

'Because when an alarm sounds, it's usually a good idea to run.'

I frowned at him, then remembered Jack. 'Where's Jack? Will he be all right?'

'He'll be fine.'

But he was already pulling out his phone. He hit the speed dial and then was speaking to the other person, Jack I presumed, as his first words were, 'Yes, she's with me. She's fine. Yes . . . On the bike . . . Yeah. Definitely the last time.'

He looked up suddenly and scanned the street. I followed his gaze to the black SUV sitting on the kerb with its windows up. 'Yes, they're here. I'll let them know. Call me when you have something. I'll stay till you're back.'

He hung up. 'Stay here,' he said.

So he really was babysitting me – Rachel had been right. And now he was ordering me around like a child. My nostrils flared but Alex didn't notice, he was already striding towards the car. Maybe I was just a burden to them. Both he and Jack had made it clear that they didn't really want me here. But I didn't need this level of looking after. It made me want to scream.

The window of the car whirred down and I saw Alex bend his blond head to speak to the driver.

I looked around me and thought about it for one second. Then I stood up and walked to the front door, pulling out my key. I unlocked the door and went inside. As I tapped in the security code on the alarm, Alex ran up the steps and into the house.

'I told you to wait for me.'

'I know.'

'So next time wait for me.' His eyes were granite-hard.

I glared at him. 'I'm not a child, Alex. You can't tell me what to do.'

He ignored me, pushing past into the kitchen. He shoved the door, letting it fly into the wall, and then crossed quickly to the back door, checking it. I rolled my eyes at the dramatics and walked up the stairs towards the shower. I was hot, angry and tired – but most of all I was heartbroken. A shower wasn't going to fix that.

The bathroom door slammed behind me and the shower started running before I realised what I was doing. I sank to my knees in disgust at myself. I couldn't even manage to keep control of my ability. This day couldn't get much worse. I stripped off my jogging gear and climbed into the shower, drenching myself and letting the grime run off me. Rachel's perfect glistening smile and seductively half-closed eyes appeared in my head. *Enjoy your babysitting*. I was still fuming when I got out. I wiped the mirror with the back of my arm and looked at myself. I was no competition for Rachel. She was a perfect match for Alex. They had looked like a golden couple standing next to each other. And she had another major advantage that I lacked – he was allowed to date her.

A knock on the door interrupted my musings.

'Are you OK in there?' Alex sounded tense.

'Fine.'

I could have sworn the doorknob turned a fraction of an inch.

I got up before he could come in to check and yanked open the door. Alex was leaning against the frame. He looked tired, stress etched around his mouth. Babysitting me must be such a chore.

'How are your hands and knees?'

I had forgotten all about them when Rachel had appeared. Now I turned my palms over and saw the blanched skin flapping free in places.

'OK,' I said, walking straight past him to my room and closing the door behind me. He didn't follow. I wondered if he would just hand over his duty to one of the 'guards' outside. I sank onto the bed, pulling the towel around me, and felt tears well up out of nowhere.

The hairbrush on top of the dresser began to move, pretty much of its own accord. I wasn't even aware that I was doing it until it was hovering in mid-air by my head. By then it was too late. It hurtled through the window like a missile. The smash, when it came, threw me sideways off the bed, glass splintering at my feet.

I stood for one moment, frozen, waiting for Alex's footsteps on the stairs and for him to burst angrily in on me – but nothing happened. I tiptoed to the door and eased it open. I could hear Alex's voice but it was muffled. He was pacing the front veranda talking on his phone. Probably to Rachel. Organising a date no doubt, for when he was done with babysitting.

I turned back into the room. This was my chance. I threw on a clean pair of shorts and a T-shirt, and with one backwards glance at the football-sized hole in the window, I was out of there.

I took the stairs as quickly as I could, jumping the step that squeaked the loudest. Then I snuck through to the kitchen, unlocked the back door, stepped out and closed it gently behind me. I put my flip-flops on as I went down the steps and ran to the bottom of the garden. I wasn't sure what lay behind the house, probably another garden, but I planned to hop the fence and cut through to the road behind.

I didn't know where I was headed but the ocean seemed as good a place as any. At the fence, I peered back towards the house but there was no movement, no yelling, just a great big hole in the upstairs window. I grabbed a tree branch and hoisted myself up until I was perched on top of the fence and then I jumped down, landing in a crouch in the garden of a house almost identical to Jack's. I ran quickly to the side of the house and edged my way down the alley alongside it, lined with rubbish bins. I peered around the house's veranda on the lookout for any black cars with tinted windows but there were none, so I began walking west-wards fast, towards Harbour Beach.

By the time I made it to the main street, I was beginning to relax. There was no sign of Alex roaring around the bend on his bike to come and find me and bring me back. The bright green light of a Seven-Eleven over the way beckoned, so I crossed over and slipped inside the cool of the store, making my way down a skinny aisle towards the drinks.

I grabbed a can of Sprite and headed to the counter to pay. A grungy-looking old man was standing in the middle of the narrow aisle, checking out the dried noodle selection. I hovered awkwardly, hoping he would notice me and move out of the way, but he kept standing there muttering to himself.

I cleared my throat, hoping he'd take the hint, but he was engrossed in studying the ingredients list on the back of his noodle pack.

My hand was going numb holding the cold Sprite. I took a step forward.

'Excuse me,' I said, as I started to edge past the old guy, sucking in my stomach and flattening myself against the shelf as I inched by.

He suddenly looked up from his conversation with the noodle packet and fixed me with a dead stare. My earlier impression had been off; he wasn't old, perhaps only in his early forties. He was dark-skinned with a dusty grey film about him. There were concrete shadows beneath his eyes and heavy creases around his mouth.

'I need your help,' he whispered, his voice scratchy as sandpaper.

My eyes flitted to the round mirror angled in the right-hand corner of the shop. The shopkeeper reflected back at me was oblivious, I could see the top of his bald head serving another customer. I really didn't need to be helping out a crazy person conflicted over his choice of pot noodle.

'Er . . . I'm not sure I'm the right person,' I told him.

'Yes, yes, you are,' he said.

The man's eyes were fevered and his breath in my face was smoke-hazed. I flinched slightly and edged further past him. I just wanted to pay for my can of Sprite and get out of here. The man twisted, blocking my path with his body, and I felt myself take a step backwards, the hairs rising on the nape of my neck. Something wasn't right. He took a step towards me, his hand outstretched as though he was going to grab me, but then he paused, his head jerking up, looking at something over my shoulder. Before I could turn to follow his gaze he was off, shuffling towards the fire exit at the rear of the store, dropping his noodle packet on the floor as he went.

I turned to the front door, seeing a red shape through the stickered glass. Alex's bike. My head fell back against the shelf. I couldn't believe I hadn't even been able to make it to the beach. Busted in a Seven-Eleven. God they were well trained. I put the can back and then scuffed my way over to the door.

On the kerb directly in front of me was Alex, leaning against his motorbike, his legs stretched out across the pavement and his arms crossed against his chest. His eyebrows were raised. He didn't say anything. Just handed me a helmet. I took it and, sighing, put it on. Alex took a step forward to help me with the strap under my chin.

'Get on,' he said and I clambered on behind him.

11

As Alex accelerated off down the street, I flattened my body against his, gripping tightly around his waist. Ouch. Something was pressing against my stomach It had the pressure and bulk of ridged metal and I reared back an inch as I realised it was a gun. I was sure Alex hadn't been carrying a gun earlier – I would have felt it – so where had he got this one from? And, more worryingly, why had he felt it necessary to bring a gun when chasing after me? What was he planning to do – shoot me if I resisted?

We slowed up outside a modern apartment block that shone in the sunlight and took a sharp turn into an underground car park. Alex tapped in a code to open the barrier and then we were out of the glaring afternoon sun and into the dank gloom beneath the building. He curved the bike around a few pillars and pulled up by a lift. He got off first, but I jumped down before he could help me. He stood and watched for a few seconds while I battled with the helmet then stepped forward to help me, biting back a smile.

A question was forming on my lips and he anticipated it. 'My place,' he said simply.

I nodded. Of course, it was just the kind of place I'd imagined.

'Come on,' he said, getting into the lift and pressing the button for the sixth floor.

*   *   *

Sara had been right in her description. Alex's apartment was minimalist to the extreme. The floors were stripped pale wood. The walls were white with nothing on them. It had the echoey, freshly painted feel of a brand new apartment, right before the owners move in.

Alex walked past me, beckoning me to follow him into the living room. This was a little bit better. There was a soft black sofa, a huge flat-screen television, a cream pile rug and a glass coffee table. But my eyes were drawn to the wall facing me.

It was made up entirely of glass, with floor-to-ceiling windows. There was an amazing view of Harbour Beach and the pier. I crossed over to look and gazed down at the little people scurrying on the street below, blading along the boardwalk and laid out on the beach like rows of boiled sweets. Out of the corner of my eye I noticed a black SUV parked on the pavement opposite the main entrance. I wasn't totally sure it was the same one that had been parked outside Jack's house but it looked similar and I wondered what it was doing here, rather than keeping a lookout for Suki back at Jack's.

'I'm going to take a quick shower,' Alex said.

I turned. He was watching me carefully. 'Please don't run off while I'm having it.' The warning was implicit.

I nodded. 'I won't.'

He gave me a fleeting smile and then turned, a little wearily it seemed, towards the hallway again. I watched as he opened a door and disappeared from view. A minute later I heard the noise of a shower running. I tried not to let my imagination run off into the bathroom with him.

I hesitated for a minute and then tiptoed into the hallway, pausing in front of the open door. There was a double futon on the floor. Built-in mirrored wardrobes lined the wall opposite the bed. The only other items in the room were a stack of books skyscrapering the bed, and an alarm clock. The bathroom was en-suite and the door stood open, puffs of steam escaping. I guessed Alex was keeping both doors open so he could hear if I attempted another escape, so I tiptoed backwards into the living room and crossed over again to look out at the view.

The black car was still sitting against the kerb and, as I stood there trying to make out the number plate, the passenger door opened and a man in black combats and a black T-shirt got out. He was wearing sunglasses and he scanned the street back and forth, before throwing a glance up at the apartment. I stepped back quickly from the window, my leg banging into the glass table.

And everything suddenly became clear. The men in the black cars weren't guarding the house, they were guarding me. Otherwise why would they be here at Alex's place too? Everything fell into place and I laughed under my breath. Alex wasn't babysitting me. He was protecting me.

I thought about it some more: Jack wanting to pack me off home as soon as possible; Alex suggesting I run at the base; the two of them obsessing over alarms and security; Alex's secret service style take on babysitting. I felt such huge relief that it wasn't me, after all – that it wasn't because he saw me as a child.

Then I realised, with a bone-numbing sense of disquiet, that if they were protecting me, it had to be from something. Something so bad I required round-the-clock security from a team of highly trained men.

Suki? I laughed again and shook my head. Why would a team of men be needed to keep Suki away? Even I could probably manage to protect myself from her. It wasn't as if she could run very fast in those platform heels. I wouldn't even need to use my ability.

The shower turned off as I sat there reaching back over the last day or so and trying to remember any other suspicious moments.

A few minutes later, Alex wandered through in a clean pair of shorts and bare feet, water still trickling down his neck from his bristling hair. My stomach did a one-eighty flip as I caught sight of the ridges of muscle running down his torso. Then he pulled on a T-shirt and I sighed audibly.

'Give me your hands,' Alex said, sitting down next to me.

'What?'

'Give me your hands,' he said again.

I offered them to him tentatively, my palms facing down, and he took them in one of his. My heart started galloping at his touch. He flipped my hands over and started to dab some antiseptic cream onto the scrapes I'd forgotten all about. I flinched at the sting.

'So, are you going to tell me why you ran off like that?' he said.

I stared at my palms and his fingers rubbing in the cream and, after about ten seconds of trying to get my thoughts in order, I lifted my face to meet his eyes.

'Are you going to tell me why you followed me?'

'Because I was worried about you.' He frowned ever so slightly, as though that should have been obvious. He let go of my hands and they fell into my lap.

'What did Rachel mean when she said "enjoy your babysitting"?' I asked coolly, observing his reaction.

'What do you think she meant?' he asked. He looked like he was laughing at me and his tone suggested that I was being deliberately obtuse.

102

'Listen, Lila, I'm not babysitting you. For one, you don't need a babysitter, and two, I actually like spending time with you and Jack's not paying me, so it doesn't qualify.'

I punched him lightly on the arm and he deflected it with a laugh.

'I believe you,' I said. 'I don't think you're babysitting me.'

Alex gave me a relieved smile, his defences relaxing.

'I think you're guarding me.'

'What?' he said, the smile vanishing, but then he threw back his head and laughed.

I had seen the change in his eyes, though – the way they had frozen and a shield had come down.

I persevered. 'You're not a babysitter, you're a bodyguard.'

He stopped laughing. 'You're right.'

Now it was my turn to be surprised. He'd caved in so easily.

'Of course we're guarding you. The guys in the Unit would be all over you like lice if we gave them half a chance. Jack would kill them if he knew the way half of them were looking at you this afternoon.'

I'd been right after all. He was trying to cover it up. I didn't feel happy to be right though. Instead, I felt a slow, creeping fear. 'No, that's not what I meant.' I said, trying to stay cool. 'You're protecting me from something.'

'Like I said, the only thing we're protecting you from is the less than noble intentions of a whole lot of testosterone-charged men.'

I shook my head at him, frustrated. 'No. I'm not blind, Alex, I can figure things out. The car isn't guarding the house, it's guarding me. That's why it's outside right now.' I saw surprise flare in his eyes then disappear. 'You didn't want me to go for a run on the street, you insisted I come to the base. Neither of you will leave me alone for a minute. Jack's acting weird about me staying and you're sticking to me like glue.'

As I said this, I wished the reality was quite as literal as that. But Alex was shaking his head at me, so I continued. 'I will find out, Alex. Even if it means sneaking off on my own again.'

This last bit was a bluff. There was no way I was letting him or Jack out of my sight again until whatever was going on was not going on anymore. But it got the reaction I was hoping for. His face darkened and his eyes, vivid ice blue now, cut into me. He leaned forward across the sofa and took hold of my wrist, holding it tight, his thumbs pressing into my pulse points.

'You cannot sneak off. You can't leave my sight.'

This was good. Great, in fact. I had been right. I wasn't sure about what exactly, though it clearly involved something quite dangerous, with me as the possible target. But there was no panic at the news, only a surge of excitement at the thought of not leaving Alex's side and relief that he wasn't thinking of it as babysitting – not exactly.

'Lila. Do you hear me?' He was shaking me now and I focused back on him. His face was torn, the familiar frown line back in place. I wanted to reach out and smudge it away with my index finger.

'Yes,' I said. 'Yes, I hear you.' The seriousness in his voice pierced my buzz. Clearly some part of my brain that wasn't overtaken by Alex's presence was trying to have its say; maybe it was the survival part.

Alex let go of me then and stood up. 'Look I need to call Jack and tell him where we are and' – he looked irritated – 'I need to tell him what I'm about to do.' When he walked out into the hallway, I felt something pulling inside my chest, like a stretching elastic band.

About five minutes later, he came back into the living room. His expression was so serious, I flinched slightly at what might be coming. He crossed to the sofa and sat down on the edge, leaning forward and staring out of the window. He put his phone down on the table and then turned to face me.

'OK,' he said. 'I've told Jack what I'm about to tell you.' He paused as though replaying the conversation in his head. A little frown rippled over his forehead then disappeared.

I was still hugging my knees. The pain in my chest had eased from the minute Alex sat back down near to me, but I was still rigid with tension.

'He wasn't too happy but I convinced him it was our only option if we wanted to keep you . . .'

I thought he was going to say 'safe', but he said, 'out of trouble', and he looked up at me through his lashes. He wasn't going to let me forget about running out on him.

I remained still, my eyes locked onto his.

'You know we caught someone the other day? That first night you were here? Well, Jack's team did.'

I nodded.

'So it seems we've stirred up a hornets' nest. We hadn't thought anything of it until you told us about Suki sniffing around the house. Then we wondered what they were up to, whether they might be looking to retaliate.'

Retaliate. I let that sink in but it still didn't make much sense to me.

'But who? Who did you catch? Who are they? And what's it got to do with me?'

'It didn't have anything to do with you at all,' Alex said, shifting slightly, 'until you told Suki that you were Jack's sister.'

'But why does that matter?'

'Tit for tat. It's a possibility. We took one of theirs, they might be looking for a way to get back at us. In which case you could be – well – an option.'

'An option? What, there's a menu?' My voice was rising. 'Why me? Why not someone else – someone in the Unit or, I don't know, surely there're other people?

You can't be keeping tabs on every family member of every person in the Unit!'

'They won't take any of the men from the Unit, it's too risky for them and, more importantly, it wouldn't be worth their while.'

'Why?'

'They know we wouldn't negotiate if one of us was taken hostage.'

'What? They wouldn't negotiate if you or Jack got caught?'

'No.' He shook his head at me. I was stunned.

'But why me?' I whispered. 'What about the others and their families?'

'Lila, remember what I told you about us not being allowed girlfriends?'

I nodded my head again.

'This is why. It's always a possibility that they find a way to get to us. It's safer if none of us have family living nearby. No one is married or has children.'

I stared at him dumbfounded. Then I remembered something. 'Sara – is she safe?'

'She's safe on the base. Jack's staying with her now, though, until they find out what triggered the alarm.'

Another piece of the puzzle fell into place. 'Is that why Jack doesn't seem to want me here, either now, or when I talk about coming back for college?'

'Yes.'

Despite what Alex was telling me about me being a possible option on the hostage menu, his confirmation of my suspicions made me feel deliriously happy. It wasn't anything personal, they still liked me. Then I remembered that my whole approach to convincing Jack about coming back for college rested on my proving to him I didn't need protecting. That was going to be a little bit tricky now. Hope was dying in me today on so many levels.

I looked back at Alex. 'You still haven't told me who these people are.'

Alex didn't say anything, he was staring out the window frowning again. The possibilities were stacking up and I flicked through them in my head. I'd ruled out the drugs connection earlier, which left vice or the mafia or – I had run out of ideas. Then a sudden thought blindsided me – maybe they were my mother's killers. I dropped my head onto my knees.

'The people who killed my mother. Is it them? Are they the ones who are looking for me?'

'No,' he said.

I scanned his face for any trace of a lie. Alex held my gaze, his eyes blazing blue.

'And Lila,' he said, squeezing my collarbone, 'we honestly don't know if they are looking for you. It's pure conjecture on our part. For all we know, they've given up and are halfway to Alaska by now. If I were them, I would be.'

107

I considered this for a moment.

'You won't ever tell me anything about these people, or Suki, or about my mother's murderers, will you?'

Alex took another deep breath and looked at me, his expression torn. 'I can't, Lila. But I'll tell you when we find them and it's over. I'm so sorry that you're in the middle of all this.'

My face must have been registering the terror I was now feeling – and the irony. I had wanted so much to be in the middle again. Because he shifted towards me and put his arm around my shoulders.

'Hey,' he said. 'It's going to be fine.'

I let my head rest against him, feeling the calm descend.

'You're with me,' he murmured, 'and I won't let anything happen to you, ever.'

12

A loud buzzing noise shocked me awake, sending vibrations through my body. I felt a hand lift off my back and Alex move off the sofa where he'd been sitting next to me.

As he got up to answer the door, he looked back and said, 'Don't worry, it's just Jack and Sara.'

I uncurled my aching body, kicking the blanket off me and pushing my hair out of my face. The dying sunset threw a few last notes of colour into the room. I wondered what the time was and how long I'd been asleep.

I got up, my heart leaping as I heard Jack's voice in the corridor.

He came through into the living room, Alex and Sara following. Jack came right over to me and held me tight for a minute or two.

'You OK?' he whispered into my hair.

I just nodded my head against his shoulder.

'So, what did you find out?' Alex had crossed to the windows and pulled down the blinds. He flicked a switch and a sidelight came on, casting a warm orange glow around the room. Sara sat down next to me on the sofa, Jack perched on the arm.

'It's all good. It was a false alarm,' he said. 'We're still not sure what triggered it, but it must have been an electrical fault because there was no security breach. We checked all the surveillance films and there was no sign of anything out of the ordinary.'

'Least we know it works,' Alex said with a little shrug.

'Yeah, I guess so,' Jack said. He looked at me now. 'And you don't need to worry about anything, Lila, you're not in any danger. We've managed to pick up their trail. They've crossed the border into Mexico.'

I glanced at Alex. Did that mean he was free to let me out of his sight again?

'If you know where they are, why don't you arrest them?' I asked.

'It isn't as easy as that,' Alex said.

Man, how hard could it be? A whole unit of trained Marines hadn't been able to catch my mum's killers, and now they were telling me they couldn't stop these guys, either. I was starting to wonder how good Marine training actually was.

'Listen, can Lila stay here tonight?' Jack said, diverting the conversation. 'I have to get the window fixed in her room.'

I glanced sheepishly at Jack. He was giving me a look.

'How did you manage that one?'

'Um, well, I . . .'

'It's cool,' Alex cut in, saving me. 'Of course Lila can stay. I'll drop her back tomorrow morning.'

I peeked at him through my lashes, grateful for the save. Maybe he realised I didn't want to explain to my brother that I broke a window because I was pissed with him and his boss.

Jack stood up and motioned to Alex and the two of them wandered off into the hallway. I looked at Sara and she smiled at me.

'Jack told me you were just outside when the alarm went off, that must have been a bit of a surprise.'

I thought back to the crush of Alex's weight as I lay on the pavement and my first ride on a motorbike. 'Yeah. It was pretty exciting.'

'It's never happened before. You should have seen the reaction inside the building.'

'Really?' I asked. 'I didn't see anyone coming out to check what was going on.'

'Lockdown,' Sara explained. 'The entire building shuts down when the alarm goes off. We can't get out.'

'I'm glad I was outside, then.' If only Rachel had been a few minutes behind schedule I'd never have met her, I thought. I wouldn't have run off. But then I wouldn't have found out I was being guarded and I wouldn't be getting to spend the night with Alex.

What did it matter, anyway? Alex and Rachel obviously had a thing going on. I shut my eyes. When I opened them, I saw Sara looking at me with a concerned expression. I tried to smile but it came out as a grimace.

'Don't worry. The Unit are on top of this. You'll be perfectly safe until you go back to London.'

My jaw clenched. Go back to London. Like I needed a reminder about that.

Jack came back into the room. He strolled over and kissed me on the top of my head. 'I'm going back to the base with Sara now. We'll see you tomorrow.'

I looked quizzical. 'It's Alex's birthday tomorrow, remember? You're still on for a party, right?' she said, looking at Alex.

He looked at her. 'Do I have a choice?'

'No!' She laughed. 'But we'll do dinner beforehand. Just the four of us.'

At least it wasn't five. If I had to sit through a double date with Rachel the chances were that more than a window was going to get broken. It would be far too dangerous in a room with forks. And knives.

Alex followed them out into the hallway and I heard him setting the alarm.

'Come on, let's get you to bed,' he said, when he came back in.

'No, really, I'm fine here on the sofa,' I protested.

'Listen, if I have to pick you up and carry you in there, you're sleeping in my bed.'

The words sounded so good – it was a shame they didn't mean what I wanted them to. I thought about protesting some more, but decided it would be more dignified to walk.

In his bedroom, Alex opened the wardrobe. I stared at myself in the floor-length mirror. Still dressed in my shorts and pink vest, my hair hanging in waves down my back, I noticed the scrapes on my knees. My eyes looked tired, with faint shadows under them. I felt like I'd lived through the longest day.

Alex turned and threw me a T-shirt. 'Here, you can sleep in this if you want. Just don't go stealing it again.'

'I didn't steal it,' I stammered in protest. I had so stolen it.

'I'm just kidding with you. You can keep it if you want.' He was laughing.

I turned away so he wouldn't see my face turning beetroot.

He crossed over to the windows and drew down the blinds then came over and put his arm around me. 'Sleep well,' he said, then bent and kissed me on the top of my head.

Always the top of my head.

13

There was a soft knocking at the door. I rolled over, unwinding myself from the tangle of sheets I'd straitjacketed myself in. The door opened at the same time my eyes did and I saw a bare-chested Alex in his shorts, standing there with a steaming mug in his hand.

'Tea?' he said.

'Happy Birthday,' I replied, sitting up. The room spun a little as I did so, Alex's bare chest was like a flashing billboard in Times Square. My eyes were drawn back to it again and again, before my gaze fixed on the shallow dips on either side of his hips that were swallowed up by the waistline of his shorts. It was all I could do not to trace the shadows with the tips of my fingers.

He grinned at me a little sheepishly, setting the tea down by my side.

'I should be bringing you tea in bed,' I said, though really I was thinking that I wouldn't mind Alex serving me breakfast in bed every morning for the rest of my life . . .

He crossed over to the windows and pulled up the blinds, letting in ribbons of sunlight. Then he moved to the wardrobe, giving me a simultaneous view of his front, reflected in the mirror, and his muscled back. I bit my lip as I took in the line of his spine and the soft shadow of his ribs under his skin. He pulled a T-shirt out of a drawer and slipped it on. I sighed in disappointment.

'Did you sleep well?' he said, throwing me a glance.

'OK. You?'

'Not bad,' he said, already out the door. 'If you want to take a shower or anything, be my guest. I'll fix breakfast. Jack'll be over in about half an hour.'

I got out of bed. My legs were aching from yesterday's run. I glanced in the mirror opposite. The sunburn had eased and I had some colour across my face now, a few freckles making their comeback on my nose, but still I looked tired. No, not tired, sad. I looked sad.

I would be leaving soon and it didn't look like I'd ever be coming back. And Rachel would sink her manicured claws into Alex and that would be that. My life would be over.

Jack arrived while I was getting dressed. I heard him talking to Alex in the kitchen and followed his voice down the corridor.

'She can't come back. It isn't safe. It's never going to be safe. Not until we've caught him.' I froze mid-step. It was Jack talking.

'That might not be for a while,' Alex replied. 'You can't stop her. Lila's got a mind of her own. Maybe you should tell her the whole story. I don't like keeping it from her.'

'You know we can't. Rachel would never allow it.'

My heartbeat was so loud they must have heard it. The conversation swerved off in a different direction.

'Coffee?' I heard Alex ask.

I walked into the kitchen.

'Hey,' Jack said, looking shifty. I hoped his job never required him to do undercover work.

'Hi,' I answered.

'You ready for breakfast?' Alex asked, serving up some bacon and eggs onto a plate and pulling out a stool for me.

I contemplated him for a second. He was avoiding my eyes. I climbed onto the stool. What was the whole story? Who was the *him* they were talking about catching? Why couldn't Jack listen to Alex and just tell me? And why wouldn't Rachel allow it? Who the hell was she to tell them what to do?

Only their boss, I remembered with a sinking feeling.

As soon as I said goodbye to Alex and the door shut behind me, I could feel the pull, that elastic band around my heart being stretched again. How was it going to feel with a whole ocean separating us? It didn't bear thinking about.

Down in the car park, Alex's motorbike stood at an angle as though leaning over to be petted.

Jack saw me gazing at it lovingly. 'I hope you enjoyed your first ride on that thing,' he said, 'because it was also your last.'

Actually I'd had two rides on Alex's bike, but I didn't pull Jack up on the technicality – maybe Alex hadn't told him about me running off.

We walked over to Jack's Audi which he beeped open. I slid into the passenger seat and tried to spot what one hundred and twenty thousand dollars bought. The speed gauge went all the way to two hundred and fifty miles an hour. Maybe that was it. I wondered if I could convince Jack to show me some of that speed. I scanned the dash. There were two buttons without icons on them. Bass? Treble? On/Off? Or something more exciting, like an ejector seat? I considered pressing one but realising how that might play out if they weren't audio balance buttons gave me pause for thought.

115

We swung out of the car park and into the blazing sunshine. I turned my head, trying to spot the black car that had been waiting on the street last night. It didn't seem to be there anymore.

A few minutes later, I checked again to see if it was behind us but nothing. I chewed on my bottom lip, trying to figure out how to broach the subject once more.

'Jack,' I eventually said, 'if I leave next week, when can I come back?'

He stepped on the gas. 'Lila, you've seen what's happened just in the few days you've been here. You need to stay in London, where you can't be a target. If you're here, I can't keep you safe.'

'But you don't need to. I can look after myself,' I said, with something approaching conviction.

Jack glanced over at me with one eyebrow raised, snorted and then looked back at the road.

I glared ahead. I needed to tell him. It was suddenly so obvious. If I told him and Alex about my ability then maybe they wouldn't feel they had to keep protecting me. They might relax and let me stay. It was a long shot, and there was still a chance they might totally freak out and send me off to some secure unit for testing, but I had to rely on the fact that one of them was my brother and the other was, well, Alex, and he never overreacted to anything.

Jack had parked the car and turned the engine off before I even realised we were back at his.

'Sara's coming round later,' he said, unlocking the door to the house. 'She thought you might like to get ready for the party together.'

I smiled. It would be good to spend time with another girl, and I might be able to get more out of Sara than I'd been able to pry out of Alex. I looked at the clock on the wall. I had ten whole hours to kill before I saw Alex again. It felt like five centuries. But possibly it was just long enough to figure out a present for him, as in a real present, not one of the imaginary gifts I'd like to give him. It might also be long enough for me to figure out a way to tell them both about my ability without either of them running from me screaming.

The present-giving problem was easily resolved in the end. In the back of my diary was a strand of brown leather Alex had once given me – a hastily pulled-together goodbye present from when I left five years ago. I'd worn it on my wrist for approximately a week in London before my new teacher told me to remove it or lose it. I figured that Alex might appreciate the return gesture. There was a risk that he might look at it and wonder why I was giving him a worn-out piece of leather as a birthday present, but I'd take it. I had no money other than a pile of loose change, so it was either the strand of leather or a popsicle.

The other problem I thought I'd solved too. I figured that it was all about the way you looked at things. I could sell my ability to them as something freakish – or I could sell it to them as a super-power. The image in my head shifted from Alex staring at me in horror and running away, to him looking at me the way Jack looked at Sara, and asking me out on a date. A superpower might just put me on a par with Rachel.

I had it all planned – I would tell them tonight. After the party. The only minor spanner in the works was the fact my ability wasn't so super and neither was my control of it. Still, I'd cross that bridge when I had to.

14

A knock on my bedroom door blasted me out of my daydreams.

Sara poked her head around the door. She was wearing a little black dress with a gold detail around the edge which reflected onto her skin, making it glow. She also had a bag the size of a small suitcase in her hand.

'You look gorgeous,' she said, coming to stand next to me.

I looked in the mirror. I was wearing the blue silk dress I'd packed. Not that it mattered what I wore. If *I'm the boss* Barbie was in the room, Alex wouldn't even notice me.

'Right, let's have some fun,' Sara said, opening her bag with a flourish. It was filled with make-up and shoes. I had never felt so grateful to anyone in my whole life. Now I might actually have a shot at being noticed. Alex wouldn't be able to see me as quite so little if I was wearing heels and lipstick and Rachel, if she was there, might even think twice about making another comment about babysitting.

'So, when was the last time you three all saw each other?' Sara asked, as she brushed powder onto my cheeks.

'Three years,' I said. A long three years.

'That was in Washington, wasn't it?' She stopped what she was doing and knelt back.

'Yes. Just after they dropped out of college. My dad flew back to try to talk some sense into Jack, and I came too.'

'Yeah, he told me about that visit. He said your dad was really angry.'

That was an understatement. My dad had totally flipped. I wondered at the time how Jack could have triggered such a reaction. But I didn't complain because before I knew it we were on a plane back home and I was wishing he'd dropped out sooner.

I looked at Sara. She was giving me a funny look, like she'd lost me into daydreams.

'You know,' she said, 'Jack thinks that joining up was the best decision he ever made.'

'For him, maybe.' I couldn't help but think how much better things would have been if he hadn't. How he'd probably still be talking to my dad. How I'd actually be able to come back and stay here with him.

'I know it's really hard for anyone to understand and I'm not sure he'll ever be able to explain it properly to you, but for Jack, joining the Unit was his way of dealing with what happened to your mum.'

'I think I do understand.' More than she knew.

'Really?'

'Yes.'

She squeezed my knee. 'I'm sure he'll make up with your dad. You shouldn't worry about it. Just give him time.'

Yes, time to catch them. I wished I could be as positive as she was.

Jack came knocking as Sara was finishing up. She had insisted on lending me a pair of heels I could barely stand up in, let alone walk in. I looked in the mirror and smiled back at the stranger there. With my hair up off my face, my cheekbones stood out more prominently and my eyes looked huge.

Jack's face said it all. If his jaw could have detached, it would have hit the floor. His eyes almost popped out his head and rolled around the floor like golf balls.

'Nice top,' was all he managed to say.

'It's a dress,' I replied.

Sara's elbow made contact with Jack's ribs. 'She looks beautiful. Come on,' she said, pushing him out into the hallway, 'We can't stand Alex up on his birthday.'

The restaurant was hushed and candlelit and when we walked in I pretended we were on a double date, with my date already there, waiting for me at the table in the corner.

Alex stood up when he saw us and I almost stumbled into the back of the waiter. It was the shoes. I wasn't used to wearing heels and salivating at the same time. Alex was wearing black trousers and a dark grey shirt. He glanced at me and I caught the now familiar pulse of muscle in his jaw and a flash of something else in his eyes which glimmered sapphire in the low light of the room.

I pulled out my carefully wrapped present and handed it to him across the table.

Alex took it with a tight smile and a thank you then put it in his pocket without opening it. I stared at him, feeling my heart begin to stutter.

Jack put his menu down. 'Do you remember when we were here before? How that waiter couldn't keep his eyes off Rachel?'

I lifted my menu up to hide my face as my double-date fantasy fizzled out.

'Alex, the waiters are going to think you're the man: last week you turn up with Rachel, this month you're with another gorgeous girl!'

I could hear Sara laughing. Alex didn't reply. I moved the menu closer and scrutinised the small print. He had brought her here. On a date. I felt like I'd been cleaved in two with a blunt spoon.

The waiter came over to take our order. It was bad timing. The pen shot out of his hand like a wayward rocket. I watched it ping off the ceiling and land at his feet where he scrabbled for it.

I stole a look at the others to see if they'd noticed. Only Alex was looking bemused. When he saw me watching him though, he looked away.

Since the Rachel comment he'd gone a little quieter, no doubt wishing she was here with him instead of me. I was sure he'd be looking over in this direction more if I had her perfect face. I slid my shoes off under the table and wished I could unpin my hair and wipe off my make-up. What was the point? I could probably have been sitting here stark naked with a sign over my head saying I loved him and he still wouldn't notice me. I would always just be Jack's sister. Jack's *little* sister.

I switched my gaze away from Alex and towards the kitchen door which was swinging backwards and forwards as a steady stream of waiters came and went, with plates piled high. I knew where this was going before I could stop myself. The next waiter had his plate whipped out his hand like a torpedo had hit it. I saw the look of confusion on his face as the plate flew out of his fingers and spun across the room, depositing a tangle of spaghetti on the floor like it was a canvas and he was Jackson Pollock. The whole room turned to look, several dozen pairs of eyes flitting from the plate on the floor to the waiter with the tomato-spattered trousers. I bit my bottom lip hard.

*   *   *

The walk from the restaurant to Belushi's only helped magnify my despair. Alex had barely looked at me all through the meal and now he wasn't even speaking to me. Jack and Sara were way ahead, leaving me and Alex to bring up the rear, walking a few feet away from each other in stone-cold silence. I kicked off Sara's high heels, which were slowly crippling me, and walked in my bare feet. I could have sworn I caught a flash of a smile on Alex's face as I reached to pick up the shoes, but he kept his eyes on the road ahead and his hands shoved deep into his pockets.

I shivered in my dress and hugged myself, rubbing the goosebumps off my arms. Alex veered towards me and I thought, or maybe just hoped, that he was going to put his arm around me but his hands stayed resolutely put. The moonlight had bleached his hair white and was casting shadows onto his face. No doubt he had walked back this way with Rachel. I bet she managed to walk in heels. And that he'd put his arm around her. I managed to not bend the lamp post around.

The club was heaving. I looked around at the bodies pressed against the bar and condensing around the small cocktail tables. The whole unit was there. They weren't wearing uniform but they were so obvious they may just as well have been. The rest of the men in the place were giving them a wide berth, like you would a pack of wild dogs.

Alex walked straight over to a crowd of them at one of the tables and I stared after him feeling completely undone, like a zipper had been pulled and all of me was tumbling out.

'Hey, you're here.'

I turned around. It was the young guy from the base. What was his name? Jonas, maybe?

'Can I get you a drink?'

'Um, er—'

'No, we're good thanks, I'll get this round,' Jack half growled.

I shrugged in Jonas's direction and looked over at Sara. She rolled her eyes at me.

'What do you want?' Jack said, looking at me like I was deaf. I realised he'd already asked me twice.

What did I want? Now there was a question. I looked over at Alex, then realised he was asking me what I wanted to drink.

'Um, Coke, thanks.'

Jack pushed his way through the crowd. Jonas had taken the hint and rejoined the men from his team.

'He's pretty gorgeous, isn't he?'

I spun my head around. Sara was nodding in Jack's direction.

I looked at Jack's back. 'Um, yeah, I guess. He's my brother.'

'No. I'm not talking about him!' She laughed softly. She nodded her head across the bar and I followed her gaze as it settled on Alex.

'Oh.' My face froze as I wondered how I should react.

'So how long have you been in love with him?'

I almost fell over. 'I'm not – I – um . . .' The denial stalled on my lips. I looked over at Sara and took a deep breath. 'All my life.'

She gave me a little smile.

'Is it that obvious?' I could feel the anxiety written all over my face.

'No, not at all. Just to me. I get paid to observe people's reactions, remember.'

She lowered her voice. 'I see the way you change every time he comes near you.'

I looked at her in horror. 'What, what do I do?' I had visions of my unpoker face in a hangdog grin.

123

'Oh, it's not that bad.' She was desperately trying to calm me. 'It's very subtle. Almost like you've been given a little particle charge. You're on edge, buzzing slightly. I recognise it because it's how I feel when I'm near Jack.'

Oh God. 'Does Jack know?' I glanced once more in his direction. He was at the bar now.

'Oh. No of course not. I won't tell him, Lila. Don't worry.'

'Thanks,' I whispered, glancing around to make sure no one could hear us.

'Have you thought about telling him?'

'Who – Jack?' Was she mad? I'd sooner be tortured. 'Why would I do that? He'd—'

She interrupted me. 'Not Jack, Alex.'

'Are you kidding me? NO. Absolutely no way. No. He's totally not interested in me like that. He sees me as a sister, that's all.' I felt my face throbbing. 'And anyway, there'd be no point.'

'Why not?' She seemed genuinely interested. Like it wasn't obvious.

'Er. Well, for one, Rachel.' Hell, did I need to spell it out?

I saw her smile falter. 'Oh, yes. There is that.'

A sucker punch to the stomach. So I was right.

Sara pulled a face. 'Rachel is definitely into him. That's obvious. But I'm not sure he's actually into her.'

'Why wouldn't he be?' I asked quietly, my eyes fixed on Alex's back.

'Lots of reasons.'

'But she's beautiful.'

'Oh come on, you know Alex has a bit more to him than that. Yes, she's beautiful . . .'

'And bright.'

124

'Yes, and bright. But there's plenty about her that's not so appealing.'

Yes, she's a bitch, I thought.

'I think you should tell him.'

I laughed. 'Are you insane? I'd never be able to look him in the face again.' I shook my head violently. 'It would ruin everything, our whole friendship. He doesn't see me like that.'

'He loves you.'

My heart stopped for a few beats then started galloping. Had he said something to her? Then it tumbled to a standstill as I realised the love she was referring to was the brotherly kind.

'Exactly,' I said, swallowing hard. 'He loves me like a sister.' I tore my eyes off Alex's back.

'But he might start to see you differently if you told him how you felt.'

'Yeah, he might start to see me like a complete idiot.'

She bit back a smile. 'If you don't tell him, won't you wonder your whole life what he might have said?'

'Er, no. I have a good enough imagination.'

'It might not be that bad,' she laughed.

'Yeah, it would, it'd be worse.' My mind was conjuring several scenes that were making me want to drop to the ground right there and then and curl into a ball. 'It's impossible, totally impossible.'

'Anything's possible, Lila.' Sara paused for a second as though thinking. 'If you both really want it enough. If it was me, I'd take the risk.' I drew in a breath but she cut me off, holding her hand up to still me. 'You've loved him your whole life. I think it's safe to assume you'll love him for the rest of your life, don't you?'

I didn't reply. Of course I would love him for the rest of my life.

'So how can you not tell him?' she whispered.

She had a point.

'I'm scared.'

She glanced over at Jack, heading back towards us with the drinks, and then said, 'You know, there's this old saying, I'm not sure of the exact translation, but it's something like "he who fears to suffer, suffers from fear" – think about it.'

She turned away to give Jack a huge smile and take the drink he was offering.

I looked over again at Alex and thought about what she'd said. He still had his back to me. I imagined walking over to him, tapping him on the shoulder, waiting until he turned around and then saying, 'I love you.'

Yeah, I was happy to suffer from fear.

15

The ladies' toilets were at the back of the bar. As I walked in, the door shut behind me with a metallic bang, and I heard a bolt slam to. I spun round, my heart in my mouth. A man was leaning against the door, his hand resting on the lock.

My first and only thought was that they'd got it wrong. That the killers hadn't fled to Mexico. That they'd found me and this was going to be the retaliation Alex had warned me about.

Then the man turned around to face me and I recognised him from the Seven-Eleven. It was the crazy noodle man. I edged back against the sink, my eyes darting around the room looking for something to hurl. There was nothing. Just a pile of paper towels – they weren't going to do much damage.

'I need your help,' the man said, coming towards me.

'Who are you?' I stammered.

'I—' He took another step towards me and I flinched back against the sink. I looked over at the door and willed the bolt to move. He didn't notice my glance, and took another step towards me, his hands raised defensively. I felt the bolt start to slide back.

'I'm known as Key – I need your help, Lila.'

The bolt stopped moving when I heard him say my name. He didn't look around at the door but kept his eyes on me.

'How do you know my name?' I asked in a whisper.

'I know your name, I know who you are. I know what you can do. I know everything about you and your brother.' He spoke slowly, letting the impact of each word hit me.

'What? Who are you?' My mind was spinning. What did he know? 'I don't understand, what do you know about me? About Jack?'

'Don't panic. I'm not going to hurt you. I'm not one of them.' His hands were making a hushing gesture.

'One of who?' I said it tentatively.

'Them. The people your brother is trying to protect you from.'

My stomach folded over on itself. 'How do you know about that? You're not one of the Unit.' I was whispering now.

'No, no, I'm definitely not one of them, either.' He shook his head once, his expression grim.

'How do you know all this, then?' I asked, leaning heavily on the sink to keep me upright.

'Because I'm looking for the same people as your brother.'

'Why?'

I saw stripped pain in his dark eyes. 'Because they have my son, Nate.'

A knock on the door made us both jump. The man looked over at it and back at me, panic on his face. He was begging me silently not to give him away.

'Hang on,' I shouted out in a shaky voice.

'What's going on in there?' a woman's voice yelled back.

'There's a leak, we're just trying to fix it.'

We heard footsteps walking away. I turned back to the man. He had relaxed his posture and was slumping against a cubicle door. I tried to unscramble my thoughts.

'Why would they take your son?'

128

He looked up at me. His eyes were hooded and heavy. He didn't look like anybody significant.

'Who are you that they would take your son?'

He shook his head at me. 'It's not me they're trying to get to. They don't know about me. It's him, it's what he can do.'

Understanding crept up on me, like anaesthetic inching up a vein. 'What can he do?' I whispered.

'We're like you.' The coldness hit my core. 'We can do – things.' He didn't break eye contact with me.

I swallowed, trying to keep calm. 'What things?'

'We're the same. Well, not quite the same, but similar – we all have talents . . . I can't explain now, but I need your help.'

This was a trap. It had to be. What if he was one of the bad guys? One of the people who was after me? There was no way I was going to admit anything to him about my ability. 'I don't understand. You're not making any sense.'

He looked at me with his eyebrows raised, as though begging me to drop the pretence. If he was one of the people after me, why had he come here alone? I glanced at the door again, then back at him. His expression was silently pleading.

'Why are you telling me this? We need to tell Jack. He can help you. I don't know anything about the people who have your son.'

He took a step towards me, bounding forward from his slump. 'No. You can't tell Alex or Jack or anyone from the Unit.'

'Why? How do you know the Unit?'

'Listen to me.' He steadied his voice, but his expression was fierce. 'You cannot tell them.'

A deadening fear finally overtook me, making my voice shake. 'Why?'

129

He was only a few inches away from me now. My hands were gripping the basin, holding me up.

'Because, Lila, they've been hunting people like us for five years.'

Another knock on the door caused me to sink to the floor.

'Lila?'

My eyes flew to the door.

Jack called my name again. 'Lila?'

I froze. Key was staring down at me, his eyes round with fear. Who was this man? Why should I trust him? That was my brother out there. I hesitated, on the verge of calling out to Jack for help, but instead I held Key's gaze. What if what he was saying was true?

'I'll be out in a second,' I finally croaked.

'What's taking so long?' Jack yelled, trying the door handle. 'Why's the door locked?'

'I'm just . . .' I looked around feeling pinpricks of sweat break out all over my body. 'I'm, um – just – girl stuff.'

I closed my eyes and prayed that Jack would be too embarrassed to ask anything else and would just walk away. There was a full ten seconds of silence from the other side of the door. And then the handle lifted. 'Oh,' we finally heard him say. 'OK, I'll see you in a bit.'

He left.

I waited until Key had straightened up and then I stood. 'Like us?' I asked. 'What do you mean they're hunting people like us?'

I could see the yellow of his eyes, tinged with red streaks. 'I mean they're hunting people like you, like Nate, like me. People who have a talent. Who can use their minds in different ways. The Unit don't know about me but I'm scared they know about my son.'

I shook my head. 'I don't know what you're talking about.'

He sighed, 'Lila, I've seen you, I know what you are. I've been following you ever since I saw you at the base with your brother and that guy Alex. The spaghetti at the restaurant earlier?' He tapped the side of his head. 'You did that with your mind.'

My breath caught in my throat. How did he know this? 'How did you see any of that? You're lying.'

'I don't need to be in my body to move around. To see things and hear things.'

'Huh,' I snorted. 'Right.' What was I thinking? I should have yelled for Jack when I had the chance.

'I can project – leave my body and go places.'

This time I laughed. 'You're telling me you can fly? You honestly expect me to believe that?' The man was a lunatic. What was I doing listening to this?

'Can you move things with your mind?'

I stopped laughing. When he put it like that. I narrowed my eyes at him. He didn't look like he could fly. But then it wasn't like I looked any different to anyone else.

'So you're saying there are others, then?' I asked quietly.

He nodded, holding my gaze intently as if scared I was about to do something crazy. 'Some the same as you; some, like me, who can do different things.'

I laughed under my breath. Why had I imagined there wouldn't be others? 'So—'

Before I could get the rest of the sentence out, he cut me off, his voice urgent. 'But that doesn't matter right now. I need your help.'

I ignored him. 'And the Unit – when you said they're hunting people like us, what did you mean?'

131

He licked his lips and I found myself literally hanging on his words. 'That's what they do, Lila.' He paused. 'That's their single remit – to find those with abilities like ours and—' He broke off.

I swallowed hard. 'And what?'

Key turned away from me. 'I don't know exactly. But when they take someone onto the base at Pendleton – they call it containing them – they never come back. That's why I triggered the alarm at the base, so he wouldn't take you inside. I wasn't sure if I'd see you again if he did.'

He. He meant Alex.

'But . . .' I couldn't find the words to finish the sentence. Alex and Jack, all this time, hunting for something – and that something was me. Or people like me.

I looked up into Key's eyes. 'I don't understand. Why?'

He looked back at me and shrugged slightly. 'Fear of the unknown? Fear of what you might be able to do?'

'But why would anyone be afraid?' Then I remembered the boy whose eyeball I'd nearly skewered. He'd been pretty afraid.

'Lila, not everyone's like you, or me. Just trying to get by in life without drawing attention to what we are. The people who took my son, the people your brother is trying to catch, this man Demos, he is something to fear.'

'Demos? Who is he? And why is he something to fear?'

'Because Demos wants power – he wants control.'

Key walked over to where I was standing by the door. He was looking at me as though it should be obvious what he was talking about it, but I didn't have a clue. Power? Control? Over what? The only thing I did know was that I needed to get away and find Alex.

And then came the crushing realisation that if what Key was saying about the Unit was true, I couldn't go and find Alex. I couldn't go near him or Jack ever again. They were after me. Tears rolled down my cheeks and I bent over to suck in some air.

Key grabbed hold of my shoulders and started to shake me hard. 'I need your help!' He was shouting in my face and I flinched away from him.

'You keep saying that,' I sobbed, 'but what can I do? You're telling me there are others like me, but worse, and that my own brother would hunt me down if he knew?' I gave a hollow laugh. 'That's ridiculous, Jack's my brother. He'd never let anyone hurt me.'

Key was looking sceptical.

'Anyway,' I said, 'what do you care?'

'I care because right now you're the only person who can help me.'

I shook my head dumbly.

'Demos has my son and I don't know where they've taken him. I need to find him. I need to get him back before the Unit get to them. I can't lose my son.' A flash of pain crossed his face. He glanced up at me quickly. 'I was following the Unit and then they caught Alicia and I lost them.'

'Who's Alicia?'

'The person your brother's team caught the other night. The night you arrived.'

It took me a few seconds to process all this.

'Lila? Do you know anything?'

'Like what? This is all news to me. I don't know. I'm sorry.'

'But you might have overheard something? Has your brother mentioned anything to you – anything at all about their missions?'

I suddenly remembered something. 'They've crossed the border. Into Mexico. I don't know where exactly.'

133

'Are you sure?' He came close. 'Why would they go down south?' He turned and started pacing, kneading his head in his hands.

'I don't know, that's just what Jack said.'

Key turned back to me. 'What else did he say?'

'Nothing, he doesn't tell me anything.'

The guy was in my face again, his breath like a cigarette blowing in my eyes. 'Are they close? Is the Unit near to catching them?'

I shook my head. 'I don't know, they're following them. I don't know what's stopping the Unit from arresting them.'

'Arresting them? Is that what you think they'll do?' A harsh laugh spat from his lips. 'Lila, you can be sure they won't be arresting them – which is why I need to find them before the Unit does. I need to get my son back before your brother and his friends catch up with them.'

I felt tears slicking down my face again.

'I need you to find out where they are and what the Unit is planning.'

'How? You just expect me to ask him? Just like that?'

'No.'

I wiped the back of my arm over my face. 'If you know so much about me – about Jack and the Unit – if you can do what you say you can do and fly places . . .' he winced but I carried on, 'then why can't you find the information? Why do you need me to help?'

'I can't get into your house because of that damn alarm system.'

I drew in a sharp breath. 'Is that what it's for?' I asked. 'To keep people like you out?'

Key raised an eyebrow. 'People like us, Lila,' he said.

'Well, how come I can get in then?' I shot back.

134

'It only works – it only goes off – if we use our power. Some kind of electromagnetic sensors. No projector can get through it. Neither can a telepath.'

I thought about Suki on the doorstep peeking through the letter box. If I'd have set the alarm that morning would it have gone off? Then I remembered how I'd broken the window with a flying hairbrush and how I'd turned the light switch on and off without touching it.

'Well how come I haven't triggered it, then?' I demanded, my voice shaking. 'All the time I've been here, how come I haven't set off this so-called alarm? There's a dozen times I could have triggered it.'

'I don't know,' he said, looking bewildered, 'was it on?'

I paused with my mouth open and tried to think back. When the hairbrush flew off the dresser the alarm hadn't been on because I'd just breezed into the house and switched it off. The time with the bag, Jack had switched the alarm off when we came in the house. But there were other times – what about the time with the light switch? I frowned at Key. It seemed too random that the alarm had always been off at those moments. Too lucky. And luck wasn't exactly something I had in spades.

'Look,' said Key in a rush, 'please can you just take a look in the house? I can't risk going near the place. Not with all the security and the cars outside. I don't want the Unit knowing about me – it's too risky.'

'You think there's something in the house? Like what?' I asked.

He shrugged. 'I don't know. Maybe Jack has information on Demos and his people, information on where they are or when they're planning on making a move. I want to know if they even know about Nate. Listen, I wouldn't be coming to you if I had any other choice. But I can't get into their headquarters and I can't get into any one else's apartment. Besides, your brother's a lieutenant, he's surely got access to more information than the others.'

My mind whirled. If what Key was saying was true and Jack had information in the house somewhere, I needed to find it. I needed to know what was going on. I needed to know if any of this was true.

'OK,' I whispered. 'I'll help you.'

The relief on his face was palpable. I thought he was going to cry. 'Thank you.' He squeezed my hand.

'I've got to go,' I said. 'They'll be wondering where I am.' The words trailed off.

Key nodded. 'OK. I'll go before they come looking.' Before I could even wrap my head around what he was saying he had inched open the door, peered around it and left.

I stood staring at the spot where he'd been standing, my breath starting to come in gasps. Little black dots began jumping in front of my eyes and I staggered backwards, falling into a cubicle. I dropped onto the seat and put my head between my knees. A hacking, laboured sob burst out of my chest and I pressed my fist against my lips to stifle it.

They didn't know it but Jack and Alex were hunting me. My own brother and the person I'd been in love with since forever would kill me, or 'contain' me, whatever that meant, if they ever found out what I was. Everything I had imagined about the Unit couldn't come close to this.

I sat up and took a deep breath. Maybe Key was making it all up. He had to be. It was too absurd. It must be a wind-up.

But the voice inside my head was calm, telling me loud and clear that this was no wind-up. Because, in a messed-up way, it

136

actually made sense. The pieces were suddenly slotting together: the secrecy, the alarm, the fact they hadn't been able to catch the people they were after even though they'd had them in their sights. Because their targets had powers, abilities – just like I did.

I had to leave right now. This second. Get on a plane and get out of here before they figured it out.

But how could I just leave? I hesitated. Maybe they would never find out. Maybe I could stay.

No. I had to go. Given my lack of control and the number of alarms all over the place it was a miracle Alex and Jack didn't already know about my power. Would they have locked me up if they did? I'd been right about them thinking I was a freak and taking me to a secure unit for testing. It was hilarious. I was actually laughing out loud. No, that was hysteria. Even I could recognise it for what it was.

I heard the door open to the bathroom and the noise of the bar rushed in followed by the close-up shrieks of some women. The sound snatched me back into the present. I was sitting in a toilet cubicle in a club full of men who wanted to contain me. I needed to pull myself together and get out of there.

I stood up, straightened my dress and unlocked the door. I stopped in front of the sink and threw cold water over my face, wiping away the remains of my make-up, staring back at the wide-eyed girl in the mirror – I looked like I'd just crawled out of a car wreck.

Time to go.

I pushed the door open slowly, hovering on the precipice of the room, looking around at the members of the Unit scattered across the bar, laughing and necking their beers. A shiver ran up my spine, like someone was walking over my grave. I wouldn't stand a chance, not even with my ability, not even with all that beer taking the edge off their aim. Still, no one had missed me while I'd been stuck in the bathroom with Key, so why they would start noticing me now, I had no idea.

Then I saw Alex. It was easy to make him out in a crowd. It was the way he stood, like he was permanently on guard. Which, I now knew, he was. Against me. He turned then so I could see the side of his face, the graze of his stubble and the shadows his lashes made under the low lights. He was laughing at something the person he was talking to was saying.

And suddenly the idea was preposterous. I couldn't leave Alex. It was impossible to even contemplate. I would just tell him everything. Walk over there right now and tell him. He had promised he would never let anything happen to me. Maybe once I told him, the Unit would realise they were making a mistake trying to contain people like me. Alex would listen and make everything OK. He always made everything OK. I took a step towards him.

He turned then and I saw that the person he was talking to, laughing with, was Rachel.

She looked amazing: blonde, svelte and gleaming, like she'd been dipped in gold. I felt as if I'd been winded, like Rachel had walked over in her three-inch heels and minuscule minidress and, with a smile on her face, punched me viciously in the stomach.

They made a silent tableau: Alex bending his head towards her, hand hovering at her waist as though about to pull her into his arms. Rachel looking up at him wide-eyed, cheekbones refracting the light like prisms. They looked like they were posing for an aftershave advert. Whatever she was saying to him, he was clearly intrigued, leaning in further towards her, his expression fervent. I waited for the death strike and for her to swallow him whole.

I wanted to yell across the bar at him to evade and resist. Wasn't that what Marines were supposed to be good at? Instead I turned on my heel, stumbling through the crowd towards a blurry green light. Blurry because I was half blinded by tears. Ahead of me, the fire exit threw itself open with such force it cracked against the outside wall. I struggled to rein in my emotions before something bad happened, like a roomful of men, including my own brother, pulled out their guns or nets or whatever and aimed them at my head. The door slammed shut behind me with a metallic clunk. I found myself standing at the top of three concrete steps, looking out over a back parking lot.

I sank down onto the top step and tried to get a grip. I wished that I had the power to make the ground open up right there in front of me so I could hurl myself head first into the chasm. This was it, then. There was no point in staying. Even if I hadn't met Key there would be no point in staying. I needed to get back to the house, find whatever information I could, then leave. Tonight. There was no other choice.

I got up from the step and looked around the parking lot. There was a chain-link fence to the left, running the length of the building, and a slim alleyway leading onto the street out the front. I squeezed down it and rounded the corner.

'Lila!'

I froze at the sound of Jack's voice. He stepped out of a mass of men knotted by the door area and came towards me.

'Lila, there you are. Are you OK?' He looked away, embarrassed, as he asked.

'Yeah, fine,' I mumbled.

'We've got to go.' He gestured towards the men behind him. They were loading up into two black SUVs with tinted windows. 'The alarm's gone off again at the base. We have to respond,

139

though I'll put money on it being another false alarm. I'm really sorry to be ditching out on you.'

A car horn blared next to us and I jumped. The door of the nearest SUV stood open, dark shapes inside gesturing at Jack, the other car already heading away from the kerb, pulling into the traffic on the highway.

'Alex is staying, so are half the guys. Stick around and enjoy yourself.' He got out his wallet. 'Here, take this.' Jack shoved fifty dollars in my direction. 'Buy a round for everyone. Sara and Alex will see you get home. I'll be back in the morning.'

Then he ducked quickly into the car, the door slammed and the car manoeuvred fluidly into the traffic.

I had fifty dollars in my hand, Jack was tied up at the base, and I couldn't go back into the bar to face Alex and Rachel. I thought about it for a split second, then stuck my arm out and hailed a cab.

16

I ran up the porch steps. The security light blinked on as I unlocked and opened the door. I crossed to the alarm and deactivated it, glancing up at the sky outside, wondering if Key was up there – was that how it worked? If he was, could he come inside now without triggering it? I kicked off my shoes. I needed to focus. It would only be a matter of time before someone came looking for me and I needed to be out of here long before then.

I stood at the bottom of the stairs, frozen. I would never see Alex again. The consequences of leaving suddenly seemed more impossible to bear than the consequences of staying. I shut my eyes and felt the walls closing in on me.

My eyes snapped open. I'd find whatever information I could and then I'd decide if I was staying or going. I wasn't sure what I was looking for, though a sheaf of papers explaining why there were government-sanctioned units dedicated to eradicating us like a nasty flu virus would be handy. Or information on what they did with such people when they caught them.

'With *us*,' I said out loud, 'when they catch *us*.'

I ran into the living room. Jack's laptop was on the table and I switched it on. It asked for a password. I hesitated a few seconds then tried 'Sara' but it beeped angrily at me and demanded I try again. I tapped in the code for the alarm. Another angry beep and a warning that I only had one more try before permanent lockout. I swore loudly. Then my eye caught the photo of my mum on the bookcase. I looked back at the keyboard and typed in my mum's name: Melissa.

```
Password accepted.
```

I stared at the screen in shock for a moment then quickly scrolled across the desktop to Jack's most recent documents and clicked on the first one.

It was titled Demos.

It took me a moment to figure out the connection. Then I remembered Key's words and my heart stalled. Demos was the man Key said had taken his son. Apparently the same man the Unit had tracked to Mexico.

I clicked the file open, my hands shaking. A face expanded across the screen. The image was grainy and unfocused and it was hard to make out the details clearly. What I could see was a man with a widow's peak of black hair, a square jaw, flat blue eyes and dark stubble. My eyes flicked down to the paragraphs of text beneath the picture.

```
First name/alias: Demos
Real name: unknown.
Height: 6'
Weight: approx 180 pounds.
Known ability: Psychokenosist.
```

What the hell was a psychokenosist? I had no idea, but surely anything that required the word 'psycho' at the front could not be good. I read on –

Summary: Considered maximum risk to
national security. SOU priority one.
Extremely dangerous. Only known
Psychokenosist in USA. Failure to appre-
hend on multiple occasions. No weapons
sufficient for containment.
Convictions: Tried and found guilty in
absentia of the murders of Melissa Loveday
and Senator Andrew Burns (see crime report
and Quantico profiling and forensic
analysis).

I felt dizzy. The words jumped around in front of my eyes. I scrolled back up so I could see the photograph again. My mother's killer. I was staring right at him. The man who had broken into my house and stabbed her to death. The same man who had Key's son. The same man who may or may not have been coming after me to use me as a pawn in his game of girlfriend barter. Alex had lied to me. The people the Unit were hunting were the same people who had killed my mother. And the people who had killed her were like me.

I closed my eyes whilst the room spun and kept them closed whilst I hit the scroll down button. I didn't want to open them and see Demos's face again. I read down.

Convicted also in closed court (Fort
Bragg, SOU) in absentia of the following
crimes: Robbery, Extortion, Kidnap, First
degree murder, Attempted murder, Treason,
Conspiracy to commit treason (See court

143

```
statements, restricted personnel only).
Sentenced in absentia to death by lethal
injection. To be administered within 24
hours of capture.
```

He had already been convicted? And sentenced to death? I fell back into the chair. My eyes tracked to the text below:

```
Known associates: Leader of a highly
organised and fast expanding group of
psygens.
```

Psygens? Was I one of those? Underneath were the profiles of eight or so people. Small boxes of text with photographs sitting next to them. I scanned down the list, burning the names and faces into my memory.

```
Alicia Harmon (Telepath) CONTAINED CP
```

The picture was of a striking black woman, her eyes flashing at the camera in defiance. The background was bright, white light. There was a cut across her eyebrow and her lip looked swollen but she was still managing to tilt her chin at the camera and smile.

```
Relationship: Girlfriend
Crimes: Robbery, Treason, Conspiracy to
commit treason, Extortion.
Sentencing: In process.
```

This was the woman that Demos wanted back. That they'd thought he might want me to exchange for. I studied her picture.

'Contained' was stamped underneath it. Contained. I said it out loud. It sounded like the word exterminators used when they were done catching vermin.

I moved down the list.

```
Ryder (Sifter) Last name unknown.
```

The picture underneath was taken with a zoom lens but was better quality than the one of Demos. It was a side profile shot of a regular-looking guy walking down the street, late twenties, longish hair, slight roguish quality due to the way his lip curled, like he knew he was something special. A sifter? What was that? Why couldn't they use plain English for goodness sake – it wasn't like I could take down the dictionary and find the definitions.

```
Relationship: Long-term associate of
Demos.
Crimes: Theft, Breaking and entering,
Carjacking, Treason, Conspiracy to commit
treason, Burglary, Bank robbery, Confidence
crimes, Automobile theft, First degree
murder, Second degree murder . . .
```

The list went on for another paragraph. I got the picture loud and clear, though, so I skipped down, wondering if he was one of the people who'd come after my mum. He had to be. Another surge of anger overtook me.

```
Bill Fields (Telekinetic)
```

He was like me, then. Another person who could make things move with his mind. I should have been excited at the knowledge, but I was horrified. The man looked like a fighting dog, his neck as broad as his head, which was shaved and battered like a boiled egg that had been dropped on the floor. I scanned through his list of crimes, It was as long as Ryder's. Murder thrown in amongst the lesser crimes like an afterthought.

Underneath his entry was one for a woman: Amber Stark. She had flaming red hair, lips the colour of crushed beetles and skin so pale it was translucent. The picture was a headshot. She looked to be in her late twenties but it was hard to tell. I peered closer. Glancing down I saw that this girl's ability was listed as Reader. Clearly nothing to do with books.

Beneath Amber was a man called Thomas Taylor. They were calling him a Projector. Thomas had been contained too. Key's statement that when people got caught they didn't come back was looking fairly accurate.

Beneath Thomas was Harvey James. The photo showed a man in his early thirties. He had a cigarette in his mouth and was wearing Ray-Bans. He could have passed for one of the Unit. He was telekinetic. The record said he had done time for bank robbery, aggravated assault, breaking and entering and that he was suspected of murder. Who wasn't? I thought. Stamped at the bottom of the page were the words: *Escaped San Quentin Prison*.

The last photo was of a girl: Japanese, beautiful, and grinning like a Cheshire cat posing for Mario Testino. I looked at the name under the photo feeling like my world was crumbling around me; it was already half in ruins, but this was the final tremor to bring everything tumbling down.

She was a mind-reader, then.

A hand suddenly slapped over my mouth and my feet were lifted off the floor. My nose was half covered by rough fingers. I gasped in a lungful of air, my brain one step ahead of my thoughts and gearing up for a scream before I had even processed what was happening. But no air could get through and all I could do was choke.

A man's voice whispered in my ear, 'Shut up, be quiet!'

I struggled to obey, panic causing tears to spring up in my eyes. I tried to scan the room to find an object that I could smash into him but I couldn't calm myself enough to focus on my surroundings. What an idiot, I thought. One of the only people on the planet with a special ability to see off attackers and I can't even make it work.

'Shhhh, it's me, it's me. Is Jack here?' The tone was frantic.

The hand loosened its grip and I sucked in some air, gulping it down. I twisted my head, my eyes lighting on the phone. The words he'd spoken sank in about the same time I saw his face and in the second I took to compute that it was Key who was holding me, the phone came flying through the air towards his head. It fell to the floor with a crash, hitting his foot and making him swear.

I fought my way out of his arms and faced him. 'What the hell are you doing in my house?'

'Is Jack here? Is he back?' Key was jigging up and down, wired and wide-eyed.

'No.' I shook myself and wiped my face, trying to remove the taste of his hand. 'What the hell are you doing? I told you I'd help you, you don't need to break into my house and—'

He lunged towards me. 'You've got to get out now.'

'What?'

'You have to leave, right now.' He started pulling me out of the living room, tugging me by the top of my arm. I let myself be pulled.

'What? Why?' I knew the answer before he said it, dread already tunnelling through me.

'They're coming. They're on their way. They used one of them to set the alarm off on the base. It's a decoy. I can't believe your brother fell for it. And why the hell did you leave the bar? Alone! Are you insane?'

We were in the kitchen; Key was fumbling with the lock on the back door.

'But . . . how? They were in Mexico. Jack said.' Key had to be wrong.

'Well, they're not now. They're back here. As soon as I left you, I saw one of Demos's people outside the bar. Bold as brass. Like he didn't care if the Unit spotted him.'

'What was he doing there?' I asked hesitatingly.

'There was only one thing in that bar of any interest to Demos.' He gave me a look that made my blood run cold. 'Then you came swanning out on your own and jumped in a cab. And that's all it took. Demos's man jumped in a car and I followed you straight here to warn you. Sure as my mama goes to church twice on a Sunday they're coming here.'

I stared at him.

'Damn! How do you get this door open?' He was yanking it so hard, the frame was in danger of cracking.

I knelt down and slid the bolt at the bottom and the door opened.

'Come on!' He pulled me out onto the back veranda.

I flew forward onto the wooden planks, whacking my elbow on the door frame and letting out a cry. Key went tumbling over me, head first down the steps onto the lawn. And then a man was on top of him, smacking his fist into his face.

I jerked onto my knees and hauled myself up, spinning around to see whether anyone else was coming up behind him. My legs were bent as though I was on a starting block but I didn't know which way to run or what to do. Key was curled up in a ball, yelling out with each blow. I unfroze and directed my gaze at a watering can, the first thing I saw. It lifted up and I hurled it with all the force I could muster at the man on top of Key. Then I looked for something else. A wooden table at the far end of the veranda was the only other object that I thought I could lift. I stared at it hard and it flew up straight away, hovered for a split second and then rocketed towards the men on the grass.

Just before it made contact, the man rolled aside, off Key. The shock made me lose my grip and the table skidded dangerously in mid-air, coming to a rest millimetres from Alex's face. It hung there like a feather while we both watched. Time seemed to have frozen alongside the table. I looked at Alex, feeling adrenaline pump into my limbs. He was staring at the table in disbelief, then his eyes slowly tracked over to me and I saw the cog turn and the realisation sink in.

The table smashed to the ground at his side. He didn't flinch, he was already on his feet, and the look on his face was one I'd never seen before. I almost toppled backwards from the force of it. The anger was barely contained. Alex took a step towards me and I cowered back against the door frame. I'd never before felt fear like it. I'd take Demos over this.

149

I closed my eyes, waiting for him to reach me. I heard Alex swear and my eyes snapped open. Key had grabbed him by the leg and was hanging off him, being dragged along behind.

'Run, Lila!' Key was yelling, through a mouthful of blood.

Alex was trying to shake him off; I could see him about to take aim with the other leg and before I knew what I was doing I had launched myself off the top step. I collided with Alex hard, bringing him to the ground, landing with a crunch on top of him. I hadn't a hope of holding him down but I clung to him tightly, holding his arms and leaning all my weight onto his chest.

'Stop, stop, please stop,' I was begging him. 'Please don't hurt him. Please stop. He's trying to help me.'

Alex stopped pushing against me. I released my grip and sat up. I was straddling him. Key had rolled onto his hands and knees and was trying to stand.

Alex sat up and I scrambled off him, backing away fast. He drew himself up to standing, his body taut. I moved to Key's side, helping him to stand. He spat a bloody wodge of saliva into the grass and leaned heavily on me, panting. I could see Alex's hands clenching into fists but he stayed pacing the grass a few metres away from us, shooting glances between me and Key.

'Alex,' I tried to speak but it came out in a hoarse whisper, 'Alex, this is Key. He came to tell me that they're coming to the house.'

'Who's coming?' Alex stopped pacing, his eyes flashing onto me like two lightning strikes.

'Demos.' Key lifted his head to spit the word.

Alex stepped towards him and Key leaned back, making me stumble.

'What? How do you know this?' His tone was fierce, quick.

'They're on their way. You need to get her out of here. They want her.' Key coughed. 'To exchange.' He hacked more bloody spit out of his lungs.

For one second Alex stood staring at Key, then he shifted his head and I felt his eyes burning into me again. I looked back defiantly, my heart rate rising. Then I felt his hand grab me by the elbow and he was dragging me across the lawn.

Key tumbled to his knees as I lost my grip on him. I dug my bare feet into the ground and yanked my arm free from Alex's grip.

Alex turned around, his face blazing.

'Where are you taking me?' I was shouting.

He reached his hand to take hold of me again but I dodged it.

'Come on,' he said. It was an order.

I stood firm. 'I'm not leaving him. He came to help me. They have his son.'

I saw Alex waver. He glanced over at the back door and then at Key. I could see the tension in his jaw, the tendons standing up in his neck.

'Come on then, quick, into the garage, the car.' He moved towards Key and put an arm around his shoulders, hauling him to standing.

'Come on, move!' Alex shouted and I ran.

I flicked on the garage light and held the door open as Alex half carried Key through. He leaned him against the car. 'Stay here.'

I ran to Key's side to prop him up while Alex ducked through into the hallway. He was back in a second with the car keys, beeping open the doors. He took Key from me and half pushed him onto the back seat.

'Get in!' he yelled.

151

From outside we heard the sudden noise of screaming engines, of cars, or trucks. It was loud, tearing apart the still night. All three of us lifted our heads. They screeched to a stop out the front of the house.

Alex dived into the driver's seat and threw open the passenger door. He leaned over and grabbed my wrist, pulling me into the car. I slammed the door shut as the garage opened up.

The thrust of the acceleration as Alex hit his foot to the floor and reversed out threw me against the dash. I heard Key roll off the back seat and a heavy thump as he crashed onto the floor.

17

I scrabbled for the seat belt as we spun out of the drive onto the road, ripping down the kerb to get around the two cars abandoned on the pavement. Two men were already on the front lawn, one on the veranda, with his hand on the front door. The drivers of both cars were revving the engines and when they saw us fly past them I caught their looks of surprise.

'Seat belt!' Alex reached over and grabbed it from my hand, ramming it home, then spinning the car through one eighty degrees. The men on the lawn were running back to the cars but the one by the door, standing under the white security light, was motionless. It was him. I knew it.

Demos stared right back at me, a smile on his face. My mother's killer was smiling at me. My mind went blank. And the world turned to white noise. A searing pain rocketed through my eye and ground against the inside of my skull like a blunt blade. I doubled over, clutching my head, trying to make it stop, the seat-belt cutting into my neck.

'It'll stop in a minute.' Alex's voice was cold.

The pain intensified. Then suddenly it did stop.

It took a few minutes before I could sit up straight again, pressing my hand to my head above my right eye, trying to mute the ache that remained.

'What was that?' I croaked.

'A little weapon against them.'

Them. He meant me, and I shrank back against the door, my eyes on the buttons, wondering what the other one did.

'It's given us a head start.'

'How?'

'It emits a frequency that interferes with the pattern of their brainwaves. It'll have . . . incapacitated them, like it did you.' He was checking his rear-view mirror every second or so, but he hadn't looked at me once. 'They're not following. It worked.'

Fear flooded back into me. 'A head start to where? Where are we going?' Was he taking us to the base?

He didn't answer, his face as impenetrable as moulded granite. I flinched further back against the door and looked out of the window to see if we were headed north but from the road signs I could see flashing past we were on the interstate heading south. Which meant we were headed away from the base. Where were we going?

The only noise was the churning of the gears as Alex's foot stamped down on the pedals. He was driving at least double the speed of any other car on the road, weaving rhythmically in and out of the lanes. I looked at his face, set in an expression of absolute concentration, and wondered how I could still feel such an addiction to being close to him, could still feel my heart lurch at the sight of him when his hatred towards me was so strong I could almost feel it coming off him in waves.

Alex dug around in his back pocket, then threw his phone into my lap instead, along with his wallet. 'There's a SIM card in the wallet, take it out and exchange it for the one in the phone.'

I fumbled with the back of the phone, eventually managing to slide the cover off. I prised out the SIM in there and Alex snatched it out of my hand, cracked open his window and threw it out. His wallet was stuffed with notes, there was at least five hundred dollars, my fingers were shaking as I tried to find the SIM amongst them. When I found it I pushed it into place in the phone and snapped the cover back on. Alex took it straight out of my hand and the wallet from my lap and shoved them back into his pocket.

Suddenly Key spoke up from the floor of the car, his voice a croak. 'Let me out.'

Alex ignored him, so I turned round in my seat and told him, 'It's OK, we're heading south. They're not following us.'

'Let me out.' He was trying to sit up, rubbing his head. He was a mess. 'I need to get back. I need to follow them.' He looked over at Alex, put his hand on the back of his seat. Alex glared at him in the rear-view mirror. 'Please, I can help you. Let me out. I can track them for you, warn you if they are getting close.'

I looked over at Alex, waiting to see what he would say.

'How will you track them?' he asked, his eyes back on the road.

Key sighed, then looking straight at Alex in the mirror said, 'I can project. I'm not one of Demos's group,' he added quickly. 'I just want my son back before your Unit catches up with them.'

Alex's lips pressed together. I watched his jaw clench tight. Finally he spoke. 'Who's your son?'

'Nate, his name is Nathaniel Johnson.' His voice broke apart on the name.

'You said your name was Key, not Johnson,' Alex shot back.

'My real name's Johnson. Anthony Johnson. Key's a nickname since I was a kid.'

'I've never heard of you or your son. Why should I believe you?'

I heard Key sigh again. 'They took my boy because he's special. Like me. Like her.' He pointed at me, and Alex flinched. Key

155

carried on, his voice rising. 'I want my boy back. He's not one of them. He's just a kid. He's sixteen. He doesn't have anything to do with whatever it is you think they've done.'

Alex stared at him for several seconds in the mirror, then looked back at the road. 'What do you know about anything they've done?'

'Nothing. Nothing, I swear to you. I never came near them before three weeks ago when they took Nate. I followed Lila to the bar and saw one of them outside so I came to the house to warn her. That's all. I don't know anything more.' Bloody foam was bubbling at the corner of his mouth and I stared at it.

Alex snapped his head round to look at Key. 'Why were you following Lila?' I wished he would look at the road. He was topping one fifty on the speedometer. My hands were gripping the edges of the seat.

'It's a long story.'

'He wanted my help.' I spoke up. 'He thought I might be able to get some information from Jack or you.'

Alex ignored me but his eyes skipped back to the road ahead.

'Look,' Key said. 'Why don't we help each other? If you let me out now I can go back, catch up with them and warn you if they're getting close. I can tell you where they're going, what they're planning, what their next move is. You need someone who can get close to them.'

'That relies on you being able to communicate with me. How will you be able to? What, are you telepathic too?' Scorn dripped off his words.

Key's eyes narrowed, 'You really don't know much about us, do you?' he said, sounding surprised. 'I can get back to my body instantly, well almost instantly, a matter of seconds. Don't matter where I am, could be another continent, only takes me to think about it and I'm there, back, right in my body. So you give me your phone number and you got instantaneous updates. I'm better than CNN.'

I couldn't even imagine what he was talking about. I really wanted to ask what happened to his body when he was out floating about, but was too scared to interrupt the conversation.

Alex swerved into the fast lane, stepping on the gas some more. 'Why? What's in it for you?'

'You help me get my son back. You and the Unit stop Demos but you find a way of keeping the Unit away from my son.'

'You could go now – project from here. That way I know right where you are,' Alex said.

'You think I trust you?' Key shot back. 'No offence. But you're one of them.'

Alex frowned, looking like he was weighing the pros against the cons. After a few more seconds he gave Key a cellphone number. I heard Key repeating it over and over, memorising it.

'You got it?' Alex asked.

'Yeah, I got it. And you? I do this, you going to keep your promise to help me get my son back?'

The silence rolled around the car. Then Alex nodded, just once, his eyes not leaving the road. He pulled across to the hard shoulder and slowed to a stop. Cars whizzed past in the inside lane.

Key seemed to relax slightly, he wiped the spit at the side of his mouth and moved to the door, as though he was about to open it and dive right out. Then he looked back at Alex and nodded in my direction. 'You need to get her as far away as you can. As in, international-sized distances.'

Alex looked round at him now, turning to face him. 'Why?' he asked, suddenly wary.

Key shook his head, grimacing through his busted lip. 'Suki will be able to trace her. Now she's seen Lila, read her mind, it'll be easy enough, given time. Or my son could trace her. If they can make him.'

'He can do that? Trace others?' Alex took the words out of my mouth.

'Yes. Others like him. From what I can tell, Suki has to read someone's mind before she can find them. Nate can just see others.'

'How?' It was me asking this time.

'It's hard to explain.' He didn't look like he was about to elaborate, as he glanced out of the window, chewing his lip, and bouncing on the seat. His body language screamed that he wanted to get out.

'Try.' Alex wasn't asking too politely.

Key looked at him and sighed like he was giving away a trade secret. 'When we project we can see auras around people, like a light.'

My mouth fell open.

'It's how I knew Lila was one of us. It's like she's wearing a sign. The colour of the aura is brighter, the light shimmering, more intense. And the stronger the ability, the brighter it burns.' It was like he was an art historian explaining the brushstrokes of a masterpiece. 'They'll find you. Believe me, they'll find you. And they want you bad.'

Key's hand was on the door handle, already opening it.

'Why are they still coming for me? Why do they want me so badly? Why don't they give up?' I could hear the creeping hysteria in my voice.

Key looked at me like I was stupid. 'Because, Lila, they want you to exchange for Alicia. They know if they got you Alex and Jack will give them whatever they want.'

I swallowed hard, avoiding Alex's eye. 'Are you sure about that?' Wasn't that before Alex knew what I was? I doubted I held the same ransom value now.

Key suddenly seemed to realised what I was getting at. He shrugged. 'Well maybe Demos just wants you then to join his little army? What do I know? All I know is they won't stop until they find you.'

And with that he pushed open the back door and was out, limping to the line of trees and bushes on the side of the road. Then he was gone.

Alex had already put the car in gear and now he pulled out into the traffic again. Within a few seconds the arm of the speedometer was stroking the one hundred mark.

With just the two of us left, the atmosphere became so intense it felt like the slightest noise or movement would ignite the car into a blue ball of flames. My whole body was rigid, poised for flight or fight, though realistically flight was not an option unless I fancied being roadkill.

'Alex,' I took a deep breath, 'why aren't you taking me to the base?'

He thought about it before answering, his voice terse when he did. 'The alarm's gone off. It's not safe.'

'No, that's not what I meant.' I couldn't look at him, choosing my words carefully. 'I don't want to be anywhere near the base or the Unit, obviously, knowing what I do about what it is you do there and how you feel about us.'

I saw his face darken with what looked like anger. He would be wondering what I knew and how. I struggled on. 'What I don't understand is why you aren't handing me over, "containing" me or whatever it is you do.'

I felt the engine growl deep as Alex pressed down the accelerator. His foot would be through the floor soon. If looks could kill, the road would be dead. I was glad he wasn't looking at me, and that he hadn't looked at me since we got in the car. And just as I was thinking that, he did look at me. His eyes were in shadow but the tone of his voice was enough to let me know he was tipping over the brink of calm.

'Jack will think Demos got to us both. He'll go after them. Either he'll catch Demos or he'll slow him down, which might give us the chance to get you out of the country to someplace safe before either the Unit or Demos catches up with you.'

It didn't answer my question but it did open up a whole load more. Out of the country? How was he going to explain that to Jack? And where was he planning on sending me? I couldn't go back to London, where they wouldn't need Suki to find me, just a phone book. So where could I go? Where on the planet would be safe?

I looked out of the windows at the red and white lights of cars making constellations in the distance and played Alex's words over in my mind, trying to imagine Jack's response. Then something registered and I stared at him wide-eyed. Had he meant he wasn't coming with me when he said it would give us a chance to get me out of the country? That was crazy. I couldn't go alone, I wouldn't make it as far as check-in before getting caught. For a moment I considered pleading with him, actually begging him, to come with me but the scowl on his face dissolved the words before I could even speak them.

The clock on the dash showed the time was now 3.06 a.m.

'Alex,' I said, when it hit 3.30. 'Why are you doing this? Why are you . . . helping me?'

His face was disappearing in and out of the strobing shadows and I couldn't see his expression.

'What?' he asked, as though he hadn't heard the question.

'Why are you helping me?' I said again, my voice shaking. If he hated us – me – so much, why all this effort to protect me?

He turned back to the wheel, slamming through the gears. 'I didn't have a choice,' he said, his voice a low snarl.

I looked away too, counting the white lines on the road as they blurred into one. As if I had a choice, I thought, as if I chose to be like this. Did he think I would choose to have him and Jack hate me?

I smacked my palm down on the door handle in frustration. Alex's arm shot across me, pressing me hard into the seat. He was looking at me like I was insane and I realised he'd thought I was trying to open the door. I stared at him in shock and he slowly moved his hand back to the wheel, giving me a look that fell somewhere between a warning and a threat. So now he thought I was suicidal too. Great. Telekinetic and suicidal. Just great.

18

When I opened my eyes I was staring at the seat buckle, my head and body twisted into the side of the car door and my hand resting on the handle, as though in my sleep I'd been trying to hide, or escape.

I glanced up and out of the window. We weren't moving anymore, we were just sitting on the side of the road as the dawn broke around us. There was no movement, no people, no cars and no noise – it was like the hiatus between breaths. I tried to work out where we were.

It looked like a desert town, flat and arid with dust already layering the windscreen, and even at this hour the road was throwing up a long-distance shimmer. Through the tinted window I could see a couple of buildings, mainly hardware and building supply stores spaced out at intervals. I had no idea what we were doing here other than maybe that Alex had pulled over to sleep.

I shifted slowly in my seat and turned towards him. He was staring out of his window and I felt both relief that he was still in the car and a shot of pain when I remembered that he wasn't here out of love or friendship but out of some dubious code of honour. That's what he had meant when he'd said he had no choice. It was so obvious. And so Alex.

I followed his gaze across the street. We were sitting opposite a second-hand car dealership. About forty cars plastered with 'for sale' signs were lined up facing us, like the start of a gumball rally.

We sat in the silence of the car, the air conditioning running, for another hour and forty minutes. Neither of us said a word. I brought my legs up onto the seat and sat there holding them, freezing but too scared to touch the buttons in the car or to open my mouth. I tugged at my dress to try to pull it over my legs and realised the seam had split up my thigh. My knees were hatched with blood and dirt. There was a small rent in one of the straps too which looked like it might at any moment lead to a wardrobe mishap. I remembered my flying tackle from the night before and glanced quickly over at Alex, remembering the hatred I'd seen in his face when I'd been standing on the porch. What would he have done if he'd reached me?

Eventually, things picked up a pace, like someone hitting the forward play button. A car pulled up outside the car dealership and a man in a short-sleeved shirt and golf trousers got out and unlocked the double padlock on the chain-link fence. He pulled into the lot and Alex started the engine.

I pushed my feet down off the seat as he drove across the road and into the dealership. I had an idea of what he was about to do and I was guessing Jack was not going to be too happy about it.

The man in the chequered trousers came straight out of his little Portakabin office, a coffee mug in his hand. I saw the look of surprise on his face quickly replaced with a broad, dental-worked smile.

'Stay here,' Alex said under his breath, already opening his door.

I watched through the window as Alex started talking. He had his back to me and I couldn't hear a word. At one point I saw him gesture towards me and the man leant a little forward and glanced into the car, waving. I fidgeted with my dress, aware that I was looking exactly like someone who'd stayed out all night and then been dragged through a hedge backwards; hair all over the place, dark smudges under my eyes where my mascara must have run, and looking altogether the worse for wear. God only knew what story Alex was spinning the man. I glanced up again and caught him pointing to a car on the far side of the lot and I sat forward to get a better view. It was a little white Toyota, fairly old-looking. Not exactly Alex's style. I didn't care what it looked like, though, so long as it went fast.

The man started to circle Jack's car. He opened the driver's door and got in next to me, giving me a grin.

'Hi there,' he said.

I looked at him blankly then forced a smile, trying to surreptitiously smooth my hair and hold my dress together at the same time.

He wobbled the gear stick, turned on the engine, checked the speedometer. His hand hovered over the buttons by the radio and I felt sickness well up in the pit of my stomach.

Alex leant in the door. 'That's just the radio tuning.'

The man put his hands back on the wheel. He turned his head and noticed the bag on the back seat. 'So, you two lovebirds are heading to Vegas, I hear. Congratulations.'

I stared at him, wondering if I'd misheard. Alex's face appeared again behind the man's shoulder, nudging me with his eyes. I realised straightaway what the message was and looked back at the man in shock.

'Oh, er, thanks.' I looked up at Alex again, who gave me the tiniest shrug. 'It's kind of sudden.'

'Well, good luck to you both,' he said, shaking my hand.

He got out of the car and I sat there in shock. I'd dreamt quite a lot when I was younger about marrying Alex. When I was nine I'd scrawled *Lila Wakeman* all over my diary about six hundred times. I'd even designed my wedding dress and practised saying 'I do' to a photo of Alex propped up on my dresser. Our wedding would have taken place in my parents' garden or a little white church. There was probably a pony in there somewhere, too. But never in all those imaginings had I imagined Vegas and a getaway car. I had to laugh at the irony of Alex now being the one pretending we were getting married.

When I glanced up I saw the man indicating his Portakabin. Alex shook his head and the man shrugged and walked inside by himself.

The next thing I knew, Alex had opened my door and pulled me out. Then he walked to the trunk and grabbed a black holdall that I assumed was Jack's.

Alex put his arm around me, his grip tight. It was pleasurable pain, my body reacting as it normally did to his touch. I was so tired I longed to put my arm around him too but I knew he was only holding me this way to keep up appearances for the car dealer. We had to look like we were in love, not like we were on the run from a secretive government unit and a pack of homicidal maniacs with mind control powers.

The man came out of his Portakabin, holding some keys and several stacks of paper in his hand that I realised were hundred-dollar bills. Alex held out his hand and the man counted out five stacks into it. I shifted uncomfortably, my bare feet starting to burn on the tarmac.

'Fifty, and I throw in the Toyota.'

Fifty thousand? Jack had said it was worth one twenty. But that was with extras that Alex couldn't demonstrate, unless he thought the man might up his price if he saw me flop to the pavement clutching my head. So fifty was probably a good amount. Jack would still go mad.

Alex took the keys from the man and handed him the Audi's in exchange.

'The paperwork's all in the glove box.'

'OK, sir, if I can just get you to sign this here piece of paper and check your licence we're all done.'

I couldn't see Alex's face because he was holding me so tight, I could only look up at his chin. He had to let me go though to reach for his licence in his pocket. I felt him edge ever so slightly towards me so his body was still touching mine. He was clearly nervous about me doing a runner. I instinctively leant into him to close the distance. I was definitely through with running away from Alex.

'OK, Mr . . .' the man peered more closely at the document in Alex's hand, 'Hunt. It's been a pleasure doing business with you.' I looked up in surprise. He turned to me. 'And the soon-to-be-Mrs-Hunt, a pleasure.'

He held out his hand and I looked at it until I felt Alex gently nudging my back. I took the hand and shook it, murmuring my thanks.

'Mr Hunt?' I asked. We were walking fast towards the Toyota. Alex had picked up the holdall and slung it over his shoulder, his other arm around me. I was walking awkwardly over the ground and he hadn't seemed to notice that I wasn't wearing any shoes. 'How do you have fake ID?'

Alex was unlocking the car and popping the trunk. He let go of me.

'How do you think I have fake ID? It's just a shame I don't have one for you, too. It would be a big help right now.'

He opened the passenger door for me and I got in. The white leather seats stuck to the back of my bare legs and the inside smelt of stale beer with overtones of upholstery cleaner.

'Nice choice,' I said, when Alex got in his side.

He looked over at me briefly and I thought I detected the start of a smile at the corner of his mouth. My stomach muscles contracted with it. It was the first sign of warmth he'd shown me. The arm around me didn't count, that had been acting. I let my eyes travel all over his face. He was busy reversing out of the space, looking over his shoulder. Maybe it was because it was daylight and the shadows were gone but the anger from last night seemed to have dissipated. He was still tense, I could tell from the furrows in his brow and the way his mouth was set in a line, but he didn't seem angry anymore, just very focused.

'Why did you sell Jack's car?'

'We're going to need the money. Plus they'll have an APB out on us. Every cop in the country's going to be on the lookout for us. The Audi's fairly conspicuous.'

We drove a few miles out of the town. Alex was quiet the whole way and the air was saturated with unspoken questions. I had so many to ask I didn't know where to begin but I knew that he most certainly had questions for me too. I wondered when he would start the inquisition.

Just as I was about to test the water by asking again where we were going, Alex swung into the car park of a giant mall. He pulled into a space away from the entrance, between two big SUVs. Before I could ask what we were doing there, Alex started unbuttoning his shirt. My jaw went slack as I watched. When he was done with the buttons he pulled it off. He was wearing a white vest underneath and I couldn't help but stare at his bare arms and shoulders, wondering what on earth he was doing.

'Here, put this on.' He chucked the shirt at me.

I looked at him with a question in my eyes.

'You can't walk into a mall like that,' he said indicating my ripped dress.

He had a point. I didn't reply, just put the shirt on over my dress, my fingers mangling the buttons they were shaking so much.

I peeked up at him when I was done. The sleeves were much too long, hanging over my hands. Alex took my arm and started rolling one sleeve up.

His eyes, I noticed, were back to their normal cool blue but they were shuttered and I couldn't read his mood. When he was done he got out of the car and I took a second to look at myself in the little mirror on the inside of the visor. Eyes like a raccoon, hair like it had been dreaded. There was little I could do besides wipe some of the black soot from under my eyes. I got out of the car.

'Can you make it in bare feet?' He was nodding towards the entrance.

I nodded back. We crossed quickly to the front of the mall and walked into the air-conditioned cool. Alex didn't put his arm around me this time, though he stayed close. I was super-conscious of how we looked, the shirt not being much of an improvement. I'd gone from looking like a dirty stop-out to looking like a dirty stop-out wearing the shirt of the man I'd stopped out with. Still, I wasn't going to take it off. Actually, the Vegas line had been kind of genius. That was exactly what we looked like. Two hungover, partied out people on their way to or from Vegas.

168

We went into the first store we came to, a Gap. Alex strode through it, clearly in a hurry, and I jogged after him. He was in the women's section picking out T-shirts. He crossed to the jeans and held up a pair, threw them down and picked up another pair, examined them for a second then threw them over his arm. He seemed to remember I was there and looked around.

'Shoes,' he said, as though he thought I'd have already figured out that's what I should have been looking for.

I turned around and saw a rack of flip-flops by the till. I grabbed the first pair in my size and turned back to him. He was standing by the underwear section now.

I hurried over, feeling my cheeks burn. I hoped to God he wasn't going to estimate my size in this department too, but when I came up to his side he said, 'You'd better get some things. I'll be just over there.'

He walked off to the men's section. I panicked at the few feet he was putting between us and reached out and snatched hold of the first things I could see then scurried over to where he was.

'Did you get a sweater? You're going to need something warm.'

Where were we going? Alaska? I turned around again and ran over to the table with the sweaters on. It was the desert, they didn't sell many sweaters in this store, at least not ones that would keep me warm if I was Arctic-bound. I pulled one from the pile and rushed back to Alex. The woman behind the counter handed Alex some scissors so he could snip the tag attaching my flip-flops. She looked like she would have liked to hand him a whole lot more, like her naked body across the counter. I slipped the shoes on while glaring at her.

Alex took me by the arm and marched me out the store. 'You hungry?'

It wasn't so much a question. We were already walking towards a fast food restaurant. I hadn't thought about it until that point. My stomach had been in so many knots but now he'd said the word it growled like a wolf to the moon. I clutched it and looked up at Alex nodding.

We ordered enough to feed about ten men and a large, black coffee, which Alex piled sugar into. I felt bad at how little sleep he'd had. And on his birthday, which I realised I had totally ruined.

We sat at a table out of the way, near to the fire exit. Alex kept his back to the wall, eating like he didn't know what he was putting in his mouth, not looking at it once, his eyes too busy moving over the restaurant. I ate until I was full and then leant back in the chair, suddenly feeling the smack of exhaustion hit me full on. I could have put my head on the table right there and fallen into a coma without caring an ounce whether Demos found me. Or the Unit for that matter.

I rested my chin on my hand and watched Alex scanning the room. Circles were starting to shadow his eyes.

'Why are you doing this?' I asked.

'What?' Alex moved his eyes back to me. The frown line, the same one I usually caused, was back.

'I still don't understand why you're helping me.'

He looked away again, over to the entrance, at a couple of noisy teenagers who had just come in. 'I told you, I didn't have a choice.' His voice was neutral, no anger in it, just stating a simple fact.

I carried on. 'But I know what you think about people like me.'

He shook his head and a half-smile, slightly sad, pulled at the side of his mouth. 'You don't know what I'm thinking.'

That was true, but last night I hadn't needed to be telepathic to know how much he despised me. 'You hate me.'

170

I waited to see what he would say. He was looking over at the entrance again, as though fully expecting to see Demos breeze through at any moment. After a couple of seconds he turned his head slowly to look at me again. 'Lila, I don't hate you.'

I picked up on the slight emphasis he put on the word 'hate' as though he was denying the one word while replacing it with another in his mind, like 'loathe' or 'despise'. It was just semantics, though.

I looked at the table and picked up a napkin, twisting it into a rope. 'Why did you lie?'

He frowned at me. 'Lie? About what?'

'About Demos. I know he killed my mother. I know that he's the one after me. But you told me it wasn't the same people. That I didn't need to worry. And you said that Suki had no connection to the people who did it and I know she does.' An associate sure as hell was a connection.

For a moment, Alex's brows drew together and he narrowed his eyes at me. I felt myself flushing under his examination. His expression calmed after a moment, his forehead uncreased. 'I'm guessing you know all this through Key?'

'Something like that.' Best leave out the hacking.

He nodded. 'I'm sorry I lied to you.'

I was thrown a bit by his apology, it was so unexpected. I shook my head as though it didn't matter. An apology was nice but I wanted to know why he had done it.

He looked at the table for an instant, then back towards the door, then finally back at me.

'Would you believe me if I told you that I was doing it to keep you safe?'

I raised my eyebrows to indicate no, I wouldn't believe him.

171

He sighed. 'I thought that if you knew the same people who killed your mum were after you, you might try to do something stupid. Like act as bait. Or that you'd run away, thinking we couldn't protect you. You looked so scared.'

'You thought I'd run away?' Before last night, I'd never have run away from Alex. I'd run to him all the way from London in the first place.

'It has been known, Lila, it's not that absurd a conclusion to draw.' He took a sip of coffee.

He had a point, so I pressed my lips together and let him carry on.

'I thought you deserved to know about Jack and your father – the reason Jack was appearing so unreasonable.' He placed his hands on the table. 'But I didn't think you deserved to know that the same people were after you as killed your mother. Why would you deserve the fear that would cause? When the threat wasn't even established—' He ran a hand through his cropped hair then put it back on the table, around his coffee. He looked up at me through his dark gold lashes and he was suddenly my Alex again. The boy who was holding my hand at the funeral, keeping strangers at bay. 'Lila, I hate seeing you scared or hurt and I wanted to protect you. It's as simple as that.'

I nodded. He hadn't used the past tense. He had said *I hate seeing you scared*. It was enough to spark a flame of hope that he didn't despise me after all.

'Why did you leave the bar and run off like that?'

'Key was there. He told me – he told me what you and Jack do for a living.'

I didn't need to tell him that the deciding factor was not that but seeing him with Rachel.

Alex was glaring at me. 'What did Key tell you?'

I started tearing the napkin into little pieces and scattering them over the table. 'That the Unit's mission was to hunt down people like me and that they – that they disappeared and didn't come back once you caught them.'

'How does he know that?' Alex said under his breath.

I shot back in my seat. If I'd wanted a confirmation about what the Unit was doing, here it was.

When we got outside, Alex became quiet. He scanned the car park several times before stepping out of the shadows by the entrance. He took my hand this time, pulling me along behind him. I was holding the shopping and he had his other hand resting behind his back on his gun. My heart was racing; coming outside again felt like being a rabbit out of a hole.

We got back to the Toyota and I waited for him to unlock the door, bouncing on the balls of my feet. But Alex didn't unlock the doors, he just opened the trunk, took the holdall out, then shut it again.

'Come on,' he said.

We walked several rows down and stopped by a brand new black Lexus. I hoped that we were just admiring it but I had a sinking feeling I knew what he was about to do. He slipped down the side of the car, pushing me ahead of him. My eyes darted around the car park to see if anyone was coming, adrenaline starting to pump. Alex stayed as cool as ice. In one fluid movement he pulled something out of the holdall and held it against the key lock. The thing in his hand beeped and the electric locks on the car flipped up.

He looked at me and tilted his head. 'Coming?'

I swallowed, looked around me again and jumped into the passenger seat which he was holding open. He walked quickly

173

around to the other side, threw the bags into the back and got in. The same machine, held by the ignition, switched the engine on. I stared at him in disbelief as we swung out of the car park, and slid down in my seat as far as I could go. It wasn't enough that we had Demos and the Unit after us, Alex had to bring the police into the equation too?

19

From the signs on the interstate, we were headed north towards Palm Springs. Alex had, at some point in the night, doubled back and headed north-east.

'What are we doing?' I asked. 'What's the plan?' I hoped that he had one, and that it was a good one – and that it involved him coming with me all the way, not just to drop me off at an airport. Then I remembered that I didn't have a passport. Alex might have a whole bag stuffed full of useful toys, gadgets and fake IDs but he didn't have a passport for me. So I wouldn't be going anywhere.

'We're going to find a motel and get some sleep.'

Apart from a motel. 'OK . . . and after?' I asked.

'One thing at a time.' He glanced at me and I felt my heart skip a beat. I wished he'd tell me what was going on and what he was thinking.

He kept his speed down in this car, brushing the limit. An hour later, on the road into Palm Springs, he pulled up at a motel, one of several lining the road. It had palm trees out the front and a square pool with railings around it. The rooms were laid out in an L shape over two floors. He drove in and pulled up next to a car with a trailer, well hidden from the road.

'Let's go,' he said, turning off the engine.

He paid for a twin room on the ground floor. Alex unlocked the door, letting me in first. I hovered in the middle of the room, unsure what to do next. He came and piled the bags onto the chair by the door.

'Why don't you take a shower? Here.' Alex handed me the bags with my clothes in.

I took them and closed the bathroom door behind me. The mirror was not kind. I looked awful. I eased off Alex's shirt and my dress, catching sight of the fading, green-tinted bruise on my thigh. For a few seconds I stood there experiencing déjà vu, reliving the exact moment that had set in motion this whole chain of events. I'd been standing in a bathroom then too, in a pretty similar state. Though in retrospect that situation was a kids' ride compared to the roller coaster I was now on.

It was a quick shower – I felt too scared to stay in it long, conscious that if Demos chose to find me now, I didn't want to have to put up a fight while naked.

When I was done, I towelled off quickly and threw on a vest and the jeans that Alex had picked out. They fitted perfectly. He had chosen my exact size.

Alex was standing by the window looking out through a crack in the curtain when I came out. He looked round at me and said, 'Come here.'

I came towards him slowly. His face was hard again and I was scared suddenly. He looked like he was going to interrogate me.

When I was standing in front of him he reached behind and my stomach dropped – he was going for his gun. He didn't need a gun, I would tell him whatever he wanted to know. He took it out, keeping the barrel pointed down.

176

And then he handed it to me. 'Do you know how to use this?'

I shook my head.

'Here.' He pressed my hands around the grip. The gun was heavier than I expected and warmer, from where it had been pressed against his back. 'This is the safety catch. It's on now, click it down to release it.' He pushed the catch with his thumb over mine and, standing behind me with his arm over my shoulder, he pulled the gun up so it was pointing at a painting on the opposite wall. 'Point and fire.'

He clicked the safety back on and took his hand off mine. The weight of the gun dropped my hand a few inches; he lifted it back up to chest height. 'Aim high, but for the chest. I guess you don't need much help in the way of weapons, but just in case.'

I felt my cheeks start to burn but chose to ignore the comment. 'Just in case what?'

'I'd just feel better knowing you know how to shoot. Just don't shoot me while I'm in the shower.' I didn't know how he could joke. Or was he joking? Did he think I would do that? If he did he wouldn't give me his gun, surely?

Alex walked into the bathroom but kept the door cracked open. I stood by the window, looking out, the gun hanging in my hand, pointing at the floor. I wanted to put it down but I also felt oddly comforted holding it.

The shower started to run. I turned from the window just as Alex walked back into the room. He was wearing a towel around his waist and had his clothes in his hands. He dropped them onto the bed and took a few new clothes out of one of the bags. Then he walked back into the bathroom without a second glance at me. I commanded myself to breathe.

I heard Alex get into the shower and I walked over to the

177

window, looking out across the parking lot to the empty, leaf-strewn pool. There was no sign of the police, no sirens, no black SUVs screeching up the road. I rested my head against the glass. When would this chase ever stop? And who was going to win?

A hand closed over mine and I almost jumped out of my skin. I hadn't heard him even come out of the bathroom.

Alex prised the gun out of my hand. 'Lila, I give you a gun and you don't even hear me coming.'

'I haven't done three years of Marine training, I don't have special . . .' I trailed off. I had been going to say 'skills'. Alex was cocking an eyebrow at me.

I sank down onto the bed. He stayed standing, watching me carefully. He looked like he was about to ask me something and I readied myself for the question about to come.

'You should sleep. I'll keep watch.'

I looked up at him confused. 'No, you need to sleep. You're exhausted.' He looked so tired, the circles under his eyes darkening, a day's worth of stubble giving his face a golden glow.

'It's OK. You go first. I'll wake you in a few hours,' he said, already turning away.

I lay down on the bed – I didn't have the energy to argue. Alex shifted the chair nearer the window and sat down in it, the gun in his hand pointed at the door. I rolled over so my back was turned and stared at the other wall, trying not to think about anything, trying to breathe through my fear. I had given up trying to figure out what Alex was thinking or feeling.

This time, the men in my nightmare had faces.

As I followed the path of blood I noticed the smashed vase on the floor by the front door and the table overturned in the living

178

room. My mum lay on the stairs like a broken doll, blood pumping from her chest, and I dropped to my knees, my hands turning red as I tried to scoop her life-blood up and push it back.

A sudden noise made me turn my head. Demos was standing right next to me, a knife in his hand. Behind him were three other men, the men whose photos I'd seen in the file. One flicked his cigarette butt towards me, smiling. Suki was a blur behind them, skipping in a puddle of blood. I started to scream and tried to lunge towards Demos to knock the knife from his hand, but my arms wouldn't move, they were held so tightly.

'Shhhh, shhhh, it's OK.'

I was pulling and pulling, trying to get free.

'Lila, it's OK. Calm down.'

My eyes snapped open at the voice. Alex was sitting on the edge of the bed holding my wrists in his hands. I was reaching towards him as though I was trying to strangle him. I stopped fighting and let my arms go limp. Then, without thinking, I fell forward towards him. There was no movement on his part to catch me and I remembered too late, as my head collided with his chest, that Alex didn't think of me as Lila anymore, that he was repulsed by me. I started to pull myself up and roll away when I felt his arms suddenly wrap around me and his hands in my hair, stroking it back. The feeling was so electric that I wondered if I was still dreaming. It was like a cotton reel inside me was being unspooled. Everything, all the dread and the fear and the humiliation was spinning away, leaving me feeling like I'd just inhaled a tank of gas and air.

'It's OK.' He was saying it over and over again and I started to believe him, to calm down and let his touch sedate me. Then I remembered the dream and the fear rolled back in, waves and waves of it, drowning me.

179

I started crying hard into his shoulder, shaking my head. 'No, it's not OK, it's not OK. They're going to find me.' How could they not? There were two of us and lots of them, with abilities far beyond mine and weapons far beyond Alex's.

Alex's arms tightened around me and I shrank into him, trying to limpet myself onto him, terrified he'd let me go. I couldn't believe he was this close to me, let alone pulling me closer. What had changed while I'd been sleeping? Since last night, when he'd come towards me in the backyard looking like he wanted to kill me?

'I'll get you away . . .' He was murmuring the words and where his lips brushed my hair my scalp was left tingling. 'I'll get you somewhere safe, I promise. Then we'll stop them.' His voice was calm and the warmth in it was such a contrast to the cold front of the anger I'd been dealing with until now, that it started me crying again.

I wished I could believe him. It would be so easy to let him hypnotise me with his words but I pushed away slightly so I could look him in the face. 'What's a psychokenosist?'

His hands tightened on my arms. 'How do you—' Then he stopped and disentangled himself, stood up and walked away.

My whole body went cold and started to shake, like shock was setting in. Delayed shock, from all the way back to the mugging, like it had been storing itself up for the last week. I hugged my arms around myself, trying to get warm and to stop my teeth chattering.

'It derives from the Greek. *Psyche* meaning "mind", and *Kenosis*, meaning "to empty".' Alex waited to gauge my reaction.

'Mind empty?'

'Yes. Demos's power is unique. He can literally empty your mind of every thought and every feeling you possess. He can

180

effectively stop anyone from doing anything.' He paused to see that I had understood. 'Demos is the most powerful one of your kind that we know of.'

My kind? So that was how he saw me.

'How many do you know of?' I asked in a whisper.

'Nine. Well, twelve now if I count you and Key and his son. But the Unit doesn't know about you three. Yet.' He was pacing the small square of area between the bed and the bathroom door.

Yet? Was he planning on telling them? How else would they find out?

'Just nine? How many more do you think there are?'

'Conservative estimate? We think there are probably two hundred or so in the United States. Based on the numbers so far. But maybe it's higher.'

Two hundred? Two hundred people like me. What were the odds, then? It wasn't many. But it was actually quite a lot of people, if you put them all together in one place.

I was still shaking. 'How long has the Unit been hunting them – I mean us?'

A scowl made its way onto Alex's face. The anger was back and I instinctively flinched away, edging into the headboard. He must have seen my expression, because his scowl disappeared. He yanked the cover off the other bed and sat down on the edge of mine, wrapping it around my shoulders.

'About five years.' It was said through gritted teeth.

Five years was how long it had been since my mother died. 'And you've only found nine?'

'You're good at keeping what you can do below the radar.'

I couldn't interpret the look on his face. Rancour, impatience, maybe. He carried on. 'Our focus is on Demos. And his people.'

181

The scowl was easier to interpret, and this time I recognised it wasn't about me.

'Why? Why the focus on him? You said that the Unit's mission wasn't to find my mum's killers.'

'It isn't. I didn't lie. The mission is to stop them, yes, but it's not about solving a homicide.'

I frowned at his casual use of the word homicide. This was my mum's murder he was talking about.

He hurried on, as though wanting to explain. 'When we joined the Unit all we cared about was getting justice for what he did to your mum. But after a while it became more than that. When we saw what he was capable of, and what he was planning, it stopped being all about our vendetta and became more about stopping him before he could do far worse.'

I swallowed. What could be worse than murder? 'This thing that he's planning, could it have something to do with why he killed my mum? Because she found out about it? Is that why he killed the senator too?'

Alex looked at me in shock. 'You know about him?'

'Yes.' I ignored the questions in his eyes, forming on his lip. 'Why did he kill her? Them, I mean. What's he planning?' I needed to know what worse could look like. I might be on the receiving end of it.

Alex bit his lip and paused, then shook his head slowly, looking at me with an odd expression on his face. 'You know what? I thought I knew. I was so sure – we were all so sure. Jack too. But now I don't know if everything the Unit has been telling me is the truth or a lie.'

I stared at him, stunned. After a minute or so I broke the silence. 'What were you told?'

'Lila, it's going to sound so crazy.'

'Yes, because my life is so completely sane right now. Tell me.'

'OK, well, the Unit – our whole mission – is basically counter-terrorism. With a twist.'

'Terrorism?'

'Yes.'

'So what are you saying? That Demos is a terrorist? I'm sorry, but you've lost me.'

'Listen, when the Unit found out about Demos it was because he had been using one of his associates, a telepath, to access information from a senator working on nuclear defence. This was during the Bush administration. Remember those rumours about the design of new nuclear weapons after 9/11?'

I looked at him blankly.

'Maybe you were too young. Well, it wasn't a rumour. It was the truth. The project was so secret that only a few people were involved in the initial research. A small team within the Department for Homeland Security.'

'My mother—'

'No. Not at this stage. Your mum had nothing to do with the initial research and development. The rumours that weapons were being built kept circulating around Washington and further afield. It's difficult to keep something that huge a secret. In 2004 your mother was asked to sit on a secret committee that was looking at the issue of weapon stockpiling.'

'She was? But I don't get it—'

'This is where the information starts to become more vague. Somehow in that process she discovered what Demos was doing. That he was using his telepathy to gain access to information about the stockpiles.'

'Please tell me why he would want information on nuclear stockpiles.'

'Why does anyone want a nuclear weapon? For control, for power. With a threat like that at his fingertips he could create chaos.'

'You know what? You're right, this does sound crazy. Why? Why would he want to do that?'

'Money probably, power definitely.'

'But you can't just waltz off with a nuclear weapon and take over the world. What can you do with a nuclear weapon, anyway? Load it into a catapult and fire? Fire it where?'

A smile twitched at the corner of his mouth and suddenly I didn't want to talk anymore. I just wanted to watch him. He was smiling at me. First hugs, now smiles. Maybe he really didn't hate me. Maybe I could convince him that I wasn't subhuman or whatever he thought about me exactly; that I was still Lila.

'He wouldn't need to fire it – it's just the threat of it – that would be enough.'

'But we have a whole army – why just go after him with twenty-four men? Why not put the whole army on to him if he's such a threat?'

For a moment I thought whoever was in charge needed to be fired. They clearly weren't a very good strategist.

'None of this can be made public knowledge, Lila. Do you want the general public to know about what you can do? What do you think would happen if people thought that people like you existed? That there were people out there who could control their thoughts and their actions, who could read their minds, or rearrange their memories?'

Was that what a sifter was? I wasn't too sure what would happen if it became public knowledge – was he talking lynchings? Men in white coats carrying out vivisections on us? Other sorts of testing?

From the look on Alex's face he thought it would be bad. I thought about how I'd instinctively hidden my ability from everyone, even the people I loved. Something inside me had known, without needing to be told, that exposing it would be dangerous. But then again, keeping it hidden didn't seem to be much safer. The Unit were after us like we were stray rodents and being contained didn't sound like a much better option – in fact, it sounded worse.

'I'm not sure,' I said finally. 'If the option is being hunted down by the Unit or having the public know about me – I think right now I'm going with the public vote.'

Alex looked at me with an expression I could only place as anguish. 'Well, you've no choice on that one. It's coming down from the highest authority. It stays secret.'

'What authority? Like the President?'

'No. Higher.'

There was a higher authority? Wasn't that supposed to be God or someone?

He saw my face, my glance up at the ceiling, and laughed at me. 'No, not that kind of authority. You don't honestly think that the President is in charge, do you?'

'Er, isn't he?' If he wasn't in charge, who the heck was?

'Lila, we're a black op. Even the President doesn't know about black ops.'

I stared at him with my eyebrows raised.

'The only option we've been told is to keep going after them. Stop them. Anytime there's any threat of public exposure it gets covered up fast. The same way other terrorist threats do. It's all kept under the radar.'

I stared at him open-mouthed, feeling my naïvety falling away from me like a layer of clothing.

'We're getting closer to them. The Unit have got three of them now. They'll get Demos eventually. Then we'll start focusing on the others – on getting them all.'

He realised what he'd said and stopped abruptly, looking at me with a guilty expression. Neither of us spoke for a few seconds. I looked away from him and tried to swallow and breathe and not cry.

'Lila, I don't mean, I'm . . .'

I shut my eyes. I didn't want to hear it.

I didn't hear him move but I felt him put his hand on my shoulder. I shrugged it off. It was clear where he stood on the matter.

'How will you stop Demos? You said he had a special power.'

Alex hesitated before speaking. 'He can only focus it on a few people at a time. Which is why he needs an army. With the abilities he's collecting around him it's getting harder to find him and harder still to fight him. Our weapons are limited – you've seen the extent of them.'

Yes, big guns and loud alarms.

'We can only use them in short bursts and his people are usually able to stop us before we can set it off. They see us coming – that girl Suki can hear us from a mile off. There are others who can pick up on the atmosphere, sense us when we get close, and now, I guess, with Key's son, it explains how they're able to predict our moves, stay one step ahead of us. He's following us and letting them know what we're planning. As fast as we take one of his people out, he recruits another.' He looked at me with a little shrug.

'And all of this, everything you've just told me about Demos and this so-called terrorist plot; you're telling me that now you're not actually sure it's the truth?' I shook my head at him, confused. 'Why not?'

Alex dropped his gaze to the floor, frowning, then looked up and met my eyes. 'Because if they could lie to me about you, then they can lie about anything.'

20

I held Alex's gaze, my breathing running rapid. 'Lie about me? What do you mean?' I stuttered.

Alex shook his head. 'The things we've been made to believe about people like you – it – it just doesn't make sense to me anymore. I look at you and I start questioning everything I've been told.'

Once more he'd stunned me into silence. Clearly the picture they'd painted of us was not that warm and fuzzy. They really believed they were hunting monsters. And in Demos's case, they obviously were.

'But you believed them before yesterday – why?'

He looked away again and I could see the frustration etched on his face. 'Because, when Jack and I were recruited at Washington State, they offered us the chance for revenge. And we believed them because we wanted to.'

'What did they tell you? How did they recruit you?'

'Two men showed up on campus one day. They wouldn't tell us who they were working for. At first we assumed CIA but I don't think they were. They showed us the information they had on Melissa's – sorry – on your mother's murder. They showed us everything they had on Demos: photographs, crime reports, trials in absentia, a whole raft of reports and evidence on other psys. At first we thought they were making it up. You have to understand, for us, it was like discovering aliens existed and were living among us. We didn't believe it. So they took us to Pendleton, to the Unit, and showed us. They had one, someone they'd captured. We saw it with our own eyes. He could do what Key can do. We started to believe them, to ask questions. They told us that the Unit's mission was to catch people like your mother's killers. We didn't need any other incentive. We signed the papers right there and then. It seems crazy now, but at the time there was no other option for either of us. We had to do it.'

It didn't seem crazy at all. I loved them both for it. I just wished I hadn't ended up being on their hit list.

'Can I ask you a question now?' Alex was looking at me, his blue eyes piercing right through me. I readied myself. 'How did it happen?'

I leaned back against the headboard and hugged my knees tighter. 'I don't know. I thought you might be able to tell me that.'

He thought about it for a moment. 'We don't know. All we've managed to do is isolate the gene. We're not sure what triggers it, though. Some people have the gene but it just lies dormant.'

It was genetic? Wow. Why wasn't Jack like me, then?

'When did it start?' Alex suddenly asked.

It felt so strange to be admitting any of this, to be talking about it so openly. But at the same time, if there was anyone on the planet I wanted to tell, it was Alex. Just not under these circumstances.

I took a few breaths then started. 'Three years ago. Well, actually there was one incident before then but I didn't realise it was me . . .'

Alex waited for me to continue.

189

'When I came to London it was really difficult. In my first week at school I got mad with a teacher. She, um, she . . .' I looked down at the sheet, stroking the hem with my finger. 'She asked me to take off the bracelet you'd given me. You remember it?' I glanced up and met Alex's eyes but he showed no flicker of recognition. Maybe he hadn't opened my present.

I carried on. 'I said no. She told me again to take it off or she'd cut it off and I said no. So she came towards me with these scissors . . . and I don't know what happened. One minute the scissors were in her hand and the next they'd flown halfway across the room and were sticking out of the blackboard.'

I looked back up at Alex. He was pressing his lips together, reining in whatever he wanted to say. It was actually quite funny that my ability had, in a way, been triggered by his present to me.

I hurried on. 'I had no idea I had made it happen. People looked at me weirdly but I honestly didn't have a clue was me.'

'And then?'

I realised I'd stopped talking. I'd been thinking back to that moment and the teacher's face as the scissors flew out of her hand. I frowned as I fast-forwarded to the first proper time I'd been conscious of.

'Well, the next time it really happened was a year or so later. At school, in the dining room someone made a comment about my mum and I just lost it.'

I bit my lip. I didn't need him thinking I was unstable or unable to control my ability. Which would be correct, but he didn't need to know that.

'I didn't usually mind the comments – I mean, I guess I was a little weird; a little distant, uninterested – but it wasn't a good time. I was missing my mum so much. I was missing you and

Jack.' I felt my stomach tighten. 'So this girl said something and I threw a jam roly-poly at her head.' There was a silence, so I added, 'Not using my hands, obviously.'

'You did what?' He burst out laughing. It wasn't the reaction I'd expected. I started laughing too.

'Yeah, it was pretty stupid. But she deserved it. Anyway, after that, everyone pretty much avoided me. They thought I'd actually chucked it, that it had been in my hand. You would, right? I got into trouble. But I didn't care – I was just utterly amazed that I could do this, this thing. So I started to practise. You know, with pencils and books and small things. It took ages to get a grip on it. I thought maybe it was all in my mind at first, that I was imagining it, and then, it was a bit like riding a bike, I just got it one day. Moving things without, um, actually touching them, was like the most natural thing in the world.'

I didn't mention that it was a bit like riding a bike with no brakes, down a very steep hill.

'And does it have anything to do with why you came here? Did you really get mugged?'

'Yes. That was the truth. I just didn't tell you the whole story.' I paused; Alex was looking at me with a face like thunder. 'I – I didn't hurt them.'

'What did they do to you?'

I realised he wasn't angry with me, he was angry with them. This was good – anywhere his anger could be directed other than at me was good.

'Nothing. Well, I mean, they were just trying to take my bag. But they held a knife to me and, I don't know what happened, but the next second I was holding the knife. Well, not holding it exactly. It was—' I couldn't accurately describe it, so I stopped.

Alex put his head in his hands. I hadn't thought it was that bad. Oh God, he did think I was a sociopath.

'I didn't mean to do it. I didn't hurt them. I know it was bad. I tried to stop. I did stop. I promised myself I wouldn't do it again. Then all this happened and . . .' I ran out of steam.

He looked up at me with an expression I really couldn't read. Like someone had told him his motorbike had been stolen.

'Will you tell Jack?' I asked.

His expression settled. 'I think he needs to know.'

'Why?' I didn't want to tell Jack. I knew he'd make Alex's reaction look like a peace meditation.

'Because, Lila, you're his sister. And I have to get you out of the country and I need his help to do it.'

I threw off the blanket and stood up off the bed. 'But he'll hate me, he'll look at me like you just did. Like I'm some kind of monster, something awful. Like the people who killed Mum.'

Suddenly he was on his feet. 'Lila, that's not what I think. I told you I don't believe it. It's not what Jack will think, either, once we explain.'

'But you're still not sure about me – I can see the doubt. And the way you're looking at me now . . . it's obvious.'

'No – no, that's not it. I'm angry now, for sure. But not with you. I'm furious with those kids for mugging you. I could kill them. You had far more self-control than Jack or I would have done.'

He sat back down on the bed, facing me. 'I'm sorry about last night, and today. The way I've been treating you,' he said. 'It was a shock.' He paused, trying to think what to say. 'It's what I was trying to tell you before. For the last three years I've been programmed to think of you, of people like you, rather, as something less than human. As all bad. It was as if the gene that triggers this was a rogue gene, like a cancer, wiping out all the good in people – and then I see you . . . It was, it was a bit like losing gravity.' He ran his hands down his face, pressed his fingers into his temples. 'Everything's changed. I no longer know what to think or who to trust.'

I stared straight at him. Did he trust me? The silence started to thump like it had its own heartbeat. Neither of us moved or said anything for a long time. I was trying to reconstruct the whole night from this new perspective.

'Is that why you almost killed Key too? Because you thought he was like me?' Was their automatic reaction to try to exterminate us on sight?

'What?' His eyes flashed, his voice was low but angry. 'I almost killed him because I saw him dragging you out of the house.'

'Oh.' I sank down onto the opposite bed.

'I had no idea who he was – I just saw him with you and—' He looked up at me apologetically and I felt my heart do a little jump. He'd been trying to save me. Put like that, it was swoonworthy stuff, though I doubted Key's face agreed.

All of a sudden, none of it mattered anymore. The whole of last night could be rewritten in my head. He wasn't angry with me. He didn't hate me. Now all I needed was for him to tell me he was coming with me.

'Where am I going to go?'

His eyes met mine. He really looked so tired. Like he didn't have the energy to stand. He hadn't slept yet. 'I don't know yet. I'm thinking about it.'

A thought bubbled to the surface. 'What about my dad? What will we tell him if I just disappear?'

'We'll make something up. You can see him again when this is over. When it's safe.'

'You know he's not going to be that happy about me missing my exams.' It seemed ridiculous to be worrying about tests when I was potentially about to be killed, but I knew how my dad's mind worked.

'Yes, I realise that. I'm sorry. Maybe you can take them in a few months' time.'

'Hmmm. Maybe.' I didn't mind. Not taking exams and heading off into the sunset with Alex was a pretty amazing deal. I'd take it every time.

A thought was scuttling around my head, though, and I couldn't shake it. I heard myself voice it quietly. 'Are you coming with me?'

He took a while to answer, then he said, 'You think I'd let you go alone?' My heart leapt.

Alex stood up and came towards me and then knelt down in front of me. 'Lila, when you asked me earlier why I was helping you and I told you I had no choice I meant I have no choice because you are—'

The trilling of a phone interrupted. I hung on to the last words, I am what? I am WHAT?

He was gone, though, over to the table, where his phone was vibrating.

'Hello . . .? We're good. Where are you? Did you find them?'

It had to be Key. There was a pause.

'OK. OK. No, that's good. Yes. I'll call him later. We're going to be gone in twenty-four hours. Is that long enough?'

'Yes, I promise. Yes – I will be.' A pause. 'No. Not on her own.' Another pause. 'Yes. And Key – thank you.'

He hung up and turned towards me. I waited. He put the phone down on the table.

194

'He's followed them. They're in San Diego. They're trying to find us there. The Unit are closing in. They think we're with them.' He stopped and I caught the worry on his face. 'I hope he doesn't get caught. There's not much I can do from here.'

I felt all the air come out of me. So we were safe for the moment. The fear wasn't gone but it was muted. No one was about to come racing through the door. Apart from maybe the police but I was sure that Alex could handle them. He probably had some gadget in his bag that would persuade them to put their guns away and leave us in peace. For the first time in almost twenty-four hours, I felt myself relax, and my muscles started to scream as they uncramped.

'I need to call Jack.'

My head jerked up. 'Now?'

No, he couldn't call Jack now. He needed to finish his sentence. I was what? He seemed to have forgotten our conversation, though. Instead, he crossed over to the chair where the holdall was still sitting and started rifling through it. He pulled out a small metallic-looking object and crossed to the phone that sat on the table between the two beds. He lifted the phone and attached the metal thing to the wires at the base. Then, glancing at me quickly, he dialled a number.

In the ten seconds it took for the call to connect, I held my breath, drawing my knees to my chest. My eyes didn't leave Alex's back.

'Hey, Jack – no, listen, listen. Yes, no, don't worry – she's here – OK, here . . .' He turned and held the phone out to me. 'Tell him you're all right.'

I clutched the phone. 'Hi, Jack, it's me.'

'Jesus, Lila, where the hell are you? Are you OK? Where have you been?'

195

'Er—'

Alex snatched the receiver back and I was grateful. I hadn't been sure where to begin on that one.

'We're fine,' I heard Alex say. 'No. I can explain. It wasn't Demos. We're not with them.' There was a pause.

'Flank two.'

Flank what?

'Seriously. They came to the house. I had to get her away and I couldn't take her to the base. It wasn't safe – the alarm – yes, I know. OK – how close are you?'

My breathing caught like it was snagged on barbed wire.

'Right. Good. That's good. Keep on them. Keep them south.'

Another pause. I could hear Jack's voice getting louder.

'The truck? Yeah, that was the idea. I'll explain when I see you. The car? Yeah, I'll explain that later too . . . No. No. It's fine.'

Uh-oh.

'No, I think it's best we stay as far away from San Diego and the base as possible. Can you meet us? Alone. You need to come alone – any more of you and they'll suspect something. You come alone and let the Unit take care of business. I'm serious, Jack. Don't even tell them where you're going. Demos is getting intel from the inside. I can't tell you over the phone.'

Alex dropped his voice, shouldering me out. 'I need to talk to you face-to-face.'

There was a hugely long pause and I started to fidget. Alex's shoulders were tensing, I could see that even from behind. He was running his hand over his close-cropped hair. I remembered how it had felt; soft, like dandelion quills. Wow, I really needed to focus.

'Just her passport. And some papers for you and me.'

Both of them?

'When's the earliest you can meet us?'

'OK. Eight a.m. Near Palm Springs. I'll call you and tell you where to go.'

I glanced at the clock. It was flashing 23.13.

Alex hung up and turned to me. My face was expectant. His lips were pursed.

'What did he say about Demos?'

'As Key said, they're in San Diego, the Unit are on them. They thought Demos had us both. It caused a major panic. The whole Unit deployed after them.'

'But I thought you said they wouldn't do anything if anyone from the Unit got taken?'

'It's not about me,' he said, looking at me pointedly.

I continued staring at him.

Alex carried on, 'He wanted to know about the car.'

I bet. I didn't want to be nearby when Alex told him the truth about that.

'And flank two?' I asked. 'What does that mean?'

He smiled. 'Just a code word, to let him know we're not under duress.'

'Why did you say Demos was getting intel from the inside?'

'So he wouldn't tell anyone what he was doing and would come alone.'

Oh.

I frowned. 'So we're meeting Jack tomorrow?' It felt suddenly like the night before an exam. I was sweating fear. 'Are you sure we have to tell him? I'm not so—'

'Yes, we have to tell him.'

I glared at him. 'Why?'

'For lots of reasons. Mainly because I need him to know the truth.'

'What about me? I don't want him to know the truth. Does that count? Don't I get a say in this?'

'Lila, it'll be fine. It's Jack. I'll talk to him – he needs to know.' Alex was deploying the tone he usually used to defuse situations, soft and smooth and stomach-flipping.

Great. Well, I hoped wherever we were going was in public so Jack couldn't do anything to me without witnesses.

Alex seemed subdued once more, wrapped up in his thoughts, and I wondered whether they were about how to tell Jack about my ability without him killing or containing me.

'Come on, let's both get some sleep while we can. We need to be up before dawn – I need to steal another car.'

He crossed to the second bed and flopped onto it, pushing his gun half under the pillow with his hand resting on it. He was on his side, his eyes already closed.

I stood stranded, knowing I needed to go and lie down on the other bed but wanting so much to crawl into his bed and curl up against him.

'Can I sleep with you?' I asked. My hand flew to my mouth. It had just come out. A bit like my ability just came out when I was tired or otherwise emotional.

Alex opened one eye and gave me a long, guarded look but then finally he lifted his arm and I went and slid under it.

21

I was lying on my side and Alex's arm was wound tight around me, the weight of it across my waist and hip. I opened my eyes a crack and saw his hand on the sheet in front of me, the gun cradled in his palm still. I could feel the warmth of his chest radiating against my back, although he wasn't pressed against me – there must have been a centimetre of two of space between us – and I fought hard against the temptation to nudge myself back and close the distance. I concentrated on keeping my breathing steady.

I turned slowly, shifting my weight, trying not to wake him, I didn't want to risk having him remove his arm or twist away from me. Once I was lying on my back, his bare arm fell across my stomach. I glanced through my lashes. Alex in sleep was even more beautiful to look at than awake. I had never been quite this close to him before, or seen him asleep. Sleepovers at seven didn't count. And then he'd been in the top bunk.

I was glad my arms were bound by the dead weight of his arm because otherwise I would have moved my hand right now to stroke his face, trace his eyelashes, follow the line of his lips. I tried very hard to still my frayed breathing. His body seemed to tense for a second, then relaxed again. His breathing stayed even and I stayed staring at his lips thinking about what they'd feel like if I moved an inch and pressed mine to them. It really was like leaving a feast in front of a starving man. I even began licking my lips in anticipation.

Then suddenly Alex's eyes were open. One second he'd been sleeping and the next his blue eyes were boring into mine. I drew in a breath. We stared at each other in the closing gloom of the room. I was lost. Gone. No hope. I could feel my heart stammering jagged beats and was sure he could hear it too.

Then, just like that, Alex moved his arm from my waist. Where the weight had been was now just empty space. I felt unfettered, like I might float up to the ceiling. I waited for him to roll away but, very slowly, very gently, he laid his hand on my cheek, his thumb near the corner of my mouth. If I'd thought his arm across my waist was electric, this was like shock therapy. My brain went blank, just aware of an intense pulsing beat in my cheek. He kept his eyes on mine, his gaze unblinking, and I stared right back into the blue. He moved almost imperceptibly and in the space between a heartbeat his lips touched mine.

The whole world opened up. It was like it exploded, drawing me down into a black hole where nothing was solid or real anymore. I felt boneless, weightless, free. Lights were beginning to flash in my head. Probably from the lack of oxygen. I had a desperate urge to feel Alex's skin against mine. All those times he'd been within reaching distance and I'd not been allowed to touch him, all those hours I'd daydreamed through lessons about being this close to him – I was making up for them all now – and then some.

The real thing was so much better than all those daydreams, infinitely, incredibly better. My hands slid up under Alex's T-shirt. It was such an overwhelming desire I couldn't have stopped myself if I'd tried. The T-shirt was lifting without me even touching it. Wonderful, useful power, I thought. And then my fingers were against the warm flatness of his stomach. I could feel the ridges of muscle beneath my hands and I heard my breathing pick up a pace.

Then Alex froze, his hand suddenly gripping my wrist, and he started tugging it away.

I opened my eyes. The flashing lights hadn't been a figment of my imagination or due to lack of oxygen. The room light was blinking on and off repeatedly. It stopped as soon as I noticed, leaving us in darkness, with just the dim light from the street shining through the crack in the curtains.

'I'm sorry,' he said, letting go of my wrist and rolling away from me.

His words spun around me, pinging off my skull, my brain disconnected, the synapses still firing around other parts of my body. I felt the flames flicker out.

Alex sat up and swung his feet to the floor, putting his back to me. I drew myself onto my knees and tried to shake the feeling back into my body.

'Why are you sorry?' I asked in a shaking voice. My hand hovered over his shoulder, too uncertain to close the distance and touch him.

Alex stood up and walked away. 'Lila, this is not right.'

Not right? Was he kidding? It was so right. So, so, so right.

'What are you saying? I don't understand. Is this about my ability?'

He'd stopped kissing me because of the light. I could see how it might be a little off-putting, but it wasn't like I'd fired his gun at the ceiling rodeo-style.

201

Alex whipped around. 'No. Don't ever think that. It's nothing to do with that. Whatever you can do, whatever ability you have, you're still Lila. It's part of you – who you are. And I wouldn't change anything about you – other than maybe your proclivity for running off,' he added as an afterthought.

My hand dropped. I swallowed hard. Then reached forward slowly to take his hand. He stepped back out of range and panic started to weave through my limbs like poison, deadening them. Without looking at me he walked into the bathroom and closed the door. I heard the sound of the lock turning.

I sat on the raft of the bed wondering which way to paddle to safety. My hand was pressed to my lips. I was trying to commit to memory the pressure of his lips, the way he'd tasted. I stared at the bathroom door speechless, my brain trying to compute what had just happened.

About five minutes later he came out. He avoided making eye contact and glanced at his watch. 'We may as well get going while it's still dark.' He moved to the chair in the corner and started rummaging around in the bag.

I stared at him, my mouth half open. That was it? That was all he had to say? I looked down at the bedcover, rucked up under my feet. At least when there was rage and anger I had known where I stood – more or less. Now I was sinking, not knowing what to think. We had just kissed, hadn't we? That had happened, hadn't it?

The sound of a zipper closing made me look up. Alex was throwing the bag over his shoulder. I watched as he pushed his gun down the back of his jeans. He glanced up at me and I was sure I detected a faint flare of embarrassment. He grabbed the keys and jerked his head towards the door. 'Ready?'

I stumbled off the bed feeling woozy and slipped on my shoes. My face was burning, my breathing still haphazard, my lips on fire. I could feel my emotions starting to flare. I couldn't understand why he was ignoring what had happened and I wasn't sure how to broach the subject. How did people do this? I had no clue what the protocol was. Was he embarassed because I was Jack's sister? Was he disgusted by me? No, I couldn't believe it. There had been no disgust in that kiss. So what else was it? Guilt, maybe? Because I was Jack's sister?

Oh no. Rachel. Of course. How on earth had I managed to forget about her? Selective amnesia, obviously. Or just complete denial.

The bag Alex was holding suddenly slam-dunked into the bed. I bit my bottom lip and looked at him wide-eyed, waiting for his reaction. He was looking at the bag in bewildered shock. Then he looked over at me with disbelief painted on his face. *Eeek.* He looked back at the bag, lying on its side by the foot of the bed. I guessed it was lucky Rachel wasn't actually there in the room because, for sure, furniture would have been flying, not just a bag.

'Did you just do that?' His voice was calm.

'Um. Maybe.'

'Lila?'

It was just like the time I got called to the headmistress's office about the flying jam roly-poly.

'Yes. OK. I did it. It was an accident. I told you, sometimes it just happens.'

'Like the scissors?'

Crap. 'Yes.'

He nodded his head slowly. 'I see.' He looked up at me now and I felt a cramp of butterflies. 'Maybe I shouldn't have taught you how to take the safety off a gun. Do I need to watch my back?'

He gave me a little smile, his eyes crinkling at the corners. He was trying to joke but I didn't feel like it. I was mad at him. Why had he kissed me if he liked Rachel?

'Why are you here with me?'

'Excuse me?' He looked properly confused. 'I thought I'd answered that one.'

'I mean,' I continued, my voice rising, 'why are you here with me when clearly you would rather be with Rachel?' I didn't really mean here. I meant why was he kissing me if, he had a thing going on with *I'm the boss don't mess with me* Barbie?

'Rachel?' He looked really confused now.

'Yes. Rachel. Why don't you go back to her? You have a choice. You don't need to be here with me.' I sounded so jealous and ridiculous. I wanted to slam-dunk myself with the bag and knock myself out.

'Don't be ridiculous.'

Oh, he agreed with me about the ridiculousness. Great. I turned away so he wouldn't see the tears of anger that were starting to prick behind my eyes.

'You think I like Rachel?' Alex said to my back. He sounded surprised.

I turned around, suddenly furious that he was making me spell it out. 'You went on a date with her, didn't you?' I was thinking about the restaurant we'd been to for Alex's birthday, but Alex seemed to be drawing a blank. He was frowning. 'I saw you in the bar,' I added, 'I saw you laughing and joking with her. So, why are you here with me?'

Suddenly the penny seemed to drop. I could see the moment of realisation and then his face turned serious. He brought his hands to my shoulders and this time I didn't try to dodge them, they weighed me down like a diver's belt.

'Lila,' he said, his eyes holding mine, 'I don't like Rachel. And I am here with you because it's where I want to be.'

He didn't like her?

'You don't like her?' I stammered.

He shook his head once, firmly. 'Not like that.'

Oh. I took a moment to compute. This was quite embarrassing, then.

Alex let his hands drop from my shoulders. 'I've never been on a date with Rachel. If you're talking about the comment Jack made at the restaurant, he was talking about a business lunch. All the team leaders were there.'

Oh again.

He waited a beat. 'And what you saw in the bar was not what you think. When you saw me with Rachel, she was telling me something that I didn't believe. That's why I was laughing. Then I saw you and . . .' He tailed off.

Telling him what? A joke? Something about changes to the working hours directive? What could she possibly be telling him that was so funny? She was his boss. Bosses shouldn't tell jokes. Especially black ops bosses.

'What was she telling you?' I asked, confused myself now.

Alex looked at the ground then his blue eyes flashed to me and I braced myself. 'She was telling me that she thought you had feelings for me.'

I swallowed and tried to keep my face neutral. 'Feelings?' My heart rate started to accelerate like it was pumping amphetamine not blood round my body.

205

He took in a deep breath. 'She told me that she overheard you in the bar telling Sara you loved me.'

Sounded out, echoing around the room, the love word settled on us both like a layer of ash after a fire. I couldn't meet Alex's eyes. I just stared at the floor in horror. Rachel had overheard that? Where had she been? The bar had been crowded but how had I not noticed her?

Perhaps because I was only ever aware of Alex. So, Rachel had heard – but why had she told him? Why would she do that?

Because she was a total bitch. That's why.

I replayed the scene from the bar in my head. Alex had been laughing because he'd just found out that I loved him. It put a new slant on things certainly, but not a better one. He found it hilarious that I loved him. I looked at the ground and visualised a hole. Nothing happened. Useless power.

I needed to get into the bathroom. Somewhere I could lock the door and hide. I didn't care about meeting Jack. Alex could go on his own. I'd wait in the bathroom for the Unit instead.

But Alex got to the door before me, blocking my way. I tried to walk past him but he feinted and I couldn't get around him. I spun round and crossed to the bed, dropping onto it like a rock and burying my head in my arms.

There was a moment of silence and I heard my breathing loud and uneven in the cave of my arms. I waited, hoping Alex would just pick up the bag and leave. But he didn't. He came and sat down next to me and I felt his hand on my back.

'Lila,' he said. 'Please. Can we talk?'

His voice was so gentle I felt myself start to turn, my body wanting to roll into him and find comfort. I stopped myself. I stayed quiet and held my breath. I really didn't know what to say.

He didn't either obviously as he sat there in silence for another minute.

Eventually, he spoke again, quietly. 'When I said I had no choice about helping you, I meant it. There was no other option because you are the only option. I don't trust anything at the moment. But the one thing I am sure of, the one thing that I do trust . . .' he paused for a fraction of a second, 'is the way I feel about you.'

He stopped and my eyes flew open. How did he feel about me? I didn't understand what he was saying. I rolled over slowly to look at him and his hand fell away, off my back. My voice when I found it was raspy. 'I don't – what are you saying?'

Alex frowned, his jaw clenching then unclenching, like he was saying the words against his better judgement. 'I'm saying that the way I feel about you is not the way I should be feeling about you.'

'What do you mean not the way you should be feeling?' I could feel my body starting to shake.

He rubbed a hand across his forehead like he had a migraine. 'I like you. Too much.'

I took in such a huge gulp of oxygen that the air turned thin around me. He liked me? Alex, who I had loved my entire life, liked me. And, from the sound of it, he meant like as in like. Not as in liking a great aunt or tea with sugar. But it didn't make sense for him to like me. It didn't add up. I sat up.

'But you laughed. When she told you, you laughed.'

Alex shut his eyes for a few seconds and when he opened them he seemed to have decided something. 'I was laughing, Lila, because I didn't believe her. I thought Rachel had to be joking.'

Suddenly nothing mattered anymore. Not Rachel. Not the Unit. Not Demos. Alex liked me. He liked me. He liked me too much. I couldn't keep the smile off my face. It was cracking it in two.

'But Lila, like I said before, it's not right. I'm not going to take advantage of you.' He stood up.

My smile dissolved. Was he kidding? I leapt off the bed towards him. 'Take it. Take the advantage. You can have it. I'm giving it to you. It's yours.'

He took a step back. 'No, Lila. You're Jack's sister.'

I stopped in my tracks. 'This is about Jack?'

I couldn't believe it. As if Jack would extend the same courtesy to Alex if the situation was reversed.

'It's a part of it. He'd kill me if he knew.'

I couldn't disagree with any vehemence. But it wasn't Jack's life. It wasn't his business.

Before I could put any of this into words, though, Alex carried on. 'It's more than just Jack. I can't see you hurt and this – this will end badly.'

What, he could see the future now?

'This as in, this,' I pointed at him and then me, 'or this as in Demos and the situation we're in? What's going to end badly?'

He gave a faint shrug. 'I won't hurt you.' It was said like a promise. 'And this is going to hurt you.' He said it so finally. As though he had already made up his mind.

The panic finally made it to my chest, filling my lungs with tar so I couldn't breathe. 'No it isn't,' I whispered. 'Stopping is going to hurt me.'

He couldn't just tell me he liked me, kiss me and then take it all away.

Considering everything else in my life I'd had taken away from me it really wasn't fair. But this time I wasn't going to let it happen.

208

Alex was shaking his head. 'I'm sorry, Lila. I really shouldn't have kissed you.' He was running a hand over his head as though trying to erase the memory. I stood there open-mouthed. 'It was wrong of me. And I shouldn't have told you how I was feeling. I just wanted you to know that what you were thinking wasn't the case. I could see what was going through your head. And none of it was true.'

'But if you feel something how can you just stop? How can you?' My voice was shaking and I tried to still it.

'Because it isn't about what I want. It's about what's for the best.'

'So you do want this? You do want me?' Did he? I still didn't know what he wanted.

Alex paused. 'I want you to be happy and I want you to be safe,' he said finally.

'I'm both those things with you.'

Alex looked pained, his face reminding me of how I had felt when he hit the button in the car and everything turned to shattering white noise. When he noticed my face though, looking like I'd had my heart torn from my chest and wrung out in front of me, he reacted quickly. 'Come on,' he said, holding out his hand, 'let's talk about this later. Now's not the time. We need to get out of here.'

He pulled me over to the door, pausing to pick up the bag. I let him. Of course I let him, even though I wanted to resist and face him and demand to know when the right time was going to be. I was desperate to get him to promise he wasn't going to stop anything, least of all the kissing, or the liking. I needed to convince him Jack wouldn't kill him, which he probably would, that he wasn't taking advantage and that he couldn't just stop, because I

209

needed him. Absolutely and completely needed him. I couldn't imagine surviving a single second in the world without him next to me. And by that, I didn't just mean in a world where the Unit was chasing me, I meant in any world.

22

We were at the base of the Palm Springs Aerial Tramway, near to the ticket booth. I looked up at the mountain rising out of the desert like a giant's table. The cable car looked flimsy, like a child's toy, next to it.

I glanced at Alex. 'We're going on that thing?'

'Yes, we are.'

'Cool,' and then, after a moment's pause, 'Will there be lots of people at the top?'

'No. That's the point.'

'I think people around us would be good.'

'Oh really? You want to demonstrate your ability to an audience?'

'What do you mean, demonstrate my ability?'

'Lila, you're going to need to show Jack. He's not going to believe us unless you do.'

'No way.'

'It's the only way. Do you want to get out of the country? Do you want to be safe from Demos?'

I sighed. 'Yes.'

'Well, then, come on. Let's go.'

Alex nudged me into the ticket booth. I stood there, staring up at the top of the mountain and then at the flat of the desert, wondering how this would play out. It was an awfully long drop. We had driven into Palm Springs, stopping for some breakfast at a roadside diner. Then Alex had called Jack from a payphone and arranged to meet him here. Or rather at the top of the cable car ride in the San Jacinto State Park, to be exact.

When he had the tickets, Alex walked back towards the car.

I followed after him. 'Where are you going? Aren't we going up? Did you change your mind?' I was hopeful.

'We're waiting,' he said to me over his shoulder.

I glanced back towards the cable car entrance. 'What for? There's no queue.'

'For Jack – I want to see he's alone first. We'll let him head on up first and then we'll follow him.'

We got in the car and I felt the first spirals of angst start to wind their way up my body. My feet started to tap the floor, my fingers playing a melody on the window ledge. Alex glanced over at me a few times and I gave him fleeting smiles that didn't kid him for a second.

'It'll be OK,' he said.

I just nodded and kept on tapping.

At midday we saw a red blur on the horizon. It looked familiar.

Alex sat up in his seat slightly and I kept following the blur as it became clearer. It was Alex's bike. Jack was riding it. I hoped he'd give Alex the keys to it before he asked about the Audi. I sank down in my seat, hiding behind the dash.

We waited while he parked up and my heart started to gallop. Jack pulled off his helmet and looked up, scanning the car park. No doubt looking for the Audi. Finally, he gave up the search and stalked over to the ticket booth and we watched him disappear inside.

I looked over at Alex. 'So, he's alone – are we going?'

'No, we'll follow him up.'

Fifteen minutes later we got out of the car. Jack was already dangling some two hundred or so metres above us in one of the cable cars. I wondered if he'd spotted us down below.

Waving in the breeze, two hundred metres up, suspended on a wire in a little glass and metal box, I felt dangerously close to the edge of something – not the top of the mountain, something more like hysteria. My brother was waiting at the summit and I could feel the anxiety building with every metre we got closer to him.

'Lila.'

I looked up. Alex was standing over in one corner. I lurched over to him, feeling the car rock beneath me. When I got to him he stepped closer, so we were brushing arms. I didn't know what he was doing at first, not until he'd wrapped something around my wrist. Then he moved his hand away and I saw it was the strand of leather I'd given to him for his birthday.

I looked up at his face and felt the blood rush from my cheeks to my head. I'd never tire of looking at him and for a few seconds my mind went completely blank with amazement that someone so beautiful liked me right back. He finished tying the knot and looked me in the face and I felt my gaze fall from his eyes to his lips and back again.

'Why are you giving it back to me?' I asked.

He pressed his thumb to my bottom lip and I heard an intake of air. That was me, I thought, before my head started to spin.

Then he bent his head and kissed me. Just lightly, for a short few seconds, before drawing away again. My bottom lip began to throb where the pressure of his thumb and lips had been. I looked down, only to catch sight of the ground about three hundred metres below, and felt myself start to sway. Alex caught me around the waist, holding me firm. I leant into him, pressing my forehead against his chest. *What was going on?* Not two hours ago he'd claimed this was wrong and told me he wasn't going to take advantage – and now here he was happily taking it. I didn't want to do anything that might make him reconsider, though, so I stayed perfectly still, breathing in his now familiar smell.

The car jolted into the landing station at the top of the mountain and Alex took hold of my hand, giving it a squeeze.

It felt like I had sea legs – they were wobbly and unsteady on the metal walkway that took us into the building and then out onto the mountain top. The air was cool, much cooler than down on the desert floor. Like being in the Alps. It was fresh and stinging and thin. I pulled on my sweater. Had Alex known back at the mall that we'd end up here? What *else* had he planned?

We were standing amidst pine trees that were stretching up into the blue and all around was such quietness that it seemed to sing. It would have been somewhere mystical or other-worldly if it hadn't been for the odd tourist milling about and a couple eating their lunch at one of the picnic tables.

And Jack. Standing there in front of me. It was a shock, despite knowing he would be waiting for us. He grabbed me in a massive bear hug, lifting me off the ground. I went tense in his arms, wanting to hug him back but too frozen with fear to do anything. Even to blink.

He let me go suddenly and turned to Alex, stepped slightly in front of me, putting himself between me and his best friend.

'So, what the hell?' he asked.

I felt my stomach begin to clench at the imminent confrontation, all the muscles going hard across my abdomen.

'We had to get away, Jack. They came to the house.' Alex gave a faint sigh.

'But why didn't you bring her back to the base where we could keep her safe? You're just one guy against a whole load of them. If anything had happened to her, I swear to God I'd—'

'She's fine, Jack. No harm. I couldn't take her to the base. Come on – I'll explain.'

Alex strode off down one of the trails into the woods. I watched him go and felt a tug of pain between my ribs, like my muscles were being stretched on a rack.

I started off after him, Jack following behind me.

'Where's my car?' he said to my back.

Why'd he have to ask me that? I so wasn't going to be the one to tell him. 'It's somewhere safe,' I stuttered. 'It was kind of conspicuous so we left it somewhere.' It wasn't *exactly* a lie.

'He didn't crash it, did he?'

'No. He didn't crash it.'

He sold it but he didn't crash it.

We followed Alex for a few minutes until we were in a clearing of pine trees. It was so silent and still that I could hear the crunch of pine needles under our feet, but not a whisper of wind or a leaf stirring.

Alex looked over at me and gave me a reassuring smile. I couldn't respond. I wanted really badly to cross the small space between us and take his hand again. But Jack's stance towards Alex

215

was telling me not to – he was simmering. Giving him any more ammunition right now would be like adding a grenade to a bonfire. I wondered again at the wisdom of unveiling my freakish ability to him. He'd probably try to taser me or something.

'Did you bring Lila's passport?' Alex asked.

'Yes, it's here.' Jack indicated the bag at his feet.

'I've got your IDs here,' Alex said, tapping the black holdall with his foot.

I frowned – something wasn't right.

Jack nodded. 'But why do I need them? Are you going to tell me what's going on?'

I edged backwards towards the tree line, in case Alex was wrong and I needed to run fast.

Alex took a deep breath. 'There's a reason we didn't go to the base, Jack. It's why I asked you to come on your own. You need to be quiet and listen to everything I'm about to tell you before you make any judgements.'

Jack didn't hear him. Or chose not to. 'What's going on?' he shouted. 'Why didn't you call me sooner? I was worried sick. The whole Unit's been on the case. Have you any idea what kind of a manhunt you've kick-started?'

I looked around me and up at the sky, half expecting to see helicopters buzzing overhead and men in black rappelling down amidst the trees.

'You didn't tell them you were meeting us, did you?' Alex took the words out of my mouth.

Jack's eyes flashed anger. 'No. I promised you I wouldn't. But I want answers. I had to lie to Sara and to Rachel. Why didn't you come back to the base? Where have you been?' I could have sworn he looked between us then with a glimmer of suspicion in his eyes. 'What the hell are you doing up a mountain in the desert with my sister?'

'We had to get away fast from Demos. And I told you on the phone, the base wasn't an option. We needed to steer clear of the Unit.'

I saw Jack trying to compute Alex's words. He shook his head, his brows pulled together into a frown. 'Steer clear of the Unit? Why?'

'Lila's one of them, Jack.'

My eyes flew to Alex's face. That was how he planned on easing Jack into the secret? His eyes met mine and I saw the instant apology in them, for the way he'd referred to me as one of them.

'What are you talking about?'

Alex interrupted, 'Jack, Lila's a psy.'

Jack's eyes tracked back to me and I gave him a nervous smile. My feet started to scuff the dirt but my calf muscles were locked and ready to sprint.

'No way.' The look on Jack's face was dead calm. 'Tell me he's joking, Lila.'

I gulped, taking in the hardness that had settled on his face. 'He isn't joking, Jack.'

I saw the way his face started to unscroll. A muscle began to twitch beneath his eye and suddenly Alex was there, right there next to me, putting himself between us, one arm half raised and reaching behind and to the side as though to shield me.

'I don't believe it.' Jack seemed to have steadied himself. His voice was calmer.

'Lila, I think you're going to have to show him,' Alex said.

I hesitated for about ten seconds, weighing up the options. But it was too late for denial. So I looked around the shrubby

217

landscape until I spied a chocolate wrapper lying on the ground and let it fly. It zoomed towards Jack, floated in front of him then came towards me. I held out my hand and let it settle on my palm, like catching a feather in the wind.

I looked up. Jack's face was torn between shock and horror. On balance, it was more horror.

'You – you . . .' Jack couldn't seem to articulate the sentence, for which I was glad.

He turned away and marched towards the nearest tree. I wondered what he was doing. Then he lifted his arm and threw a punch at the bark with all his strength. I flinched at the crack.

'Jack, calm down.' Alex took a step towards him, hesitated, seeming not to want to put too much distance between himself and me. 'She's your sister. She's still Lila. Believe me, I was just as shocked as you – probably more so. When I found out, she was launching a table at my head.'

Jack was crouching down now at the base of the tree, his back turned away from us, cradling his fist.

Alex continued. 'It's *Lila*, Jack. Whatever we've been made to think about them, we're wrong.'

Jack spun around and up, then marched towards us. I ducked closer towards Alex, sheltering behind the wall of his back. 'How did it happen?' he demanded.

He would have been in my face if Alex hadn't have been there, a solid screen of muscle between us. I flinched back from the venom in his voice.

'She doesn't know,' Alex answered for me. 'The gene just triggered somehow. Look, Jack, we're wrong. We *must* be wrong. What do we really know about all this? Just what we've been told. And we've believed it – believed everything. But what if it isn't true?'

Jack's face twisted with anger and he squared his shoulders. '*Isn't true?* Are you telling me that what we know about Demos is a lie? Are you saying that he didn't kill my mum?' He was yelling now. 'Are you telling me that every single one of the – Jesus – what are they even? They're not human! You're telling me that they're . . . what? *Misunderstood?*' Jack's face was blazing. 'You've seen the psych reports – they're off the scale – they're a whole new subcategory of sociopath.' He looked at me then and his expression was pure, unadulterated hatred.

I felt my knees start to give. First I was a freak and now I was a sociopath? An *off-the-scale* sociopath. Oh God. Alex reached behind me and I felt his hand against my back. It was the only thing that stopped me crumpling to the ground.

Alex's voice stayed calm. 'Yes. I've seen what I've been shown. But that doesn't make it real. It doesn't add up.'

'It doesn't add up? All the work Sara's been doing – have you even read it? What more proof do you need?' Jack yelled.

I could see Alex's jaw tensing. 'Yes, I've read it. But since when do you believe everything you read? And now I've got evidence to the contrary.' He nodded his head in my direction.

Jack rounded on him, practically spitting the words out. 'So, what, Sara's making this stuff up? You think her team are just sitting around fabricating entire reports?' He let out a bitter laugh that shattered off the trees around us. 'Suddenly you know better than the professionals? You always think you know best, Alex.'

I saw Alex wince, then his face smoothed out again, back in placatory mode. 'I'm not saying I know best. And I have no idea why they might be lying to us. What the point would be or what Sara's part in it is, I don't know. I just know what my instinct is telling me about your sister.'

'Oh right. You have an instinct about my sister now?' Jack pressed his lips together but I could see the way his nostrils were flaring.

'Yes.' Alex chose to ignore Jack's tone. 'My instinct is telling me something's not adding up. Maybe the Unit has it wrong. What if there isn't a hard and fast rule? What if we're making dangerous assumptions about them that need to be tested? The powers that be have done a damn good job of convincing us that we're fighting something less than human, but take a look at what's in front of you and make a judgement, Jack. It's Lila – come *on*, Jack. She might be a little impulsive but that doesn't make her a sociopath.'

I swivelled my gaze to Jack, trying my best not to look like a sociopath. Jack's eyes were so narrowed I could barely see the irises. It didn't look like there was any doubt in them, though.

Alex pulled me out from behind his back, holding me by the arm. 'Lila's your *sister*. Do you really think she's one of them, that she's honestly like that? Lila is *not* bad. Look at her. She's incapable of doing anything remotely evil – she can't even lie properly.'

I thought about the mugging and all the things I'd wanted to do to Rachel and wondered about that. Maybe Alex shouldn't be so quick to make such statements. Maybe they *should* take me back to the Unit and start running some tests.

Alex continued. 'It doesn't make sense, Jack. And if they're lying to us about this, what *else* are they lying to us about?'

Jack looked at me, our eyes caught like Velcro. He frowned slightly and I saw him processing everything he'd been told. His eyes dropped to my feet, where the chocolate wrapper was now lying, and when he looked up at me there was confusion in his eyes, like a kid who's just found out that Santa Claus doesn't exist. His belief system was shattering like a sheet of glass in front of him, as though Alex had fired a bullet right through it. He rubbed a hand over his face and I saw the purple blue welt on his knuckles where he'd punched the tree.

Finally he opened his mouth. 'OK, I'm not saying I believe everything you're saying. There's no way Sara's made anything up, but you're right about Lila. She's a terrible liar.'

I grinned at him, feeling the first faint flutter of hope that everything might turn out all right. But Jack wouldn't catch my eye and I felt my momentary blast of happiness dredge away.

'So, what are you proposing?' Jack asked.

Alex visibly relaxed, his shoulders dropping. He walked towards Jack and, taking him by the elbow, propelled him towards the tree line.

'Stay here,' Alex said, turning briefly towards me. His face was drawn and pale under the tan.

I recognised the stress etched into the lines around his mouth. I nodded silently, hoping he wouldn't be going far. He gave me a smile that faded as soon as it appeared.

As they walked away, my stomach clutched with unease. They stopped about ten metres off and Alex turned his body so all I could see was his back, his arms gesticulating, and the side of Jack's head silhouetted behind him.

I looked over my shoulder at the wide spaces between the pines circling us and then up at the blue arching sky wide above me. I thought about what Alex had said about the Unit and the research they were doing. That Sara was doing. What if it was actually true and I *was* bad? Maybe it was in me, hidden deep. Maybe every time I lost control and a bag or a knife or scissors went flying, that was me, the real me. The *bad* me, taking over. Maybe Sara and the Unit were right to be hunting us down after all.

After a few minutes I looked over and saw Jack looking straight at me. The razor's edge of his gaze was blunted. His arms were crossed across his chest and he was nodding. He turned back to Alex and then glanced over at me once more. I saw him frown at something Alex was saying, then suddenly Jack's voice was cracking like a bullet across the open space between us.

'No way!'

The air reverberated with the noise and the eagle overhead shrieked in response. It left a vacuum of silence in the air when it died away. Had Alex just told him about the car? I edged closer towards them, feeling my unease deepen.

'You have to, Jack. It's the only way,' Alex was saying. Then he handed the black holdall and the keys to our car to Jack.

I took several more steps towards them, trying not to crunch on the pine cones littering the ground. They were talking so loudly now they didn't notice me coming closer. Alex was shaking his head, his voice low but determined. He wasn't inviting debate on whatever they were talking about. Jack was staring back at him, his green eyes darkening, but I could see that whatever Alex was saying was starting to filter through, because he seemed somehow defeated.

Alex was still talking and I caught the urgency saturating his voice. 'You need to go now. Take Lila and head for South America. Don't tell me where. I don't need to know.'

'What?' My voice was a broken whisper.

I saw Alex's back freeze. The muscles in his shoulders hardened to stone. He turned slowly to face me. I could see the effort he was

222

making to keep his expression even but his eyes were giving him away. Normally so guarded, now they were telling a whole story and I didn't want to hear it.

He took a deep breath, his shoulders rising and falling, his eyes not leaving my face. He took a step forward, one hand reaching out towards me. I took a step back.

'What's going on?' I asked quietly.

I saw Alex flinch slightly. His hand dropped. 'Jack's going to take you away, somewhere safe—'

'No. *No.*' My head was shaking, trying to shake the words out of my ears.

'I can't go with you, Lila.'

'Why?'

'Because Jack is your brother and you need to be together. You are each other's only family. Other than your dad, you're all you've both got.'

All? I had thought I had Alex too. Realising he didn't see it like that made me turn away from him.

Alex caught me by my arm and spun me around to face him.

'Lila, please don't walk away. It isn't that I don't *want* to come with you.'

I stayed looking at the ground. 'Then why aren't you? You told me you would.'

'I told you I wouldn't let you go alone.'

I shook my head at him. It was a shallow deceit. He had known all along. He had planned everything, I realised, even this conversation, no doubt. It explained his comment last night about things ending badly. It was only prophetic because he'd already written the script. I looked down at the bracelet on my wrist. It explained why he'd given it back to me. It had been a goodbye present five years ago and so it was again. I bit my lip, cursing my stupidity, that I hadn't seen it coming.

'I'm sorry, Lila. One of us has to stay. One of us has to stop them.'

And he thought he could stop them on his own? It had taken five years and a whole unit and they'd still only managed to catch a few. Alex himself had admitted how impossible they were to hunt or to catch. He'd spend his life trying. And now I'd never see him again.

'Lila,' he carried on, 'we need to find out what's really going on with the Unit, find out the truth. And, more than that, we need to stop either them or Demos finding you.' Alex was still talking, shaking my shoulders softly, 'Which is why you need to go now.'

I felt myself stumble against him, trying to hold on to him.

He turned to Jack. 'You need to get her out of here. Now. Far away, where the Unit and Demos can't find her. Because you know what they're capable of if they do.'

Shivers ran up my spine, like I was suffering a heavy bout of flu. Was he talking about Demos or the Unit? I looked over at Jack. A dark shadow rippled across his face. His whole body seemed to adjust in its wake. That's when he looked at me and I saw the anxiety pass across his face. Alex had pressed him on his Achilles heel – his guilt over what had happened to our mum. Despite everything he might feel about what I was, he'd never let the people who did that to our mum have a chance to do the same to me. He hated them more than he hated me.

I looked back at Alex. 'I won't go. I won't go without you.'

Jack fired a glance in my direction, his green eyes burning with suspicion. Then he looked at Alex, a scowl starting to form on his face.

'Lila—' Alex's face was so torn that I knew if I pressed him I had a chance of keeping him here with me.

224

'You don't need to find out what's going on at the Unit. It doesn't matter. Nothing matters.' Except us, I wanted to say, but Jack was right there and I couldn't. 'I don't want you to leave me. Please.'

'It does matter, Lila. If I don't stay, if I come with you, we'll spend our whole lives being hunted. If I stay I can make sure that doesn't happen to Jack and you.'

'How? You're one person.'

'I can do my best. At least I can cover for you two until you disappear. Try to keep the Unit from finding out about you. Listen to me, I promised you I'd keep you safe and this is the only way I know how to. Let me do it. One of us has to stay and it has to be me.

'Jack, you need to go now.' Alex said it while still looking at me.

Jack took a step towards us. He was pulling his rucksack onto his back.

'No!' I grabbed for Alex's wrist.

I felt his other hand sear hot against my cheek. He bent his head, and in a voice that Jack couldn't hear, said, 'When you came down the stairs and fell into me, that was the moment.' Then his lips pressed against mine.

I heard an intake of breath from Jack.

Alex stepped back, his eyes on me the whole time. 'Take care of her,' he said.

'She's my sister,' Jack growled at him. His fists were curled tight at his side.

Alex glanced at Jack and nodded once. Then he turned around and started jogging back towards the park entrance.

My legs stumbled forward, automatically trying to follow him, and I felt Jack's hand on my arm like a clamp.

'No, Lila,' he said.

23

Then I realised there was no hand on my arm. My whole body was frozen. I tried to move my legs, but it was like trying to wade through wet concrete. Nothing happened. I couldn't even turn my head.

'Don't move.' The voice came from behind and shocked the hell out of me. It wasn't Jack. It was a girl.

'They can't,' someone answered. It was a man's voice and it caused a spasm of shudders to ride up my spine.

'I know – I just like saying it.' Suki danced in front of me, giggling delightedly like I was an eagerly anticipated birthday present. 'Hi, Lila,' she said.

I opened my mouth to scream but it was as though someone had hit a delete button in my brain. My mind went blank.

'Oh, Demos, don't do that – it's no fun. It's just Lila. Let her talk. Go on, last time I learnt so much. I didn't even need to read her mind.'

I heard someone expel a laugh. Demos. He was so close I could feel his breath on the back of my neck. Adrenaline cascaded through my body but just as it reached the part of my brain that controls reflexes it stopped. Like the tap had turned off. I was suddenly so calm I felt like I'd had a bottle of Valium injected straight into my cerebral cortex.

A thought poked through the fog of my brain. Where was Jack? Was he still behind me? Then I remembered Alex. I tried to swivel my neck to see where he was. He'd been leaving me. I couldn't remember why, though. Where was he now? Was he safe?

'Ahh, how sweet, she's looking for Alex. She's worrying about him.' Suki skipped into my field of vision again, pouting.

I frowned at her. How dare she read my thoughts?

'Oh come on, you would too, if you could.' Suki shrugged at me and cocked her head to one side.

I noticed she was wearing another pair of unfeasibly high, totally impractical shoes for being up a mountain and a dress that clung so tightly to her body it was a wonder she could move.

I narrowed my eyes, willing her to go to hell.

She flinched back, her eyebrows pulling together into one neat line.

I heard Demos's footsteps crunching on pine needles before I saw him. He meandered into view, smiling, and stopped dead in front of me. He was wearing a dark suit and a white shirt with an open-neck collar and looked like he was on his way from, or to, a funeral. He studied me for a few long seconds then he laughed a little laugh, as though I'd cracked a joke, and nodded his head.

My first instinct was to lash out. When my limbs wouldn't obey I looked around for something, anything, to throw at him. There was nothing. Just trees. I chose the smallest and focused on it, willing it to uproot so I could use it like a battering ram through his skull. I saw the leaves tremble but it stayed firmly gripped by the ground.

'Uh-oh, Demos. She doesn't like you very much.'

I brought my eyes back to the two of them. Suki had linked her arm through Demos's and was leaning into him.

'Hardly a surprise.' Demos was fixing me with eyes as flat and blue as a November sky. 'I'm going to let you go, but don't try anything, Lila. There's no point. I think you see that now. And besides, Jack's right behind you. And I know you wouldn't want anything to happen to him, would you?'

It felt like being untethered from iron bindings. My limbs were suddenly free, my voice back. I turned my head slowly to see behind me. Jack was on his knees, his hands by his side, frozen like he'd been set in carbon. Though from Jack's expression, Demos wasn't cutting off any of his thoughts. His face was a picture of agony.

I dropped straight to his side, wrapping my arms around him. 'Stop hurting him!' I screamed.

'I'm not hurting him,' Demos said, laughing.

'Then let him go.'

'No, not yet.'

I looked up at him standing over us and willed him to die. I tried to imagine his head parting company with his body, his limbs detaching from his torso. But nothing happened. My mother's killer was standing a few metres in front of me, threatening my brother, and I could do nothing about it. A feeling of helplessness started to overwhelm me, then receded, ebbing away as suddenly as it had come.

'He's not in pain. Well, not physical pain.' Suki had moved forward, closer to Jack, and I twisted my body to shield him.

She skipped back a few steps towards Demos. 'Wow, he's properly furious. About a lot of things. He can't believe he led us here. He's blaming himself.'

She came forward again, bending down to speak to Jack face to face. 'Don't blame yourself, Jack. It's not your fault. We would have found you anyway. Eventually.'

'No. He didn't. Sorry.' She was answering an unspoken question. I saw Jack's eyes fill like acid was burning them.

'See, here he is.' Suki moved aside and pointed past Demos.

I looked up, following her outstretched hand, and saw Alex walking towards us. My heart leapt at the sight of him. At first I thought maybe he was coming back to rescue us and hope rocketed through me. Then I noticed the two men on either side of him and the gun hanging in mid-air, resting against his head as he walked.

I was on my feet and tearing off towards him before they could stop me, but as I got close to Alex, my feet suddenly jammed into the earth like I'd been lassoed around the ankles. I would have fallen to the ground but my body slammed into thin air like I'd been thrown against a concrete block and I was frozen there, at an acute angle, only a few metres away from Alex's arms.

A trickle of blood was running down his cheek and his eyes, locked onto mine, were kaleidoscopic with anger. They had hurt him. Fury filled my head. I saw the gun resting just above his temple and in a heartbeat it was hurtling through the clearing like a boomerang. A split second before it hit the branch I was aiming at, it jolted to a stop, spun around and came bombing back in our direction. I didn't have time to figure out how. My mind went blank again and I looked back at Alex – how had he got that cut on his cheek?

The man next to him was holding the gun again – aiming it at Alex's head but scowling in my direction as though he wished it was pointed at mine. I recognised him. He was one of the men from the file on Jack's computer. The one who looked like a bulldog. What was his name again?

'Bill, try to keep a grip. You know who we're dealing with.' It was Demos. He was at my side.

Bill, that was it. He was telekinetic, like me.

'Sorry, boss.' He scowled at me some more.

The sound of a mobile ringing made me jump. I realised I could move my arms and legs once more.

'Get that, would you?' Demos said to the man on Alex's other side, a man in his mid-twenties with longish hair and a rakish look about him. I knew him, too. He was called Ryder. I remembered the list of crimes under his name, as long as *War and Peace*, and the fact he was a sifter.

Ryder reached into Alex's back pocket and pulled out his mobile which was trilling away innocently. He handed it to Demos, who took it and hit the speaker button.

'Hello?'

Key's voice echoed around the clearing. 'Alex, it's me. Go. You gotta go! They're on their way. They're coming for you – at the cable car. They've found you.'

'Whoever you are, thank you. But you're a little late.' Demos flipped the phone shut. He turned to Alex. 'So, it looks like we'd better hurry up and do business, then.'

From behind, I heard Jack's raised voice. 'Get your hands off me!'

I turned around. He was being manhandled to a standing position by someone. My mind raced through the photos I'd memorised from Jack's computer. I knew this one. Harvey James. As he came closer I saw he even had a cigarette dangling from his lip like he did in the photo. Jack was walking a few paces ahead and Harvey and Suki were sauntering along behind him. I noticed that Jack was holding his hands up with the palms forward, the international sign for surrender.

When they reached us, the gun hovering against Jack's back, right between the shoulder blades, became visible. Harvey was telekinetic too. I wondered if I could get the gun off him.

'Uh-uh. I can't read minds, Lila, but you're pretty obvious.'

I whipped around. Demos was looking at me from under heavy lids, his eyebrows raised in a lazy threat.

I turned back to Jack. I could see the effort it was taking for him to stand there and not lose control.

'Sorry,' he said, looking at me, his eyes glistening green.

I shook my head at him, my eyes filling too. 'No, it's not your fault.'

'Take me. Don't hurt her.' It was Alex.

I drew in a breath and turned back towards him. No way was he giving himself up for me. Not that I thought any of us was going to have a chance to walk away from this. It was bad. Demos and his people had formed a rough circle around the three of us and at the edges, by the trees, I spotted a couple of others. There was no way we were getting out of this one.

'While I appreciate the offer, I don't want you. I want her. I know what you two will do for her. But don't worry, I'm not planning on hurting her. Unless, of course, you mess up. So I guess you'd better not mess up.'

'You want us to swop Lila for Alicia?' Alex said.

'Very good, Alex. Never underestimate you – that's what I've learnt over the years.'

'No need to swear.'

We all looked at Suki. Alex shot her a look that was colder than liquid nitrogen.

Demos leant a little down towards her and said quietly, 'He didn't, Suki.'

231

She looked at Demos. 'Oh, sorry.' She turned to Alex. 'Sometimes I can't tell what's internal and what's not. But still, no need to swear.'

Demos carried on. He took a pace so he was standing between Jack and Alex, like a football coach prepping his team at half-time. 'So, at least I don't need to spell it out. You boys head on back to the base. I'm sure between you you can figure out a way of breaking and entering. I'm confident in you both and it's amazing how something like this can force the mind to focus.'

He wandered to my side and put an arm around my back. It was meant to be proprietary. I felt my spine arch away from his touch and saw Jack start to bubble with rage, the tendons in his neck beginning to bulge. Alex raised his arm a fraction to hold Jack back.

Demos seemed to be enjoying the effect he was having. 'Bring back Alicia and you get your sister back alive. I don't care how you do it. It's a good deal, I think.'

I let my eyes track from Alex to Jack. They were both looking at me. Both of them trying to convey to me that I shouldn't worry, that everything would be just fine. I gave them a washed-out smile, trying to convince them that I believed them. The trickle of blood on Alex's cheek had dried to a crust and a reddish bruise was swelling his cheekbone.

Jack turned his head to look at Alex and Alex dragged his eyes off me and looked over at Jack. I saw the silent communication happening between them. The nod of their heads. They didn't need to be like Suki, they knew each other so well. Plus Jack had his unpoker face on. I could see they were agreeing to do whatever Demos wanted, and my stomach knotted itself in fear. Heading back to the base and trying to break someone out sounded like suicide.

Alex turned to Demos. Took a step towards him. I noticed the gun still hovering at his back but Demos didn't try to stop him. He stood his ground, his eyes watchful.

'If we do what you say – if we get Alicia – you'll give us Lila. Do you swear it?'

Demos nodded. 'I'm a man of my word, Alex. You should know that.'

Jack took a step now too, the gun nudging his head. I saw a smile curl on Ryder's lip. 'I swear to God if you try anything . . .'

'Save it, Jack. If anyone's going to try anything, we both know it'll be you. You're impulsive – like your sister. Like your mother was, too.' It was said almost with affection.

My body recoiled like a snake had reared up and bitten me. Jack's reaction was the complete opposite. He darted forward so fast that his hand made contact with Demos's throat, his fingers closing around the soft flesh before Demos even had time to react.

In the next instant Alex and I lunged for the gun at Jack's head. Alex's hand knocked it out of the way and I spun it up into the tree branches and out of the clearing.

I heard a grunt from Bill and watched as Ryder smacked his elbow hard into Alex's ribs. Alex folded over, hugging his body, and I let out a yell that mingled with Suki's screams. But then there was silence all around.

Harvey stepped forward with the other gun in his hand and brought it to rest against the base of Jack's skull. My heart stopped in my throat.

Demos stepped back from Jack's outstretched and frozen hand, his fingers massaging the red bruises rising on his neck. Alex stood up straight, nursing his ribs, but with a confused frown on his face. His eyes tracked straight to me. I wasn't frozen. I could still think.

'Are you OK?' he mouthed.

All I could do was nod. Then he looked over at Jack and I saw the question in his eyes and the flash of anger that came in its wake.

Demos was frowning at Jack now. His brow so heavy it looked like it might cave in at any moment. 'Trying to prove my point, Jack?' he asked. Then he turned to Bill and Harvey. 'This is a seventeen-year-old girl,' he said, nodding his head in my direction. 'Can you, or can you not, handle a seventeen-year-old girl?'

They looked sheepish.

'I told you she was strong,' Suki piped up from behind Demos.

'Maybe she could give those two some lessons.' He turned back to them. 'Watch her please.'

Then he turned on me. 'Lila, please rein in your talents. Or I will have to stop you from thinking. And I really don't want to have to do that.'

There was a pause and I realised he was waiting for me to respond. I nodded at him through clenched teeth.

'So where was I? I believe I was telling Jack not to try anything. That fell on deaf ears, didn't it, Jack?' He pushed his face into Jack's frozen one. 'So I'll say it again, to be clear. Do. Not. Try. Anything. Don't even think about bringing the Unit into this. It won't end well.'

I remembered Alex's words along the same lines. It was as though he had prophesied this.

Then I heard a clicking noise and saw Harvey cocking the gun against Jack's head. I struggled to keep my panic and rage under

234

control, terrified that I'd knock the gun again and it would go off accidentally and shoot Jack's brains out.

'Move the gun, Harvey, it's freaking her out.' It was Suki.

Harvey scowled at her but did as he was told, pulling it back but keeping it trained on Jack's back. I felt my panic ebb a notch and wondered if it was because of that or whether Demos had had a hand in it. He hadn't let Jack go, though, his body still forming an awkward statue in front of us, his face strangely peaceful-looking.

Demos turned to Suki. 'What's he thinking?' He was indicating Alex. God, I had longed for that ability only a few hours ago – it was so ironic. 'Is he going to bring us Alicia? Or is he planning on bringing the Unit?'

Suki paused, listening in silence to Alex's thoughts. I could see Alex's brow furrow at the violation. 'No. From what I can tell, he won't do anything that might put Lila in danger.' She paused. 'Well, any more danger. He doesn't know how they'll get back onto the base, though. Yet. Or how they'll break Alicia out. The security is heavy. I . . .' She shook her head. 'He's . . .'

I could see her frowning and then her eyes grew wide. She stretched up and whispered something in Demos's ear. He cricked his head to listen, his eyebrows raised in interest, and then flicked me a glance.

He turned back to Alex. 'That's interesting, Alex. Thanks for the information.'

I wondered what on earth Suki had heard Alex saying. He didn't look annoyed at her. On the contrary, he gave an almost imperceptible nod.

'Amber!' Demos was calling to a figure at the edge of the clearing.

235

She lifted her head at the name and walked towards us fast. All I could see was a haze of red hair blazing in the afternoon sunshine and a pair of statuesque legs clad in tight black leather. She created much the same impact as Rachel did on a group, and a hush descended.

'Amber, what do you sense – is he telling the truth?' Demos asked when she got near.

She turned towards Alex, who met her gaze coolly. She smiled at him as though they were old friends. 'Hey, Alex, are you telling the truth?'

I watched as Alex's brow furrowed at the question. What was she, a human lie detector?

'Yes,' he answered firmly.

Amber stood there for five long seconds, her eyes tracing Alex's body and a smile fluttering on her lips. I shuffled uneasily. I knew a look like that when I saw one. I coughed under my breath and she broke out of her private reverie.

'Yes, he's telling the truth,' she said to Demos. 'That was amazing.'

What was amazing? What had she been doing to him with her mind? I looked at him in horror but Alex seemed as confused as I was. Amber walked to Ryder's side and slipped her arm over his shoulder, whispering in his ear. He glanced up at Alex and over at me.

'Good. I don't like liars,' Demos said. 'And as regards getting onto the base and into the building, you're a resourceful guy, Alex. I'm sure you'll figure something out. And don't worry – we'll take good care of her.'

A sly smile slashed Suki's face in half. 'He says he'll kill you if you don't.'

236

'I'd like to see him try,' said a voice.

'Quite,' said Demos. 'Right, Jack, can you hear me?'

Jack's face suddenly transformed from its nirvana-like expression into stone-cold hate.

'I'm going to unfreeze you but remember there's a gun at your back so you need to behave.'

With that Jack fell forward, stumbling to standing. The tendons on his neck were taut as wires and you could have struck a light off his eyes.

'Alex and I were just discussing details. He's trying to work out how you'll break Alicia out. And I was saying that I had no doubt you two would manage it somehow. Though it's a shame and rather surprising that you don't have a special talent like your sister. You do know it's genetic, don't you?'

Jack made no response.

Demos laughed suddenly. 'It's ironic, isn't it? Your sister being a psy. Being one of us. You gotta find that funny.'

Jack continued to ignore him, staring right through him.

'No? Not funny?' He glanced at Suki and sighed. 'What's he thinking?'

She didn't take her eyes off Jack. 'He's thinking that no matter what his sister is, she'll never be like us. That she's not a killer – oh, that's interesting.'

Her head tipped up like a dog hearing a sound and trying to figure out where it was coming from.

'What?' Demos asked.

'Not him. Her.' She pointed at me. 'She's worrying that she is just like us. Something about an eyeball?'

Everyone shifted to stare at me and I shuffled my feet and tried to make my mind go blank. God, she was so annoying.

237

Demos considered me for a moment before turning back to Jack. 'You know we've known all along about Lila? We've been watching her. We had Harvey here disable the alarm system at your house so Lila didn't trigger it accidentally. We didn't think it would be helpful for any of us if you contained your own sister. We'd be without collateral, you'd be without a sister, and probably without a job.'

Jack's jaw looked like it might be about to dislocate. I shook my head. At least I knew now why I'd had luck on my side.

'Well, Jack, Alex,' Demos sighed, 'time you were on your way. I'll give you twelve hours. Here,' he threw a phone towards Alex who caught it in his left hand, his eyes not leaving Demos's face, 'take this. Call the last number dialled when you have her. Then I'll tell you where to come.'

Alex barely nodded at him.

Demos turned back to Jack. 'It's a shame we can't have more time together. But at least I'll have the pleasure of your sister's company for the foreseeable future, if not yours.'

Amber hopped a few steps back and away. 'Demos, seriously, stop it right now, you're going to give him an aneurysm or something. All I can see is red, red, red. It's giving me a headache. I don't like it.'

'You don't much like him chasing you either, darling.' He turned to Jack. 'You'd better hurry, the clock's ticking.'

My legs started to shake. I looked at Alex, but his eyes were already on me.

'I'll come back, I promise you. I won't let them hurt you,' he whispered to me, as though no one else was around to hear.

Then Jack was blocking my view, his arms wrapped tight around me. 'I love you,' he whispered into my ear. 'I'm sorry. I'll fix this.'

238

A hand tugged him away. It was Ryder.

'We'll be sending someone with you.' Demos twisted around and beckoned someone over who I hadn't noticed until now. He was just a kid wearing a Metallica T-shirt and a pair of beaten-up Converse. He was even younger than me. It had to be Nate. I wondered if Key was around.

'How do you know his name? Who's Key?' It was Suki asking. She was looking at me curiously.

The others all turned to stare again. The boy Nate was suddenly alert.

I tried to make my mind go blank. La la la la la la la la.

'You can't keep that up forever,' Suki said, with a touch of menace.

La la la la la la la.

'Oh, Demos, make her stop.'

La—

Suki was looking at me with relief on her face. Why was she looking at me like that?

'Key's my father.' A boy was speaking up from behind Demos's back. It had to be Nate. 'He can project. He's probably here right now.'

As one, we all scanned the clearing from left to right, our eyes peering up into the branches and amongst the trees, looking for a ghost.

'And why would he do that?' asked Demos.

'Apparently he thinks his son is here under duress,' said Suki, laughing.

'Well, you tell this Key when you see him that I'm taking good care of his son. He's happy – as you can see.' Demos looked at Alex and gestured at Nate, who was hanging his head at the

239

sudden attention. 'Come out come out wherever you are.' Demos laughed. 'I know you can't show yourself. But if you can hear me Mr Johnson I'm taking good care of your son. He's happy – you can see. And not here under duress.'

'Oh really?' I spoke up. 'Because you aren't physically touching him, just controlling his mind, he's not under duress?'

Demos turned to me angrily, and I heard a growling noise that I thought came from Alex's direction. 'No – I'm not controlling him. That would be too much effort. He's here because he wants to be.' He turned back to the clearing, calling out to the emptiness between the sky and the trees. 'Hang around, Key, maybe you'll discover something that'll make you change your mind. Maybe you would be happy joining us, too, and Lila – I could always use another projector' – he looked at me – 'and someone with telekinetic ability.'

'Over my dead body,' I replied.

Demos frowned and then turned to Alex and Jack once more. 'I think it's time you two were on your way. Take Alex's bike – it'll be faster. Remember, Nate'll project and follow you, so don't try anything, OK? See you in twelve hours.'

He walked to me and put his hand on my shoulder, his fingers as heavy as slabs of lead. My whole body turned rigid and I thought he was doing something to me again, until I realised it was just my natural reaction to his touch. I fought down every instinct to shrug him off and mouthed the word 'go' at Alex.

He hesitated, his lips parted, and for a split second it looked like he was about to say something, but then he grabbed Jack by the elbow. 'Let's go,' he said, and tugged him backwards out of the clearing.

They gave me one last glance before twisting around and starting to jog towards the cable car. I swallowed hard several

240

times, feeling the violent stretch of the invisible elastic tying me to Alex and then the sudden whiplash against my insides as it snapped in two.

I stood there watching after them, in the middle of a circle made up of my mother's killers, and wondered if it was the last time I would ever see them.

Out of nowhere, Suki suddenly appeared at my side and put her arm around my shoulders. 'Don't be sad,' she whispered in my ear. 'He loves you. He's sorry that he never told you.'

24

I'd seen eyes like his on a dead shark carcass once. That was all I could think of as we sat opposite each other at the picnic table. It was an unlikely location for a head-to-head with a murderer. Too light. Too peaceful. Like a scene from *Bambi*.

I shifted uncomfortably on the wooden planks of my seat and looked around. I wondered where Jack and Alex were by now. Probably just getting to the bottom in the cable car, or possibly already on the road. It was pointless I knew, but I glanced over my shoulder to look for them, half hoping they were still up the mountain and were about to launch a rescue mission. But the pain I was feeling inside and the ache between my ribs told me loud and clear that Alex was really gone.

I scanned the clearing again anyway. Amber and Ryder were taking a stroll arm in arm down one of the many paths that led off the picnic area. Harvey and Bill were rolling cigarettes at a table twenty metres away to our right. Nate's body was slumped over the table between them. He looked like he was sleeping off a hangover. As I watched, Bill took a sweater, rolled it up and placed it under Nate's head.

Suki was sitting next to Demos, eyeing me through those spider-leg lashes of hers. I could feel her rooting around inside my head, making my scalp tingle. Or maybe I was just imagining it. I looked away from her, trying to block her out, if that was even possible.

After half a minute more of absolute silence, she turned to Demos, shaking her head. 'They've told her all sorts. Something about you wanting to steal nuclear weapons? It's like an L. Ron Hubbard story in there.'

I stared at her, my lips parting.

'I'm going to get something to eat. Leave you two to it,' she said, leaping up from the bench and skipping off towards the café. I watched her go.

'I'm guilty of maybe half of what they say.'

I swivelled my head back to Demos. He had his hands clasped in front of him on the table. I considered his words for a few seconds. 'Which half?' I asked.

He snorted. I guessed it was laughter. 'I like you. You're feisty,' he said. 'Just like your mother.'

I gripped the edge of the table until I felt a splinter dig under the skin of my thumb. 'Do not talk to me about my mother.' My voice came out as a hiss.

'I'm sorry.' A deep furrow formed between his brows. 'You're just so like her – I mean the way you look, your mannerisms. It's . . .' He shook his head and stared at me in what I took to be amazement.

I sat for a few seconds in a state of total shock. 'How do you know what my mother was like? You only knew her long enough to kill her.'

The furrow in his brow had become a trough. He looked down at the table, then back up at me. 'Lila, I did not kill your mother.'

I stared at him unmoving, unblinking, unbelieving.

243

'I admit I am guilty of some of the crimes they accuse me of. The breaking and entering, probably the treason, certainly one murder.'

I inhaled sharply.

'But I'm definitely not interested in stealing nuclear weapons,' he said, raising his eyebrows in obvious amusement. 'And I did not kill your mother.'

I wasn't sure if Demos was stilling my voice or whether my brain just didn't know how to function anymore. I could still hear myself thinking though, turning circles, running after questions, so he couldn't be. And my feelings were still there. I tried to decipher them. There was definitely anger. But mostly pain. And a whole lot of confusion. I didn't think he could be doing anything to me.

'I knew your mother.'

I looked up, startled. 'How?'

'She was a friend of mine.'

'Of course she was. And Nate's not here under duress and you're not holding me hostage. And really you're a nice guy – I bet you like puppies and teach Sunday School. When you're not killing people on your day off.'

His fists hit the table, making me jump, but he was laughing, his body shaking.

'Wow, Suki was right, they really have done a number on you.'

I ignored him. I knew what I'd read. But Alex had told Jack not to believe everything he read. Damn, I didn't know what to believe anymore. But then I looked at Demos and I knew for sure there was no way my mother would have been friends with him.

'My mother would never, in a million years, have been friends with you,' I said, but my power of conviction was already starting to waver.

He stopped laughing. 'She was, Lila.'

'You're lying. Why are you lying to me?'

'For a time she was more than just a friend.'

I shook my head and laughed.

'I loved her very much.'

My laughter died as abruptly as his had. My hands automatically moved to cover my ears. 'Stop it!' I shouted. 'Why are you doing this?'

'I'm telling the truth, Lila. I loved your mother and for a time she loved me back.' He pressed his hands against his forehead and closed his eyes. 'Then I did something stupid and she wouldn't forgive me – not that I blame her.' He opened his eyes again. 'She met your father and . . .' he took a deep breath, 'not long after that she was expecting your brother. It was too late.'

'You – and my mother? You expect me to believe that?' I pushed back from the table to standing. I had to get away from him.

Before I could go anywhere he reached into his back pocket and I fell back onto the seat, suddenly afraid. But he was just taking out his wallet. He slipped a square of paper out from inside and handed it across the table to me. I took it from him slowly.

It was a photograph. Black-and-white, taken in a photo booth. A tiny square holding two familiar faces. Only I couldn't quite make sense of it. I stared at the person smiling at the camera, long hair cascading down her back, her eyes just like mine. It was my mum, no doubt about it. And she looked so happy. The other person wasn't my dad, though. It was Demos. No question about it, albeit a lot younger. He had his arms wrapped around my mum and he was nuzzling – there was no other word for it – nuzzling her neck.

I put it down on the table and pushed it back towards him with my index finger. I noticed my hand was trembling. A splash of rain plopped onto the table in front of me and I looked at it in surprise before realising I was crying.

Demos started speaking softly now, almost fervently. 'I loved her. I loved how she was passionate and idealistic and impulsive. I loved how she always wanted to do the right thing, no matter what it cost. How she always knew the right thing to say. I loved the way she used to push her hair back out her face, just like you're doing now, and the way she would smile and her whole face would light up.'

I took several breaths before I could get the words out: 'You didn't kill her?'

'That's what I've been trying to tell you.'

'But if you didn't, who did?'

I could hear my heartbeat rushing in my ears like a waterfall.

'The senator she was working for. He had her killed.'

Several seconds expanded and contracted in front of me. Andrew Burns? But he'd been killed too. I'd seen the report. Demos had been tried and convicted of his murder. I wondered if he knew that there was an electric chair plumped and waiting for him at the base.

I narrowed my eyes in suspicion. 'Why would he have wanted her dead?'

His brow furrowed again and his eyes became even more hooded under the weight. 'Because, Lila, your mother was unique – like you. She had a very special gift.'

I stood up again, struggling to unknot my legs from under the bench. Then I was stumbling and tripping over the packed earth. The next instant I was kneeling on the ground and Demos was by my side.

'Stop doing that to me. Stop controlling me!' It came out as a half-cry, half-growl.

'I'm not, Lila. I'm not doing anything, I swear. Here . . .' He held out a hand and I looked at it.

Then I reached out slowly and let him pull me up to standing. Once on my feet, I tore my hand away and we stood there for a long while just watching each other.

'What could she do?' I asked finally.

'She could read minds – like Suki.'

My mouth fell open. Demos put a hand out to me. 'I'm sorry. I realise that must be a shock.'

A shock? He was king of understatement. I was getting fairly adept at handling the surprises, revelations, muggings and kidnappings that were occurring on an hourly basis, but this – this was straight out of left field. How could my mum have hidden a secret like that for so long? I had only been keeping my ability secret for four years and already it felt like half the world knew. Yet Jack and I had never known. I wondered if my dad had.

'Now you know your mum was one of us, do you still believe that rubbish they're feeding you about us being subhuman monsters?' He rolled his eyes. 'Seriously? Come on.' He was looking at me like he was trying to assess exactly how gullible I was.

I thought back to the conversation I'd had with Alex in the motel. He had said he didn't believe the Unit anymore. Because of me. A pain that seemed to strip the muscle from the bone peeled through me. I wanted him here with me so much right now. I wanted him to help me make sense of everything.

I looked at Demos, struggling to find an answer. 'I . . .'

'I brought you two some food.' Suki appeared suddenly by the picnic table. She was holding up a brown paper bag and beckoning us over.

247

I looked at Demos. I wanted to finish the conversation, preferably not with her anywhere near me.

'Come on, sit down. Have something to eat.' He put his hand in the small of my back and started to lead me to the table.

I knocked his hand away. 'I don't want to eat. I want you to tell me what happened to my mother.'

'I will tell you, Lila. Just come and sit down.'

I let him push me back towards the table and sat down in a huff. Suki sat opposite me, next to Demos. I gave her one of my best scowls. I didn't need her reading my thoughts just now. Or ever, in fact. How did the others stand it? She handed me a sandwich silently, the smile gone from her face. When I ignored the offering, she placed it on the table in front of me.

'Your mother was a remarkable woman, Lila.' Demos was looking at me so lovingly that I was in no doubt that he was seeing my mother in front of him. At least I hoped he was. I arched an eyebrow and crossed my arms over my chest.

'I'm sorry – you know this. You don't need me to tell you. It's just uncanny seeing you right here in front of me.' He shook his head. 'It's making it all seem so real again. Like it was just yesterday.' He stopped and took a breath. 'I met her when she was not much older than you are now. We were freshmen at Stanford. We met on campus in the first week – for me it was love at first sight. She was beautiful.'

My nostrils flared. I did not want to listen to this.

He noted my reaction with a smile and a nod, but carried on anyway. 'She was really something special – and she saw through me straightaway . . .' He laughed under his breath at the memory and it felt like a horse kick in my gut.

'A talent like your mother's is a difficult one to handle.' I saw him throw a glance in Suki's direction and registered her half-smile back at him. 'I've seen it drive people mad. Usually listening to your own inner voice is enough to push you over the edge – imagine what it does to you when you're able to tune into everyone else's.'

I glanced at Suki – maybe she had been pushed over the edge. It explained a lot.

'But your mum, she was special, she saw her ability only as a good thing. Something that she could use as a gift. To help others.'

'But—'

He held up a hand. 'I'm getting to it. Your mum was an idealist. She honestly believed she could change the world. She believed that if she went into politics she could make a real difference. I guess that's what most politicians think. Well, maybe not most. But she did have an advantage over the others. She thought if she could read people's minds she'd have no problem influencing people. Believe me, I saw your mum working her magic and it was impressive. She should have been a lawyer. She could have made millions. She could have turned a whole jury in seconds.'

'So why did she dump you?'

He winced. 'She met your father. I couldn't compete with his English accent.'

Or with his morals, charm or good looks, I thought.

I heard a tiny giggle emanate from Suki's direction.

'And it was over just like that.'

I was so glad my mum had come to her senses. Demos could have been my father. Not worth contemplating.

'I was madly in love with her. And when you're madly in love you do crazy things.' I could have sworn he was looking at me in a pointed way but then he carried on. 'All I could think about was stopping her from feeling anything for Michael, your dad. I thought if I could do that she'd come back to me – stupid, I know. But before I could do anything she heard me – she read my mind as soon as I had the thought. I wouldn't even have done it, I don't think. But she heard it, called me out on it and cut me off. I didn't blame her.'

He halted a moment before carrying on. 'We didn't speak for almost seventeen years. She moved to the East coast to get away from me. Married your father. Had you and Jack.'

Was he expecting sympathy for his tragic love life?

'Great. So now I know all about how much you loved my mum. It doesn't tell me why she's dead and why they're blaming you, though.'

He ignored me. 'The next time I heard from your mum, she called me up out of the blue. She was working for some senator and she'd discovered something she was really scared about. She would never have called me otherwise. We hadn't had contact for a very long time.'

'What did she say?'

'She needed my help. She said I was the only one who would know what to do. So I went straight to DC.' He frowned at the table, then at me. 'But she was dead before I even got there.'

I shut my eyes and tried to keep breathing. When I opened them again I saw him and Suki both watching me warily.

'How do you know for sure it was Burns that killed her?'

Demos leant towards me, his arms nearly touching mine. 'It was him. I got proof. I sent someone I knew, a guy called Thomas, to find out. He could project. It didn't take him long to find out. Not that there were any other suspects, anyway. I needed to know what your mum had found out, why he'd needed to kill her.' He laughed under his breath. 'I wanted to do it like your mother

250

would have. No violence. Nothing illegal. Believe me, it went against the grain. I would sooner have killed him for what he did.'

It went against my grain too. I wished he had killed him.

'Thomas sat in on some fairly interesting conversations. He managed to pass on quite a bit of information before he disappeared.'

I prised the words out of my mouth. 'What happened to him?'

'I assumed he'd been murdered too.' He looked sideways at Suki and I saw them exchange a smile.

'So what did you do?' I asked nervously.

He eyed me for a moment, weighing his words, trying to gauge my likely reaction. 'I killed Burns.'

I didn't flinch. I met his stare head on. He didn't back down. No, definitely no remorse there.

'But it was too late to stop what he'd started.'

'What do you mean? What had he started?'

Demos inhaled hard. 'The Unit. Burns was the man behind it.'

My hands fell flat onto the table and I leant forward. Our arms were touching.

'Burns was taking kickbacks from a defence company, Stirling Enterprises. They were paying six-figure bribes. Unsurprisingly the company won a very large, very lucrative military contract.'

'He killed her over money? That's what it was about?' Fury fizzed in my voice.

'It wasn't just the bribes your mum found out about. It was the details of the contract. That's what they couldn't afford to become public knowledge. On the surface it was a standard defence contract, to develop and supply new weapons to the military. But your mum found out exactly what they were researching and developing.'

I blinked at him several times as I absorbed the information.

'They're researching us, Lila. That's what your mum found out. The Unit is trying to isolate the gene that triggers our abilities so they can then use it to create new weapons.'

I threw back my head and laughed so loudly that Bill and Harvey looked over at me.

'Yeah, OK, that makes complete sense.'

'No, we're not mad.' Suki was responding to the silent accusations I was now throwing their way. 'Imagine if someone could do what Demos can do – only to hundreds or thousands of people at a time.'

'That's not possible.' I might not have listened too hard in biology lessons but I knew that it wasn't possible.

'Yes it is,' Demos interrupted. 'Gene therapy is the fastest advancing science of our time. You should see the progress they're making in medicine. It's actually quite fascinating when you have time to study it. All of this, everything we're talking about, is possible.'

OK, maybe I didn't know that much after all. 'So you're telling me that this company, the Unit, is not developing new guns or bullets, or bombs, but is, in actual fact, trying to create a super-army of mind-control freaks?'

'I wouldn't use that exact terminology, but – yes. Why else is a defence company employing geneticists and neuroscientists?'

I thought immediately of Sara. No way. Did she know what was happening? She couldn't. She was so nice. Jack was so in love with her. A split second later my body froze, the muscles contracting up my spine. 'Jack and Alex? Do they know?'

Suki shook her head, her hair slicing against her cheeks. 'No. They don't know. They think the scientists are just there to do psych evaluations. They have no idea what else is going on.'

'They're just soldiers, Lila. Pawns in a game.'

I looked at Demos.

'They were recruited on purpose. Why else would two eighteen-year-olds be approached in their freshman year? It was genius. They're exploiting your brother and Alex's obsession for revenge and using it to catch me. And they knew that recruiting Jack would give me pause for thought.'

I raised my eyebrows sceptically. It didn't seem to have given him much pause for thought.

'He's Melissa's son. They knew I wouldn't be able to hurt him.'

Yeah, I thought, that depends on how you define hurt. Kidnapping me and sending Jack on a crazy suicide mission qualifies as hurting, to my mind.

'We didn't have a choice, Lila.' It was Suki again. I kept forgetting she had access to my thoughts.

I was about to launch into a tirade but Demos interrupted, his voice so final it stopped me like a red light. 'And the real tragedy of it, the really sick thing, is that all this time, while they've been coming after me, your brother and Alex have actually been working for the very people who killed your mother. The company told Burns to do it.'

Licks of energy started to flicker up my arms and legs. The sandwich in front of me suddenly spun away across the table. Demos's hand shot out and he caught it in mid-spin. His eyes widened in a gentle warning. I worked on my breathing, trying to steady my whirring mind.

He spoke the next words slowly, watching me carefully for any more adverse reactions. 'The men who killed your mum are from the Unit. Your brother and Alex lead them.'

253

I put my head on the table, resting my forehead against the rough wood, feeling wave after wave of nausea wash over me. Prickles of sweat started to bead the back of my neck. I had probably shaken hands with the men who'd killed my mother. How could any of this be allowed to happen?

I felt a hand, Suki's I guessed, start to stroke my forearm, then her voice, light and smooth, answering my silent question. 'The Unit operates completely outside of any normal parameters.'

Demos spoke up. 'It answers to no one, Lila. It's so top secret only a few people in government know its real mission.'

I lifted my head from the table, it was heavy as marble. I remembered Alex saying the Unit operated under a higher authority even than the President. The clearing started to blur like I was on a merry-go-round. I felt myself lurch to the left, my elbow cracking against the side of the table. I put my head back down and closed my eyes.

'Why do they want you so badly? Because you killed Burns?' I asked, once the world had stopped spinning.

'No, not because of that.' He was laughing softly to himself. 'I did them a favour. Saved them a lot of money and the bother of doing it themselves.'

Suki butted in. 'They're after Demos because he's the most powerful of all of us. He's one of a kind. Not like the rest of us.' I opened my eyes and looked up. She sounded in awe of him.

I noticed the blush rising up her neck.

'It's enough that we know what the Unit is doing,' Demos said. 'But, yes, the main reason they want me – all of us, in fact – is that if they catch us, they hit the mother lode. Every known ability in one go. They'll test us like lab rats. Get what they want, then dispose of us.'

I watched as the blush drained from Suki's cheeks. Then her chin lifted and her head snapped to the side. She and Demos rose from the bench in unison, both looking over towards the table where Bill and Harvey were still sitting. I noticed that Amber and Ryder had joined them. I wondered what was going on, then saw Nate was sitting up between them. He was back.

I jogged after Demos and Suki, who by now were halfway towards him, Suki struggling to keep pace with Demos.

'What's happening?' Demos demanded as we reached them.

'They're there. They're in.'

I inhaled so loudly everyone turned to look at me.

'In the building? How'd they manage it?'

'They took Rachel.' Nate's face was fairly gleaming with exhilaration, like he'd just played a video game and had broken through to the final level.

Amber edged down her side of the bench and patted the empty space next to her while looking over at me. I studied her a while and then eased myself slowly down onto the bench. Bill grinned at me, and Harvey gave me a one-sided smile and a nod, cigarette still clamped in the corner of his mouth.

'It was really clever. They went straight to her house on the base. Alex goes strolling up and knocks on her door like he's there to watch the game or something. She's all over him as soon as she answers the door.'

I was glad I was sitting down.

'She was all "*Where have you been? Oh my God!*" Alex totally played to it. Tells her he had to go after Lila . . .' he paused to glance at me, with a slight apologetic smile, ''cos she'd run away. He said that he'd found her, given her a good talking-to and

255

packed her off on a plane home. Then the next thing he's got a gun to Rachel's head and told her to come take a ride. Seriously, it was like the coolest move, like he was Jason Bourne or something. They got her in the car. Did I mention the car? They stole it from outside the base. A hardcore 4×4 turbo engine. It's awesome.'

'Nate.' Demos's voice was hard as stone. 'What did they do?'

'Sorry.' He felt the rebuke. 'They took her to the Unit. Told her to cooperate or she was as good as dead. Jack told her that they were all going in and that she was going to authorise a prisoner swop. Something about taking Thomas and Alicia over to the Washington Head Office.'

Thomas? Thomas was dead. 'What do you mean, Thomas?'

Everyone turned to look at me, except for Demos. 'Nate,' he said, 'go back now. Tell us when they're on their way.'

Nate nodded, eager as a puppy. Ryder caught his shoulder moments before his unconscious head smacked onto the table. He replaced the rolled-up sweater gently. Suki reached over and stroked Nate's hair.

Demos was fixing me with one of his looks. 'Thomas is alive. Alex told us.'

'When did he tell you that?'

'Earlier, in the clearing. He told us Thomas was alive and that he'd bring us him and Alicia in exchange for your safe return.'

I thought back to Alex standing there with a gun against his head. The silent communication he'd had with Suki. The look in his eyes before he'd turned and left me. My fingers traced the bracelet on my wrist, remembering the way his hands had felt holding my face, the way his breath had tickled my neck, the pressure of his lips on mine.

256

And I couldn't stand it anymore. It felt like my mind was going to shut down, switch off. I lurched upright and started to back away from the table. I braced myself for the inevitable freeze but when it didn't come I turned and started to run towards the trees in the distance.

'Let her go,' I heard Demos say.

25

Suki found me. I was sitting against the base of a tree. I reckoned I'd been there about an hour. Possibly longer. The light filtering in shafts through the branches above me was almost horizontal.

'There you are,' Suki said.

'Is Nate back?' I asked.

'No. Not yet.'

I sank back against the tree. They had been shot or captured, I knew it. I covered my face with my hands and squeezed my eyes shut.

'They'll be fine, Lila. It's Alex and Jack. They're good at what they do. Let's go and wait for Nate. He might even be back already.'

I scrambled up, my legs stiff from sitting cross-legged so long. We walked back in silence. There seemed little point in talking.

The clearing was barred with shadows, the sky above us turning indigo. Everyone was gathered around watching Nate, who was still slumped over the table. Amber turned first, sensing our arrival. Everyone else looked up, following her gaze, and I saw the anxiety on their faces. They looked like family at the bedside of an intensive care patient. They smiled when they saw us and I felt myself redden. Only a few hours before I'd been doing telekinetic battle with Bill while Ryder held a gun to Jack's head. Now we were all friends, suddenly? God, what was happening? Maybe I had that thing – what was it called, Stockholm Syndrome? – where the kidnappee develops a bond with the person doing the kidnapping. Sometimes they even fall in love with the kidnapper. I looked at Demos. No, that was definitely never going to happen. What on earth had my mother been thinking?

I hesitated a few metres away from the table.

'Come on, we won't bite,' Suki whispered, brushing past me and going to stand next to Demos.

Demos nodded over at me, then went back to studying Nate's unconscious face. I stood dangling on the periphery for a minute, then went and sat down on the very edge of the bench, next to Ryder. The minutes ticked by, the sky darkening as though a pot of ink had been diffused into it.

I was beginning to feel the last strains of hope leaching away when Suki and Amber both seemed to stiffen. Amber lifted her head off Ryder's shoulder and Suki bounced forward and put her arm around Nate. We all stared at his face, waiting for signs of life. He blinked a few times then sat up, shaking his head. The dazed expression started to clear and suddenly he was grinning at us.

'They made it. They're on their way.'

The tension evaporated just like that. Harvey stubbed his cigarette out and started rolling another. Amber let out a huge sigh and I watched as Ryder gently stroked her hair. It was done with such tenderness that just watching them felt like fish hooks were being embedded into my skin. I looked at Nate instead, willing him to tell me more. To let me know how they were, whether they were hurt.

'What happened? How did they do it? Did anyone get hurt?' Suki was asking for me.

259

'No, they're fine. They're all fine. Well – kind of.' He looked at Demos and I saw his Adam's apple bob as he swallowed. 'Alicia's pretty pissed off. But she's fine. Just a few bruises. Thomas – he's not so good.'

I felt my body release like a popped balloon. My fingers uncurled from their position clutching the underside of the seat.

'Let's go,' Demos said, striding off.

Without another word everyone was up and moving after him.

Nate was walking just ahead of me, next to Suki. I hurried over to them. 'Is Alex OK? Is my brother?'

They both turned to me. 'They're fine,' Nate said, grinning widely. 'It was a breeze. They didn't even break a sweat – it was so cool.' He sounded like he had a crush on them.

'How did they do it?'

'Dunno. I couldn't go in – or near the building. I waited outside. They just went in then came out twenty minutes later with Alicia and Thomas. Then they all got in the car and drove off. I hung out for a bit with them in the car then came back here.'

'What about Rachel? What did they do with her?' I asked.

'Oh my God.' Suki stopped dead. 'Nate!'

Demos stopped still ahead of us, then marched over. 'What?'

'Rachel. They're bringing Rachel,' Suki told him.

Nate's face was stricken. 'Yeah, sorry, I forgot to tell you. They didn't want to leave her, they thought she might sound the alarm, so they brought her with them. They had to put her in the trunk.' He shrugged.

I couldn't help myself. I laughed out loud.

Demos considered the news for a minute. 'Nate, can you go back?'

Nate's shoulders sagged. 'I'm not sure. I'm really tired.'

Demos appraised him for a few seconds, then nodded. 'OK, I understand.' He put one hand on Nate's shoulder. 'You did well.'

'Maybe I can try again in a little while?'

'Maybe.' Demos nodded again, then marched off, pulling a mobile out of his pocket and dialling.

I wondered if he was calling Alex and if he'd let me speak to him but he was already out of earshot. I hung back with Nate and Suki.

'Is it the projecting that makes you tired?' I asked.

Nate looked at me and nodded. 'It's like running at warp speed. Mega fun but mega exhausting.'

We made it to the cable car just as they were closing it for the last ride down. That was good timing on Nate's part.

Once we were all inside, I inched away as casually as I could from the others and went and stood in the exact place where Alex had kissed me. I closed my eyes and tried to relive the moment, the way his thumb had touched my bottom lip. The way his lips had felt when he'd pressed them against mine, the way he'd looked at me with those velvet blue eyes. I took a deep breath and noticed the ache in my ribcage was better.

Like a bomb blast it hit me. Alex loves me. I felt the smile splitting my face in two.

It vanished when I remembered that before Demos showed up Alex had been going to leave me. In fact had actually left me. His last words had been something about being the moment. That was it: 'When you fell down the stairs,' he'd said, 'that was the moment.' The moment what?

'The moment he fell in love with you. Durr. For goodness sake, Lila. It doesn't take a mind-reader to work that out.'

I sunk down onto the bench in the middle of the car. So Alex had loved me the whole time, from the moment we'd seen each other again? All that time I'd been freaking out about Rachel? All that time I'd spent inches away from him, sleeping in his bed by myself; sitting opposite him at dinner, smashing plates; clinging to him on the back of his bike; sneaking peeks at him through a half-ajar bathroom door – and all the time he'd been in love with me? We'd wasted all that time when we could have been kissing? And he'd had to wait until two seconds before leaving me until he told me? If the Unit didn't kill him, I was going to.

The smile was back, though, pulling my face into a rictus grin. If I wasn't so ecstatically, crazily happy right now, I would most definitely kill him. Then I had another sudden realisation. Alex most definitely wouldn't be able to go back to the Unit now. He'd have to come with us. Woo-hoo.

'Are you OK, Lila?' It was Nate.

I looked over at him, startled. 'Um, yes, why?'

'Well, you were just hyperventilating, clapping and grinning like a toddler on speed.'

'She's just happy.'

I looked over at Amber. 'Keep it up. It's a pleasant relief,' she said.

Ryder wrapped his arms around her from behind and winked at me. I couldn't stop myself from grinning back. I wanted to go over and hug them both. They were in love. I loved them for being in love. The world was beautiful and Rachel was tied up in a boot and Alex was coming back to me and he loved me.

'OK, Demos, I think I need you.' Suki was calling out to Demos over her shoulder while still looking at me.

I pulled a face at her.

'Lila, please turn it down a fraction. I can't hear myself or anyone else think. He loves you. You love him. Now before you start singing about apple trees and honey bees, let's please try to think about other things.'

'How about Jack? Think about Jack.' Nate grinned wickedly at me.

I didn't want to think about Jack. I was really happy he was safe too, but when I imagined me and Alex being reunited, Jack wasn't in the picture. He was safely off to the side, with his back turned.

'Yes. Jack isn't going to want to see that.'

My attention flew straight back to Suki. 'What?'

'Jack. You're right to worry. He was pretty annoyed with Alex earlier. I heard him. In amongst all the rage against us, there was quite a bit of anger aimed at his best friend.'

Oh dear. 'What was he thinking?'

'Ooh, thinking? Girl, I know what he was saying.'

Now my attention was fully on Nate. He had one hand on his hip and the other looped over Suki's shoulder.

'When? Oh God, what happened?' I stared up at them.

'They had big-time words about you.'

'About me?'

He giggled. 'Yeah, it was hardcore.'

'What did Jack say?'

'He was like, "*Dude, what the hell with my sister?*" And Alex was all "*I love her*", and Jack was "*No way, man,*" and Alex just turned round and said "*That's the way it is. Deal,*" and that was sort of the end of it. You know, I totally get why you're in love with him by the way. He's totally gorgeous.' He rolled his eyes as though he'd just licked his favourite flavour ice cream.

'Er, OK, thanks. I think.'

'Nate – you are unbelievable.' Suki poked him with her

263

spear-like elbow, then turned to me. 'I swear he spends more time following the hot guys from the Unit than the useful ones.'

'I do not.'

'Do too.'

They were like two bickering kids.

'I am not.' Suki pouted at me. 'He is.'

'Lila . . .' I looked at Nate. His big brown eyes had gone liquid all of a sudden. 'Did you see my dad? Is he OK?'

I looked at Suki and hoped she wouldn't give me away. 'Yeah, he's fine.' I thought back to his blood-spattered face. 'Well, I mean, he's really worried about you.' I remembered the promise Alex had made to Key about protecting Nate from the Unit and getting him away from Demos. It didn't look like that was a promise Alex was going to be able to keep. It didn't look like Nate wanted to go anywhere. I lowered my voice. 'Why'd you run away in the first place?'

'I didn't run away. I'm free to make my own choices about how I live my life.'

OK, that I understood only too well. Who was I to accuse anyone of running away?

'And anyway,' he continued, 'what I'm doing now is way better than school. I get to do cool, real-life beating bad guys stuff . . .'

Didn't he think they were using him? He was just a kid.

'We're not, Lila.' Suki was frowning at me. 'And he's not a kid. He's the same age as us. We're making our own choices, aren't we? Wouldn't you fight for what you believed in?'

I'd fight for Alex. That much I knew. And for Jack.

'There you go then,' Suki said.

'But that's different. They're my family. This isn't personal for you.'

'How could it get any more personal, Lila? They're coming after people like us, containing us and even murdering us. Demos is doing this because of your mother. And we're fighting with him because we believe in him. If the Unit caught you, wouldn't you want to know that we were out there fighting for you and trying to get you back?'

I didn't have time to answer. The cable car ground to a halt and I looked around, startled. We were back in the real world. The eight of us exited the car and followed Demos across the car park. It was dark now, the lights from Palm Springs glowing like phosphorescence in the distance.

'Where are we going?'

'To the Batmobile,' laughed Suki.

26

We stopped by a huge RV bus with West Virginia plates. Harvey went to unlock the door. *This* was the Batmobile? I took another look. It was vast and cruddy-looking. There was a sticker across the bumper saying, *Honk if you love Jesus!* and a *Children on board* warning sign with a smiley face leered out at us from a side window.

'Good getaway car, huh?' said Demos in my ear.

'Er, yeah,' I mumbled, as he pulled me up into the back.

Inside was a whole other story. It looked like there was room to sleep a small army, with space for a ballroom at the back just in case they got bored with the flat-screen surround-sound home cinema system. Cream leather sofas lined two sides, and at the back was a darkened corridor that appeared to have several doors leading off it. *This must be what if feels like to be a groupie on a tour bus*, I mused as I stood there gawping, while the others started to move around and make themselves at home.

'Where are we going?' Amber asked Demos as she curled up on one of the seats.

'To Joshua Tree.'

'Cool,' squealed Nate. 'I love U2.'

Suki raised her perfect eyebrows at him and shook her head. His face fell momentarily, then he punched her lightly on the arm and they fell onto the seats and started to giggle together.

I watched as Harvey climbed into the driver's seat up front, with Bill in the passenger seat next to him. They started messing around with a sat nav screen that emerged at the press of a button from a dash lit up like the flight deck of a plane.

Demos disappeared down the corridor and into one of the rooms at the back of the bus and I looked around for somewhere to sit. Amber and Ryder were lounging on one of the sofas opposite Nate and Suki. I edged towards them. I'd take the loved-up couple over the hyped-up, mind-reading, U2-loving duo.

'Hi,' I said as I sat down. This was slightly uncomfortable.

'Hi,' they said back, smiling at me.

They were waiting for me to say something. My mind went completely blank.

'So – what's a sifter?' I blurted out.

Ryder threw his head back and laughed. 'Straight to the point. I like it.'

Amber leant her head back against his shoulder and kissed the underside of his jaw. I waited for the searing stab of envy. But it didn't come.

Amber started to laugh and shake her head, her curtain of flame-coloured hair undulating around her, if that was physically possible. 'You are so funny.'

'Huh?' I stared at her, confused.

'I get these waves and waves of emotion off you. It's never still, never one colour. It's like tuning into a rainbow. It's beautiful.'

I didn't know what to say to that. I'd never been called a rainbow before.

'Young love.' Ryder laughed and kissed Amber on the top of her head.

Young? I'd been in love with Alex for seventeen years, give or take a few. It wasn't young love.

I turned to Amber. 'So, you can see emotions like colours?'

'Mmm, colours. If I try, I can change the colours, make feelings go away. With your brother earlier, that was horrible. But with you and Alex, it's . . .' she laughed to herself, '. . . it's so . . .' She shook her head, trying to find the word. I waited with bated breath. So *what*? '. . . So extraordinarily lovely. You have to understand, I'm mostly around worry and fear, so it's nice to be around happiness once in a while.'

I looked at Ryder. It looked like she was around happiness more than just once in a while. He was good-looking. *Very* good-looking. And very adoring. I grinned at him some more. He wasn't anywhere near as good-looking as Alex, though.

He noticed me looking at him and a slow, easy smile crossed his face. 'So, Lila, Demos got you onside, then?'

The question surprised me. 'Yeah, I guess so. I mean, I don't know. It's all so confusing. So much to get my head around. But I guess so. I mean – the photo of him and my mum. And what he said about the Unit. And all of you . . .'

What I meant, was that just these few hours with them had dispelled so many fears. None of them were in any way intimidating. They were all lovely. OK, I still didn't get my mother's thing with Demos, but everyone else was so kind.

'We're not too bad,' he said, cocking a smile at me.

I was suddenly reminded of the photograph I'd seen of Ryder on Jack's computer and the list of crimes beneath it. Were any of them true?

Ryder noticed my change of mood. 'So what did Alex and Jack tell you about us?'

268

'Ryder!' Amber poked him in the ribs.

I blanched. 'Er, they didn't tell me much. What I know I heard from Key and from the files I found on the computer.' I couldn't catch his eye. 'It wasn't exactly flattering.' I looked up and saw he was looking at me quizzically. 'I thought Demos killed my mum. That's what Jack thinks too.'

'He didn't.'

'Yes. I know that now. But all the newspaper reports, what the police told us about how she was murdered . . .' I shuddered, recalling the nightmare I always had.

'Do you want me to take that away?'

I looked at Ryder, confused. 'What do you mean?'

'The image you have in your head. Do you want me to take it away?'

'That's what you do?'

'Yes. Sparingly.'

Did I want to not have the image of my mum lying dead in a pool of blood in my head?

'*Yes.*' I nodded.

Amber adjusted herself, moving along the seat to give him space. Ryder sat forward and placed one hand on the side of my head, his index and middle fingers on my temple. He stared at me and I noticed his eyes were grey. A really unusual colour, like a pebble thrown up by the waves on a stormy beach.

'OK, it's gone.'

'What?'

'Think about your mum.'

I closed my eyes. There was my mum, laughing and trying to put hair clips in my hair before my first day at school. Then a memory of her carrying a cake with eight candles on it and singing me 'Happy Birthday'. I started smiling as I recalled another memory of her lying curled up next to me reading *Harry Potter*.

'What did you just do?' I asked, looking at Ryder in wonder. I hadn't remembered any of those things in so long.

'Nothing.' Ryder leaned back into the seat, stretching his arm out, and Amber fell into him, leaning her head against his chest. They were so adorable.

Amber laughed again.

A voice interrupted the laughter. 'Do you mind if I join you?'

I looked up. Demos was standing over us.

'Not at all.' Ryder moved his feet out of the way and Demos sat down next to him.

'Everything OK?'

'I think so,' I mumbled.

He didn't seem to hear me. 'We're going to be meeting them in an hour or so.'

My heart started to skip a path through my ribcage.

'I need your help.'

I eyed him suspiciously. 'With what?'

Demos fixed me with one of his looks and I felt my muscles constrict. 'We need to stop them, Lila.'

No. I needed to be back with Alex and to go with him and Jack somewhere far away.

Suki appeared and dropped to the floor by Demos's feet.

'What do you want me to do?' I asked nervously, glancing at them both.

'We need you to convince Jack and Alex to fight on our side,' Demos said.

I felt four sets of eyes on me, and I could have sworn Harvey threw an anxious glance at me too, via the rear-view mirror. 'Fight?' I said the word as though it was an unfamiliar concept.

'Yes. Fight.'

No. I didn't like the way this conversation was going. There was going to be no fighting happening.

Demos looked over at Suki. She pressed her lips together until they went white and shook her head at him. He looked back at me.

'Lila. Please.'

I looked around me. Everyone was fixing me with pleading looks. 'How are you going to fight them?' I asked. 'What can we do? Alex said the Unit operate under an even higher authority than the President.'

A little smile started to lift the corner of Demos's mouth. 'If we have Rachel, we'll have leverage.'

'But Alex told me the Unit would never exchange or barter for anyone.'

'They will for her.'

'Why?'

'Don't you know?' Demos narrowed his eyes at me in surprise.

'Don't I know *what*?'

'No, she doesn't.' Suki was shaking her head.

'What?' I asked again.

'Rachel's father *owns* Stirling Enterprises.'

'Oh.' I wasn't sure why I was surprised. Surely my facility for surprise was totally neutralised by now. I leant back into my seat, suddenly relieved. 'Well, in that case, you don't need me. Or Jack or Alex. You have all the leverage you need. You just said so.'

'No.' Demos was shaking his head at me. 'It's not enough. We need people who know how the Unit operates, who can help us to stop them from the inside. We need Jack and Alex.'

'No.'

'Lila, I don't think you have fully understood what your life will look like if you run from this. You will spend the rest of your days hunted. You will not be able to go home. You will not be able to see your father. You will not be able to settle in one place for longer than a few days, a week at the most. You will always be looking over your shoulder, wondering if they've caught up with you. They won't leave you alone. You know too much and, genetically, you're too valuable. They *will* find you. They will kill Alex and Jack, like they killed your mother, and they will contain you.' He paused. 'Am I making myself clear?'

Crystal, I thought. I sat there, unable to move, my head whirring through the options. *Could we run? Would we have a chance?*

'You can't run, Lila,' Suki said.

I frowned at her. Why couldn't I?

'The Unit killed your mother, Lila,' Demos said. 'Don't you want revenge? Isn't that what Jack and Alex have been after all these years? Don't you think they'll want the chance to stop them?'

My head snapped up and I glared at him. He knew he had me. In that one instant, I knew I would stay. I didn't have any other option. And if Jack and Alex could be made to believe, I knew there was nothing on this earth that would stop them from going after revenge.

Demos scented victory. 'We need to fight back. And to do that we need Alex and Jack to join us.'

I stared at him for a long while until Suki started to grin. 'OK,' I said, 'I'll help. What do you want me to do?'

There was a collective unleashing of held breaths all around me.

'You need to talk to them. We need to convince them of the truth. They won't listen to me. But they trust you.'

Yeah. I could see a huge flaw with his plan. Jack would never be convinced that Demos didn't kill my mum. 'You met my brother, right?'

'Yes.'

'OK. And you realise I'm not really in his good books right now? And you – well, let's not even go there. What makes you think he'll listen to me? That he'll ever trust you?'

'You can be pretty persuasive when you want to be.'

I could? I hadn't been able to persuade Jack to let me stay in California. And I hadn't been able to persuade Alex to stay with me and not go back to stop the Unit single-handed.

'You're asking me to basically announce to them that they've been living a lie for the last three years. I have no proof other than the photo you showed me of you and my mum. And they hate you. I'm not sure I can do this. Jack will kill you before he listens to a word I say.'

'But Alex won't. He'll listen.'

Would he? I thought about it. He might. He had already started having doubts. Maybe he would listen? And maybe he could convince Jack? I certainly wouldn't have a hope on my own.

'What about Rachel?'

We all looked over at Nate, sitting on the opposite sofa, by himself. 'Why don't we get her to talk? She must know what's going on. Maybe, if they don't believe Lila, which I'm thinking they might not, Rachel could, you know, convince them.'

Demos looked at him with interest. 'Good thinking, Nate.' Then he knelt back down on the ground next to me. He rested a hand on my knee and I looked at it, thinking how weird it was that I wasn't flinching away in revulsion.

273

'When they arrive, Lila, I need you to stay back. Remember they still think we're holding you against your will. We need to make sure we get Alicia and Thomas and then you can go to them.'

'OK,' I said, almost mutely.

'We're there,' Bill yelled from up front.

27

The gate into the Joshua Tree National Park was shut and locked. It took Bill about two seconds to remove the lock and open the gate, all from the comfort of his seat upfront. Harvey revved the engine and drove straight in.

The road was rutted, unmade and it was pitch-black out there. The lights from the car dazzled several Joshua trees standing like sentries along the roadside. We rolled along the ruts for ten minutes until we were quite a way into the park. I wondered what on earth had made Demos choose this place in the middle of nowhere.

'Because it's the middle of nowhere,' Suki said.

'Yeah, OK. Would you please stop doing that?'

'Sorry.'

Harvey killed the engine. The lights started to fade in the bus. Only small footlights at the sides of the sofas stayed on – like on a plane during a night flight.

Then Demos's voice came at me out of the gloom. 'Everyone ready?'

No. I wasn't ready. I couldn't believe I had agreed to help. But what choice did I have? I wasn't sure there was such a thing as free will anymore.

'Bill, Harvey – you know what you're doing?' Demos called out.

'Yes.' They opened their doors and jumped down into the darkness. I watched them melt into the night and wondered where they were going.

'OK.' Demos turned back to the rest of us. 'I want this to go smoothly. We do the exchange. Lila goes to them. She convinces them to hear us out.'

I hoped Demos believed in the power of visualisation. I glanced around at everyone else to see how they were buying the pep talk. They all seemed pretty focused and positive. Maybe it was just me who was a quivering ball of nerves.

'Suki, I need you by me. I need you to talk to Alicia, make sure she knows what's going on. And vice versa. I need you telling *me* what they're planning. Alicia's been in the car with them all this time so she'll know if they're planning on doing anything unhelpful.'

He turned to Nate. 'Nate, stay back please, in the bus, out of harm's way. You've done enough. Get your strength back.'

'It's back already,' he said eagerly.

Demos ignored him and I saw the glower of a sulk cross Nate's face.

'Amber, Ryder – you stay with Lila. Here . . .' he handed a gun to Amber, 'take this. You have yours right, Ryder?'

'Yeah,' Ryder said, reaching around and tapping his back.

Amber pointed the gun at the floor and checked the chamber with a practised one-two movement.

I jumped up. 'Whoa – why do you need guns?'

'Just so no one tries any heroics,' Demos said, looking at me watchfully.

The gun was suddenly in my hand. Amber was standing with her finger pointed at the floor, trying to figure out what had happened. As Ryder looked over at me, I flipped his gun out of his waistband and let it smack into my other hand. I stood there like a cowboy at the OK Corral.

'No one meaning Jack or Alex?' I demanded. 'You are *not* pointing a gun at my brother again. Or Alex. Or doing your mind-control thing, either. They've done what you asked them to. They've brought you Alicia and Thomas. And pointing a gun at them isn't going to help get them onside.'

Everyone had fallen silent and was looking at me. No, not at me, I noticed. Their eyes were tracking the guns which I had started to wave about in time with my anger. I lowered them so they were pointing at the floor and pushed the safety on Amber's, glad all of a sudden that Alex had shown me how to do that – before I blew my foot or someone's head off.

Demos kept his voice soft and calm. 'Lila, they still think we killed your mother. They think I kidnapped you.'

'You did,' I pointed out.

Demos hesitated a fraction. 'What I'm saying is that they might not be so willing to let things slide once they have you back. They aren't going to be coming into this unarmed. I just want to be prepared. Can I have the guns back? Please?'

'No.'

'*Lila.*' His scowl was back. I squared my shoulders and gripped the guns more tightly. I was glad Bill and Harvey weren't there. I'd have stood no chance against them.

He tipped his head at me and raised his eyebrows. 'I can make you.'

I raised mine back at him. 'Not if you want my help you won't.'

I saw his scowl deepen then vanish. He nodded once curtly and turned away from me.

'So like your mother,' he muttered. I grabbed for one of the guns as it fell from my hand, stopping it in mid-air just before it hit the floor.

'Let's go,' he barked. I looked up and around at everyone else. Suki and Nate were watching me wide-eyed, Amber looked mildly irritated but Ryder was laughing.

'You've got balls, that's for sure.'

I took it as a compliment. He threw his arm around Amber. 'So, we're supposed to be making sure you don't go bounding off in Alex's direction when they come. But you've got the guns. Not sure how we're going to manage that one now.'

'Can we just rely on you, Lila?' Amber said.

'Yes. I promise.'

I took the clip out of Ryder's gun and pocketed it. Two guns seemed excessive. We waited in the dark envelopes of shadow on either side of the headlight beams. Bill had parked the bus so it was off the road but facing it at an angle, the headlights illuminating the route they would be coming down. I was hedged in behind Amber and Ryder. Suki was standing next to Demos to my left a few metres away and I had no clue where Harvey and Bill had disappeared to. Nate was sulking in the bus.

I looked around. The ground was pockmarked with little round holes. I stared at them, trying to figure out what they were, then did a little hopping dance when I realised they were rattlesnake holes. Suki giggled from the darkness.

'You'll hear them coming first – they rattle.'

She couldn't see the face I pulled at her.

'But I can hear you thinking it, Lila. Same difference.'

I focused instead on the blackness ahead, punctured by the

arthritic shapes of the Joshua trees and the spray of stars lighting up the sky like someone had needled holes in a blackout curtain. Two were getting bigger. They weren't stars, they were headlights. Everyone went quiet as they came towards us. I took a step forward automatically and felt myself brush up against someone.

'Lila,' Ryder said in a sing-song voice. It carried a hint of a warning.

I stepped back. 'Sorry.' I stood on tiptoe instead and peered over his shoulder to watch as the car came nearer. I could hear the engine now and the wheels tearing over rutted ground.

'It's them,' Suki and Amber said, almost at the same time.

'What are they thinking?' I whispered into the darkness where Suki was standing.

'Um, hang on, they're too far away. OK. They're just wondering why the hell Demos chose here. Alex is thinking about what he'll do if we've hurt you. Jack, well Jack's just thinking about how he can kill us. Lila, I really hope you can convince him not to try that . . .'

I felt the angry, blunt press of the gun down the back of my jeans. I hoped that I'd put the safety on properly. 'I'll try.'

The road ahead of us suddenly shone as the car they were in rounded the bend. It stopped just on the periphery of the light cast by the bus headlights. The engine cut, leaving the silence to roll back in. The lights from their car bathed the road ahead.

I tried to make out the shapes in the car but, wedged behind the wall of Amber and Ryder's backs, my view wasn't great. The doors clicked open and the internal lights turned on in the car. I couldn't see either of them though as they climbed out and stood in the shadows. On the back seat I could make out Alicia. She was smiling calmly and nodding to herself. Next to her was a slumped shape leaning against the door. I caught sight of a face, the grey, milky colour of a corpse, and heard Amber draw in a tight breath. Ryder's grip on her arm tightened.

'Alicia's fine,' Suki whispered to Demos. 'She says they're focused only on getting Lila back. No other plans. They're both armed. But she says we need to watch Jack. He's volatile. His thoughts – I can read them too. They've been jumping around a lot. He's focused now, but Alicia says he's only just keeping a grip.'

I peered like a blind person into the darkness towards where the taller of the two figures stood. My whole body was screaming with one instinct – to run towards Alex. It was like trying to force myself to stand next to a fire that was about to engulf me, rather than running to safety.

'Give me Lila,' Jack shouted across the space. My heart flew into my mouth at the familiarity of his voice.

There was a pregnant silence. 'Give us Amber and Thomas, then we will,' Demos called back across the void.

'Where is she?' Jack shouted, his anger shearing the words, making Amber reel backwards into me.

'Lila, let them see you,' Demos said, turning his head towards me, but not taking his eyes off the two of them.

'I'm here,' I called out, and stepped into the beam of the headlight so they could see me. I felt Ryder's hand on my arm, just a gentle pressure, warning me not to run. I held my other arm up to shield my eyes from the glare. There was a crunch of gravel as someone, maybe both of them, took a step towards me.

'Uh-uh,' Demos's voice called out.

I blinked in the glare of the light and looked over towards the dark shape I knew was Alex. I could see his outline, could see his hands cradling what looked like a gun.

'I'm fine,' I called out, plastering a smile onto my face to try to convince them that they could both relax and not try to kill everybody.

'Give us Alicia and Thomas. Then you can have Lila.'

'No. Alicia first. Then Lila. Then you can have Thomas.'

There was a huge sigh from Demos. 'You know, I could have them both before you could do anything about it. I'm playing fair because I promised Lila I would. So, OK, we'll do it your way. But no messing. I want us all to get what we want.'

He shouldn't have phrased it like that. I heard a snort coming from Jack's direction. We all knew what Jack wanted. How on earth was I going to stop him from doing something crazy? Was that what Harvey and Bill were doing? Were they out there in the darkness watching and waiting, ready to act if Jack or Alex tried something? I sure as hell hoped so. I wasn't sure I would be quick enough to stop a finger on a trigger. Especially in the dark.

A few seconds passed and then Jack walked to the rear door and opened it. I saw him bathed in the light from the car, saw the creases across his brow, the tension in his neck making his jaw jut out. He was furious. *Damn.* This was not going to be easy.

'Suki, tell Alicia not to do anything. Tell her what's happening.'

'I have already. She's fine.'

Jack helped Alicia out of the car. A little rougher than was necessary. He gave her a little shove and she started to edge towards us then, when she realised she was free, she started to run, but awkwardly. Her hands were tied behind her back. I felt the tension coming off the people around me in little waves.

Alicia stumbled the last few steps and Demos stepped forward into the light and caught her by the tops of her arms as she fell. She looked up at him and for a short second we all watched as Demos bent and kissed her on her lip, where it was split. She grinned back up at him. 'I knew you'd do it,' she said, laughing softly.

He pushed her behind him, and Amber took a step towards her, putting her hand on Alicia's shoulder and squeezing gently. I saw a sudden flash of metal and then heard the plastic snap of a tie breaking apart. Alicia's hands, now free, slid into the palm that Demos held out to her. She leant forward and whispered something in his ear.

'Now Lila.' It was Alex. The sound of his voice was all it took for the last licks of pain to disappear from inside me with a whoosh. Ryder's hand dropped from my arm and I was off, racing towards him.

I wasn't sure how I covered the ground between us but suddenly I was slamming against Alex's chest and his arms were around me. My feet were off the ground and his lips were hard against mine and there was nothing but him and me in a wide-open and empty space. Until I felt my feet make contact with the ground and opened my eyes to see dark shapes shuffling awkwardly and heard someone clearing their throat.

I stood unsteadily with my hands locked around Alex's waist, smiling up at him. His face was darkened by shadows but lit by the cobalt-blue of his eyes. His hands ran up my arms, as though checking I was all there, in one piece, then up my throat until they came to rest on either side of my face.

'Are you OK? Did they hurt you?'

I shook my head and clutched at his hands. 'No, no, I'm fine. Alex, I need to—'

I couldn't say another word because his mouth was on mine again and lights were dancing in my head.

He pulled away gently, just an inch, and when I opened my eyes he was staring right at me. 'I love you,' he whispered.

My stomach lurched into my mouth, my heart following swiftly behind.

'I take it my sister's OK?' Jack shouted from the other side of the car. He didn't sound too happy. Though no one could be as happy as I was right then in that moment.

'I'm fine, Jack,' I called back, trying to get my voice to work properly.

More than fine. I was flying. Alex stroked my cheekbone and then pulled me to his side, his arm binding me tight.

'Now Thomas,' Demos called.

I heard the car door crack open again and some scuffling noises as Jack reached in and pulled someone out. We watched as a thin pile of rags began to shuffle forwards. There was a collective intake of air, then Ryder stepped forward into the beam cast by the headlights and gathered up the toppling man. I watched from behind my hands as he half carried Thomas towards the bus and helped him inside.

'What did they do to him?' I said, looking up at Alex.

'I don't know,' Alex said through gritted teeth. 'Come on, we're out of here.' He opened the back door and started to push me inside the car.

I grabbed hold of the door frame and faced him. 'No, Alex, wait.'

'Lila!'

We all froze at the sound of Demos's voice. Alex turned, shielding me with his body.

'No, it's fine, Alex.' I tried to edge around him. 'I need to talk to you. You need to listen to what they've got to say.'

'Did he hurt you?' Jack yelled from the other side of the car.

'No. No. He didn't hurt me.' I pushed with both my hands against Alex, then skipped around him and ran to stand in front of the car. I wanted to step between Jack and Demos if I needed to. 'Nobody hurt me. Don't – just listen. I need to talk to you both.'

They both stepped towards me. I could see the furrows and fury in Jack's face, the fear in Alex's. I held up both hands like a traffic policeman, to try to stop them.

'We can talk in the car, Lila.' Alex's voice was subdued, and he was fixing me with one of his hypnotic gazes.

I shook my head at him. 'No. I'm not going.'

They both stopped mid-step and stared at me like I'd lost my mind.

'Listen to me,' I said. 'You've got it all wrong. They didn't kill Mum. Demos didn't do it. They lied to you. It was the Unit. It's been them all along. They killed her.'

'Get in the car now.' Jack's voice was like lightning. He stepped forwards, reaching out a hand to grab me.

I danced back a few steps, out of his way. 'No. I'm staying.'

'Lila, what are you *saying*?' It was Alex. I turned to look at him.

'I know it sounds crazy and trust me, I didn't want to believe him. But I do. I *do* believe him.' I took a step towards him, my voice dropping. 'Demos didn't kill her, Alex.'

Our eyes were locked. I reached my hand out and took hold of his, clasping his fingers.

'They want to talk to you. They want you to fight with them.'

'Fight the Unit?'

'Yes. We need your help.'

I watched as Alex's eyes narrowed at me. '*We?*'

'What the hell did you do to her?' Jack shouted at Demos. He grabbed me by the top of my arm and yanked me out of Alex's grasp. 'Lila, they've messed with your mind. Come on, we're leaving.'

He started dragging me towards the car. I fought against him, trying to prise his fingers off me. 'No, they haven't. I know it's true.'

Jack stopped pulling and I realised that Alex was blocking his way. His hand was resting on Jack's shoulder. They faced off, staring each other down.

'Listen to her,' Alex said.

I stepped between them, pushing them apart.

'Please, Jack – why won't you just listen to me?'

'Because they're lying to you, Lila. Come on, let's go.' He turned and started walking towards the car.

'We're not lying, Jack. I knew your mother.'

Demos was suddenly there, standing next to me. I felt Alex's body tense, his hand moving to his gun, holstered on his hip. I squeezed his other hand to stop him and he froze. Demos was being as good as his word. He could have stopped them both from moving another muscle, but he didn't. Jack turned slowly back towards us, his eyes blazing.

285

'He did, Jack. It's true. He didn't kill her. You've got to believe us.'

'I understand why you wouldn't trust a word I say, Jack,' Demos said, 'but at least ask Rachel – just ask her. If you still don't believe me after that, well, then you can shoot me.'

28

I held my breath. I could see the gun was still in Jack's hand, his finger on the trigger. Jack looked at me and I thought I saw a shadow of doubt flare in his eyes, or maybe it was just murderous intent. Without another word, he turned and marched to the rear of the car and popped the trunk. I heard footsteps behind me and glanced over my shoulder. The others had come to stand in a semicircle behind Demos. Ryder was back too, I noticed.

Alex pulled me closer. I gave him as reassuring a smile as I could muster. The line was back between his eyebrows. It seemed to be a permanent fixture whenever he was around me.

'Get your hands off me!'

My stomach muscles clenched on hearing her voice.

'You think you'll get away with this?' Rachel's words faltered as she came into view and saw her welcoming committee.

She was wearing a white blouse and a knee-length black skirt and only one shoe, making her attempt to stand up straight to confront us look comical. Her hands were tied in front of her and her blonde hair was tousled and falling loose from the pins that had been holding it. She still looked beautiful, but like she'd been put through a tumble dryer.

When she saw me, she threw her head back and sneered, 'Is she worth it, Alex?'

Alex laughed under his breath and stepped up to her. 'Right now, you have two choices,' he said, his voice as smooth and soft as velvet. 'You can tell me and Jack the truth about the Unit. Or I'll hand you over to Demos and you can tell him the truth.' He leant forward a little and whispered in her ear, 'And I don't think he's going to be as nice to you as I might be.'

He stepped back, letting her see Demos, who smiled at her in a way that sent chills even through me. I saw the fear start to gather in her eyes, though she kept her voice calm and almost flirtatious. I wanted to hand her straight over to Demos.

'You know the truth, Alex. Whatever they've told you, it's a lie. The Unit's just trying to stop them – you know this.' She looked at Jack. 'He killed your mother, Jack, for chrissakes.'

'No. He didn't.' I lunged towards her. 'The Unit killed my mum. Your father's company was behind it all. You've been lying to Jack and Alex the whole time. Admit it. Tell them what their precious Unit is really doing. Why you're really chasing us. What's the research for, Rachel?'

Rachel's mouth opened in surprise. She closed it quickly. 'Jack, she's talking nonsense. She's been brainwashed by them. Who knows what kind of mind-altering stuff they've done to her?'

'They've done nothing to me, which is more than I can say for what you're doing to us.' I squared up to her and heard Alex suck in a breath before I realised that I'd let myself out of the bag, so to speak.

Rachel's eyes narrowed. 'You're one of them,' she said. Her eyes flew to Jack. 'That must have been a surprise, Jack.' She sneered and Jack's expression darkened.

It didn't matter that she now knew about me. Ryder could remove that little piece of information later.

I took a step towards her. 'Tell them what the Unit's really doing.' I saw a trace of fear wash across her face. 'Tell them why they need the scientists, Rachel. Tell them why the Unit killed my mum for finding out what was going on.'

We all froze as a gun clicked. It was Jack. He was pointing it straight at Rachel's head. I backed away instantly. Alex's arm circled my waist, drawing me back even further against him.

'Is it true?' Jack spoke.

Rachel froze. So did the rest of us.

'*Is it true?*' Jack's finger was pressing on the trigger. 'You trained me, Rachel. You know that I'll do it.'

For a hideous moment we all watched Rachel's face as it transformed from her habitual iciness to a whitewash of fear. I looked at Jack, terrified at what he might be capable of.

Then Rachel spoke. 'You're right, Jack. I did train you. I made you what you are. Tell me, did it never cross your minds as to why you were both recruited? What made you two so special? Did you never ask yourselves why you were both made team leaders over all the others?' She let out a high-pitched peal of laughter and I gripped Alex's hand against my waist. 'We wanted to keep you close – you fools.' She threw her head back and laughed again.

I pressed myself against Alex's body. He felt like rock, the muscles in his chest and arms locked. No one had time to react before Jack flew forward and pushed the gun against Rachel's forehead. She stopped laughing abruptly and wobbled on her one shoe. I saw her eyes skitter around the group, looking for help. None was forthcoming.

Her blue eyes fell back on Jack, became calculating. 'If you do it,' she said quietly, 'you'll never know what happened to your mother.'

Suki gasped so loudly that I thought she'd been shot. 'No. Oh my God.' She bent over double, her hands on her knees.

'What, what is it?' Ryder had a hand on her shoulder.

'She's not dead.' Suki looked up at me and Jack. Her face was pale, her eyes glowing gold. 'She's not dead.'

Jack dropped the gun from Rachel's head and stared at Suki. '*What?*'

'I saw. I mean, I heard it. Your mum's alive. They're keeping her. Like Thomas.'

There was a silence so profound I could almost hear the earth turning. Then a world of noise and emotion rushed in to fill the void. A growl erupted from my chest and I lashed out at Rachel. Alex caught me around the waist and held me back. I fought like a crazed animal. I wasn't sure what I wanted to do in that moment but I wanted her to tell me more. I wanted to get into her head like Suki could and find out everything she knew. *My mother was alive.* The energy drained from my limbs and I felt myself go limp in Alex's arms. *My mother was alive.* I looked at Jack.

His arm was stretched out at a right angle to his body. The muzzle of his gun was flush with Rachel's forehead.

'Don't—' Demos's voice rang out.

'Jack!' Alex yelled.

'Demos! They're coming!'

I stumbled round at the sound of Amber's voice, trying to see her. She was clutching Ryder's arm. 'I can feel them.'

Demos turned immediately to Alicia. Her eyes went blank and unfocused, then suddenly opened up, startled. 'Yes, I can hear something. Lots of people. Not far off.'

'Damn,' he shouted. 'Let's go. Get Rachel. Harvey, Bill – come on!'

Two shapes emerged from the shadows on either side of the car and started running towards us.

'Rachel stays with us. I'm not finished with her.' Jack didn't let go of her arm and there was a silent stand-off between him and Ryder, who had hold of her other arm. Rachel looked between them, seeming unsure which fate would be worse.

'You can have whatever time you need with her after this is over,' Demos said, coming between them. 'Right now, you need to let us take her. You follow.'

'Come on, Jack, let her go,' Alex said, tugging at his arm.

Jack let her go with obvious reluctance and Ryder dragged Rachel kicking and yelling over to the bus and hefted her inside.

Alex started running to the car, pulling me along behind him.

We had covered about ten metres when we heard Suki calling out.

'We're too late. There's no time. They're moving too fast.'

She was pointing at something in the distance. Headlights were dicing the night sky into pieces. I heard Alex swear under his breath. His fingers tightened around my waist and he started to move fast towards the car.

'We have to stay and fight our way out.' Demos's voice pitched across the darkness towards us. He was standing still as one of the Joshua trees, his eyes calculating the shrinking distance between us and the bouncing lights on the horizon.

'How many are there, Alicia?'

'I can't get a good read. Over a dozen. Maybe fifteen.'

Demos turned to his other side. 'Suki?'

She closed her eyes for a couple of seconds. 'Yes, about that. Two cars. They've got weapons.'

'Let's go – there's still time,' Ryder shouted to them from the door of the bus.

'No,' Demos replied. 'We can't outrun them. If not here, it'll be somewhere else, a few miles down the road. Here we've the upper hand. We can fight them – slow them down enough so we can get away and they can't follow us.'

Ryder jumped down from the bus. 'Well, we need to stop them before they get close enough to hit us,' he said.

Demos turned to Alicia, his voice urgent. 'Alicia, tell me who's got what weapons.'

'Front passenger in both vehicles. Go for them.' Alex spoke up. 'They'll be the ones with the weapons that can take you down.'

I cringed as I remembered the splicing pain in my head.

'The others will be armed with guns.'

Demos turned to me. 'Lila, give Ryder and Amber back their guns, please.'

I didn't hesitate. I flew the clip towards Ryder and the gun towards Amber.

As soon as Amber caught it, Alex grabbed hold of me again and pushed me in Jack's direction. 'Jack, get Lila in the car. Get her out of here. We'll hold them off.'

I reeled around. He was checking the chamber of his gun. 'No. I'm staying. I can fight too.'

Jack interrupted. 'No way. You're coming with me. Let's go.'

'No.' I skidded away from him. 'I'm staying with them.' I looked over at the others, huddling around Demos.

I turned to Alex, who was glaring at me. I could see his jaw pulsing angrily. I squared my shoulders and stared back defiantly. There was no way he was packing me off out of this. Especially if he was staying.

He glanced at the horizon where the lights were flashing. We had about thirty seconds before they were upon us. There wasn't enough time for us to get clear. 'Stay behind me,' he growled. 'Keep back.'

Jack spat a curse into the dirt.

'Lila.' I turned to see Demos standing at my side. 'I need you to help Harvey and Bill. You need to take out the first car. Can you do that, do you think?'

Take out a car? What did he mean – flip it over? I glanced over at Harvey and Bill then swallowed hard. 'I'll try.'

'Good. Alex, you and Jack focus on anyone who gets out, especially if they manage to use their weapons. We don't have enough manpower or weapons to do anything else right now but try to stop them following us. Let's take the cars out, stop as many of them as possible and then get the hell out of here.'

The headlights from the first car bounced over the ridge before we could agree or disagree with his tactics.

'Demos – now!' Alicia called out.

Demos spun to face the cars charging towards us. But they weren't cars. They were tanks. Or close enough. Humvees – each one several heavy, brutal tonnes of metal.

Alex moved to stand in front of me and a part of me wanted to laugh at the pointlessness of the gesture. Nothing was going to stop that thing, not a bullet, not some unreliable mind power and certainly not a single person standing in the way. We had left it too late. Alex didn't flinch a muscle, though. He stood there, in the blinding white light thrown out from the Humvee, his gun raised, his stance ice-cool. Then he fired once and I heard a bullet whip past and the sound of rubber bursting.

'Come on, Lila, turn it.' He spoke through gritted teeth as the Humvee shunted to the left before righting itself and bearing down on us even faster.

I focused harder than I'd ever focused on anything in my life. The car rounded a slight curve in the road about one hundred metres away. My eyes tracked the tyres. I visualised them lifting off the ground and toppling the Humvee over, spinning it onto its roof. Nothing happened. What were Bill and Harvey doing?

'Come on!' Alex fired again and the bullet ricocheted off metal like a staple gun firing into a brick wall.

I saw Jack out of the corner of my eye, blue flashes raining out of his gun as he shot repeatedly. I refocused through my panicking, stalling heart. As though it was made of nothing more than fibre-glass, the entire metal beast suddenly lifted clean off the ground and veered violently to the left. I could feel the line between me and it like a thin silvery chain. I looped it in my mind like a whip and then gave it a long, delicious flick. The Humvee bounced into the ground, skidded and then flew up, somersaulting over on itself a half-dozen times. It skimmed the roof of the second Humvee with a scream of torn metal, and impacted with the ground so loudly I had to cover my ears. A hail of dirt and stones and tree branches came raining down out of the sky, littering the ground around.

'Oh. My. God.'

'Jeeez.' Alex was staring at me, open-mouthed.

I swallowed hard, staring in horror at the carnage – there was no movement from inside the deformed, twisted metal. *Did I just do that?*

'Let's go!' Demos was calling out to us. 'Get in the car, go, we'll cover you.'

The second Humvee had spun off the road at a hundred-and-eighty-degree angle to us. The doors were flying open and men in black combats were rolling out onto the ground and starting to run towards us, guns in hand.

'Get behind the car,' Alex ordered. His hand was on the back of my neck and he was crouched low, pushing me towards the car. Jack was following.

My whole body was shaking with the adrenaline rush. I looked over my shoulder. Ryder was covering the others as they piled into the bus. Demos was standing on the road, like a human shield between us and the approaching men. I hoped to God he could stop them. I had no idea what the range of his power was or how many he could hold at a time.

Alex flung us to the ground behind the car and reached for the door handle. I peeked over the bonnet of the car and caught sight of one of the Unit running towards us with a gun the size of a bazooka in his hands. Without even thinking about it, I wrenched it from his arms, hurling it with as much force as I could into a Joshua tree nearby. The tree toppled over onto one branch and the man who'd been carrying the gun flattened himself into the ground.

A sudden scream made me turn my head. For a moment I couldn't figure out what was happening.

Ryder was lying face down on the ground, several feet out. Demos was standing about ten metres away from him with his back turned. His gaze focused unstintingly ahead. He hadn't even turned to see what had happened. I knelt and got ready to make a dash over to Ryder but couldn't. Alex had me by the arm.

'You can't do anything,' he said, before looking back over the top of the car and starting to fire.

I looked at Demos. He was still standing there, unmoving. Then I realised he wasn't moving because he couldn't. He was holding five men frozen in mid-run. He couldn't break his concentration or turn to help Ryder. Now was the time for someone to run out there and take their guns off them and the car keys too. Why wasn't anyone helping?

I looked over at the bus. Amber was screaming from the doorway and Harvey had his arms around her from behind, like he was saving her from drowning. He was dragging her backwards out of the way and she was clawing at him desperately.

Someone had to go and help. But before I could break free from Alex's grip, Jack had gone.

'Cover me,' he called back over his shoulder.

Cover him? I turned back to Alex. He glanced at Jack, now scuttling over the darkened ground. He swore, then started firing a thick rain of bullets out into the darkness. Jack reached Ryder and rolled him over. His head lolled back into the dirt and a thin trickle of black blood spilt out down his chin. A sudden cold sickness leadened my stomach.

I turned my head back to see where Alex was firing. Four men were coming towards us, taking aim at Demos and Jack. As I counted them, one went down with a cry. Alex paused to reload. I focused on the man at the front. He fired in our direction and the windshield shattered over us.

Alex put his hand on my head and pushed me to the ground. 'Stay down!'

He opened fire again, bullets cracking all around. I spun to look at Jack out in the open. They were going to get shot.

I poked my head over the bonnet and focused on the one in front, whipping the gun out of his hand just as he pulled the trigger.

296

The bullet whistled through the air and I heard the sound of it hitting mud. The earth was dry. As I realised what that sound meant, a wrenching, twisting pain flooded through me. Turning my head to look, I saw I was right.

Jack was standing still. But he was looking at me curiously. I felt a shrieking pain in my chest, like the bullet had hit my heart. His hand dropped to his stomach, pressing against his T-shirt. I looked down at his hand. Between his splayed fingers, a spreading dark was appearing.

'Jack!' I screamed and lurched out from behind the car towards him.

Alex grabbed my shoulder and hauled me back, seizing me around the waist and holding me so tight all I could do was struggle against him. He rocked backwards with me in his arms and I kicked out at the ground, watching with horror as Jack fell to his knees and then pitched forward, his arms flung out on either side of his body.

'No, no, no!' I was sobbing and kicking and trying to get free from Alex's grasp.

'Lila, stop, stop! You'll get killed if you go out there.'

A bullet spun past my head, smacking into the ground by my ankle. Alex rolled over, pinning me with one leg to the ground as he knelt and continued firing over the bonnet of the car at the remaining two men. Tears were rolling down my face as I stared helplessly at Jack lying motionless on the ground. I could see a pool of blood seeping into the earth around him.

'Damn it. There's two still out there.' Alex was yelling to Demos, trying to be heard over the haemorrhaging roar of an engine. 'And there are more coming. We've got no chance.'

I turned my head to see. Another set of headlights had appeared in the distance.

'Go. Get out of here,' Demos yelled back. 'I'll hold them off as long as I can.'

'No!' I screamed again. 'We're not leaving Jack.'

Alex put his hand on my face, pulling me around so he could look me in the eye. 'If we leave him, Lila, he has more chance of surviving. We can't get to him without getting killed. And if we *did* get to him, there's nothing I can do for him here. He'll have more chance if they reach him.'

He glanced at Jack one more time then started firing again out into the darkness where the two remaining men had gone to ground.

I stared at Alex, not comprehending, then looked back at Jack. His eyes were open and he was looking straight at me. I felt relief but it was quickly swallowed by panic. I couldn't leave him. Then he moved one arm, the hand holding his gun, and pulled it up so it was parallel to his head.

Still looking at me, he mouthed the word 'go', then raised himself onto his elbows and started to fire.

'Open the door,' Alex shouted over the noise.

'What?' I stammered, my eyes still on Jack.

'Open the car door. I can't reach.'

I opened it without even looking at it. Then I felt myself physically lifted off the ground as Alex hauled me like I was a sack around the car door and threw me onto the front seat.

'Head down, move!' he yelled.

I obeyed instinctively, curling up into a ball and flattening myself across into the passenger seat. Alex was in after me in the next second, revving the engine. A bullet whined and smacked into the side of the car as he spun it into reverse and roared out onto the road. I gripped the dashboard and looked back at the dark shape lying abandoned on the ground. That was my brother. That was Jack. I saw him drop his gun and rest his head back on the ground. Alex pushed me down into the seat well. I felt the tears pounding down my face in time with the smack and hiss of bullets.

We veered off the road, Alex killing the lights so we were hurtling through blackness. He swerved violently, the wheel spinning beneath his hands. He wrestled with it while I clambered onto the seat and looked over my shoulder. We were heading away from the park gates, in the opposite direction to the blazing headlights of the third Humvee that had just appeared over the ridge. I willed Demos to move. Then the bus started to roll forward and Demos jumped on board, the men he'd been holding frozen suddenly reanimating and firing in all directions. I watched as two of them raced over to Jack and rolled him over onto his back, kicking the gun out of his hand.

Alex grabbed my hand, lacing his fingers through mine. 'Lila, look at me. Look at me,' he shouted.

I forced my head to turn, to look at Alex. His eyes were burning into mine. 'Don't look back. Just keep looking at me. It's going to be OK,' he said. 'Everything's going to be OK.'

Epilogue

As dawn broke, we pulled into a rest stop just off the highway.

Alex opened his door and got out. I followed after him, looking around at the half-dozen or so trucks parked around us. There was no RV with West Virginia plates amongst them.

It had been two days. Two days and two nights of not knowing. Two whole days and two whole nights running from the scene we'd left behind in Joshua Tree – from the people we'd left behind. I felt a horse-kick to my stomach every time I remembered Jack sprawled in the dirt bleeding, with Ryder lying dead beside him.

I screwed my eyes shut. When I opened them again the sun had started to stretch the shadows across the asphalt. I scanned the highway in both directions, sighing loudly. I didn't want to be here. I wanted to be in Oceanside.

I glanced over at Alex. He had his sunglasses on so I couldn't see the dark shadows or the look in his eyes, which I was grateful for. Alex, normally so impossible to read, was struggling to hide his worry. He kept reassuring me that Jack would be OK and I was trying hard to believe him but his eyes kept giving him away.

As though he sensed me studying him, Alex turned then walked around to my side of the car. He put his arms around me and I sank my head against his chest, feeling some of the anxiety immediately fade away. He lifted me up and rested me on the bonnet of the car and we stayed like that for a while, me cocooned in his arms with the sun slowly warming us.

'Will they come, do you think?' I asked eventually, my cheek still against Alex's chest.

'They'll come,' he answered, as though it wasn't up for debate.

For forty-eight hours we had been zigzagging through California and Nevada, trying to shake the Unit off our tail. Alex was convinced that Demos, either through Nate or Suki, would find us eventually. I hadn't voiced my fears – that they had been caught or that the Unit would find us before they did – because they didn't need voicing. But now we were getting into our third day since the shoot-out and there was still no sign of Demos and my fears were starting to press against the dam of my chest, threatening to burst through it.

If it wasn't for Alex's arms around me, I thought I would give up and just wait for the Unit to find me. At least then I'd get to see Jack and my mum again. But even as I thought it I knew that I would never give up – I would never give in to the Unit, not after everything they had done to my family.

I lifted my head so I could watch the road, surreptitiously scanning the rest stop and the surrounding area for missiles I could launch if I needed to.

Eventually, when the sun was brushing the bottom branches of the trees around us, we heard the grind of gears and looked up. A dirty white RV was thundering down the highway. I gripped Alex's arm. We watched as it pulled into the rest stop. It had a West Virginia number plate. I jumped down off the bonnet.

They had found us.

I spun around to Alex. A shadow of a grin passed across his face when he saw my expression. 'Told you,' he said.

I turned back and waved at the RV as it drew up in front of us. Demos and Harvey were first out, Suki and Nate stumbling down the steps behind them. The two of them looked shell-shocked. Suki's face was streaked with black lines. Alicia and Bill followed last. There was no sign of either Amber or Thomas. Alicia looked fierce. Her eye was healing but I noticed the scowl she shot at Alex. Bill seemed uneasy, like he wanted to be away from all this.

'Are you OK?' Demos asked, striding straight towards me. He put a hand on my shoulder, his eyes boring into mine.

'Yeah, I'm OK,' I said, my voice husky. 'Is Jack, though? Did you see him? Is he alive?'

'They put him in one of the Humvees,' Demos answered. 'He's alive but we didn't see what happened to him.'

My face fell. What was the point of all this waiting, then? We should have just gone straight back to the base, followed after them and found out. I couldn't wait any longer not knowing. I heard a familiar voice and looked up.

'I saw what happened to him.' Key was standing in front of me. It took me a few seconds to place him.

'Wh-what are you doing here?'

Seriously, what was he doing here? My eyes flew from Key to Demos and then back to Key. Only a few days ago Key had been warning me about Demos. Now they were on the same side? It hit me only then. Of course they were on the same side. We all were now.

'I was on the mountain, Lila,' Key said, wiping the back of his mouth. 'I heard you all talking – heard what Nate had to say, and then I followed you all to Joshua Tree. Saw that girl Rachel talking about your mother – figured you might need some help in getting her back.'

302

I stared at him, tears stinging my eyes. I couldn't speak.

'I caught up with these guys eventually but it took a while. Had to go back for my body,' he said, shrugging and smiling at the same time. He glanced over at Nate and smiled. Nate grinned back at his dad.

'And Jack? You said you saw what happened to him.' I clutched for his hand.

He looked back at me and the smile vanished. 'They took him back to the base. He's in the military hospital there. The Unit are all over him.' He paused. 'He's not in a good way, Lila.'

I felt my breathing start to hike. The ground started to shimmer and move beneath my feet. I felt Alex's hand come around my waist, rest on my hip, stilling me.

Key took a breath and I caught the wary look he flashed at Alex. 'He was hurt bad. The bullet missed all the vital organs but it's lodged near his spine. They operated. He's OK but he's in a coma. They won't know what the damage is until he wakes up.'

Alex's grip on my waist tightened and I leant into him, closing my eyes, taking in Key's words.

'He's alive,' Alex whispered into my hair.

Relief belatedly rushed through me. I straightened up, pulling away from Alex. Jack was alive. So now we needed to get him back.

I turned to Alex. 'How do we get into a military hospital?'

He hesitated. 'Not that easily,' he said finally.

I stared at him, wanting a better answer than that, but I just found myself looking at my reflection in his sunglasses. I had my hands on my hips, my hair tumbling over my shoulders, my eyes burning. I turned away, kicking the gravel with my shoe.

'And Rachel?' I heard Alex say.

I spun around.

'She's inside,' Demos answered.

'We stuck a gag in her mouth,' Suki added. 'She can really talk and Demos can't spend all day whiting her out.'

Demos gave a faint shrug.

'What are you going to do with her?' Alex asked.

Demos studied Alex hard, his gaze inscrutable. 'We'll use her. Somehow. She must have some information. Suki and Alicia are both trying to read her but she's blocking them somehow. We'll find a way in, though, or we'll use her as collateral.'

Alex frowned a little but just nodded.

'You need to get Lila out of here,' Demos said, tipping his head towards me.

'No!' I yelled, moving to stand between them. 'I need to go back. We need to get Jack. We need to get my mum.'

'We will.' Demos turned to me, his voice low. He put a hand on my arm. 'Just not now.'

Why not now?

'We'll get them back, Lila, I promise. But first we need to regroup. Ryder's gone.'

I stopped short, my protest dissolving. Ryder was dead. Demos's head was hanging down, his eyes hooded. I looked over at Suki, tears streaming down her cheeks. Nate was wiping his eyes with the back of his hand. Alicia was still glaring at Alex and Bill was just looking at the ground. This was their family. They had lost one of their own. And so had I.

'I'm sorry,' I choked out.

Demos nodded at me, his lips pressed tightly together. He looked over his shoulder at the door to the RV.

'Is everyone else OK?' I asked.

'Yeah.' Demos looked at the ground. 'No one else got hurt,' he said, under his breath.

There was a moment of stillness. Only the shudder of traffic from the road.

'You go,' Demos finally said to Alex. 'Take Lila and head south. Over the border. Keep going until you hit Mexico City. We'll find you there.'

'What are you going to do?' Alex asked.

'We're going to try to draw the Unit away from the two of you, we'll go north.'

'OK,' Alex said and started to pull open the car door. 'We'll see you in Mexico.' His eyes flashed suddenly to me. 'Then we'll take it from there.'

I considered him for a moment, considered myself in his glasses. Then I opened the door of the car.

'Wait.'

I turned around. Demos had hold of my arm. He pulled me towards him and squashed me into a massive hug. 'Stay out of trouble,' he murmured before letting me go.

I stumbled back out of his arms and stared after him as he marched back to the van. Suki held up a hand in farewell. Nate tugged her backwards and nodded a sad goodbye. I watched them go, feeling a familiar snap and ping as something inside me started to stretch.

Then I turned to Alex. His eyes were fixed straight on me, filled with anxiety and something else. Something I now recognised. Because I knew the feeling well – had known it since the day I broke my leg twelve years ago.

I smiled a weak smile. 'Come on, let's go.'

An echo of a smile turned the corner of his mouth up. He pulled me by the arm until I was tight against him and then bent to kiss me on the lips. 'We'll find your mum and Jack, I promise,' he said.

And I believed him.

**IF YOU ENJOYED *HUNTING LILA*,
LOOK OUT FOR THE NEXT HOT BOOK
FROM SARAH ALDERSON – *FATED*, COMING SOON!
TURN THE PAGE FOR A TASTER...**

'Her name is Evie Tremain. She's seventeen years old. She lives in Riverview, California. Now go and kill her.'

The stillness in the room erupted as chairs scraped the floor. There were a few hushed whispers, a stifled laugh and then the door slammed shut cutting the noise off like a guillotine.

Lucas stood slowly, taking his time. He didn't notice that the others had left the room, nor that Tristan was standing by the window watching him. All his attention was focused on the photograph he held in his hand.

It showed a girl – dark-haired, blue-eyed – looking straight at the camera. It was a close-up. He could make out the shadows her lashes were making down her cheeks. A strand of hair was caught like a web over one eye and in the corner of the shot he could see her hand, reaching up to brush it away. Her lips were slightly parted, like she'd been sighing just at the moment the lens snapped shut. Her expression was ... Lucas paused. He wasn't sure *what* her expression was. She looked unhappy, or maybe just pissed off.

She was a Hunter, though, so what did he expect? And this one had a history that would make anyone unhappy. Or pissed off.

'Is something wrong?' Tristan asked.

Lucas looked up from the photograph, then glanced over towards the door, realising that he was the only one left in the room. He looked back at the older man.

'No, nothing's wrong,' he answered quietly.

'Well, you'd best get going then,' Tristan said, his eyes not leaving Lucas's face. 'You don't want to miss out on all the fun.'

Lucas looked down once more at the picture of Evie Tremain, feeling momentarily ambivalent towards her. Then he scrunched the photograph up into a ball and dropped it on the floor. It didn't matter what lay behind that expression because soon nothing would. She was just another Hunter to be dealt with. Next week or next month there would be another. And then another. And dealing with Hunters was what the Brotherhood did.

Lucas didn't look back at Tristan but he could sense his eyes burning into his back as he left the room.

Moving away fast down the corridor, Lucas realised he could no longer hear the others. He was faster than any human - he knew because he'd had to outrun them many times – so it didn't take him long to reach the basement garage.

There was just one ride waiting for him. Caleb and Shula were sitting in the front seats, the engine revving, the back door flung open.

'Come on!' Shula yelled. 'What's keeping you? There's a Hunter to kill and the others are going to beat us to it!'

Lucas smiled and shook his head, ducking into the back seat and slamming the door shut.

He let his head relax back against the seat and watched the speedometer climb as Caleb slammed the Mercedes out of the underground garage and onto the highway. Lucas stared out of the window. This stretch of highway was always quiet, but at night it was even more so – there were only a few factories and gas stations for at least twenty miles in each direction. The Mission was a good base for the moment. Tristan had chosen well.

'She's pretty.'

Lucas turned his head. Shula was leaning across from the front seat, waving the photograph of Evie in his face. He grunted and went back to looking out the window.

'Think she'll put up a fight?'

Lucas looked back at Shula. She was studying the photo intently, as though she could will it to life. Her raven-black hair was spilling over her shoulders, her skin glowing freakishly in the green dashboard lights. He almost smirked. Shula tried so hard to fit in and yet here she was looking as unhuman as a Shapeshifter midshift.

He smiled softly. 'Let's hope so.'

Shula grinned back, then kicked her legs up onto the dash and spun the volume button on the radio to high.

***

Evie Tremain turned the lock in the café door. Main Street was dead. All the stores were dark – only the yellow street-lights were eclipsing the darkness now. Two cars were parked up in the shadows out front. Someone climbed out of the passenger seat of one and walked in her direction. She flipped the *Closed* sign quickly. There was no way she was serving another customer tonight. Not even for the chance of a twenty dollar tip.

She backed away from the door and flipped the light switch, collapsing the whole place into blackness, then headed behind the counter to gather up the trash bags. The sound of someone trying the door made her jump. She spun around, irritated. Couldn't they read? They were closed.

She saw a guy standing in front of the door looking in, staring directly at her. His hand was still on the door handle. He was about six feet tall and wearing a floor-length black leather coat. Evie took in the whole of him in one glance and felt something similar to a rock settle on her stomach. Something wasn't right about him. In fact, something was most definitely off. Then she realised he was wearing sunglasses. Ray bans. In the middle of the night.

'We're closed,' she mouthed, wondering whether he could even see her, shrouded in the shadows behind the counter.

The boy didn't respond or smile or act in any way as if he'd seen her, though his hand did drop from the door handle. He turned on his heel and strode back towards his car, coat flapping like a windsock behind him.

Evie stood there a full minute, trash bags clutched in her hand, waiting for the sound of a car engine turning over and accelerating away. Nothing. The street stayed fathomlessly silent. She edged towards the door and peered through the glass. The cars were both still sitting there, empty as far as she could tell. The guy in the long trench coat was nowhere to be seen.

A feeling of unease crept through her but she couldn't stand there all night like a total wuss, hovering in the gloom. So she took the bags and walked to the back door and opened it, annoyed with herself for getting so freaked out over a boy who looked like he'd gotten lost on the way back from Comic Con.

The back lot was empty except for the giant metal dumpster just to her right and her dusty old Ford parked a few metres to her left. There was a single light blazing above her head illuminating the door and the concrete step she was standing on. She headed straight towards the dumpster with the bags in one hand and a tin of coffee grinds in the other and that's when she saw him, on the periphery of the shadow line, his coat splayed out behind him.

The hairs on the back of her neck bristled. She drew in a breath and did a quick calculation of the distance between her, the boy and the door.

But before she could figure out where to run to, the boy in the sunglasses stepped forward into the zone of light. She saw that he was a little bit older than her, maybe twenty or twenty-one. He was wearing black jeans and leather biker boots, and a black wrinkled t-shirt with some kind of slogan on it. A part of her brain registered that he looked ridiculous, like an extra from the Matrix, but the other part warned her not to tell him so.

At least not yet.

He stopped just in front of her.

'Evie Tremain?' he asked.

She froze, her mouth falling open. How did he know her name? Who the hell *was* this guy? As she studied him she suddenly heard a voice in her head start screaming at her to run. She could hear her own heartbeat - it sounded like a horse smashing its hooves against a stable door. Her eyes darted instantly over the lot, looking for exits.

'Evie Tremain?' the boy asked again, impatient now.

'Who wants to know?' Evie asked, buying time. The back door was about ten metres behind her or she could try to get around him and head down the side alley and out onto Main Street. She took a small step backwards. The diner was closer.

'The Brotherhood,' the boy replied tonelessly, closing the distance between them in a single stride.

Evie couldn't reign in the laughter that erupted out of her. 'The Brotherhood?' she snorted. '*Seriously*? What is that? The name of your Death Metal band? Because, you know, it sounds kind of *lame*.'

The boy – whose face had been expressionless until then - suddenly frowned in confusion, as though he didn't know how to answer her. The sound of crunching gravel broke the silence. Evie's eyes flew to the far end of the lot, which was sunk in darkness. Was someone else there? The boy followed her gaze and looked over his shoulder too. Adrenaline pumped through Evie's body in one giant surge. She dropped the trash bags and took a step back, twisting her body as she moved. She brought her arm up like her dad had taught her, fingers curled into a tight fist, and in the second that the boy turned back to face her, she smashed it into the side of his head.

The boy's head spun with the force of the punch, his sunglasses flying across the lot.

Hit first, ask questions later, she murmured to herself. Her dad had always said it was better to be safe than sorry.

She turned to run back towards the door but the boy lunged for her, shrieking. She raised her arm instinctively, ready to smash it into his face again, but then stumbled backwards letting out a cry. The boy's eyes were inches from her own, his pupils fixed and dilated. And the thing that had stopped her, and made her stomach scrape the floor, was the *colour* of them. They were bright, carnation-red and totally unseeing.

The boy flailed his head from left to right as though someone had thrown acid in his face, his outstretched hand groping blindly in her direction.

He's blind, Evie realised, her thoughts assuming some sense. *He can't see me.*

Out of the corner of her eye she saw a dark shape wavering behind the boy. It seemed to extend and stretch out, like a time-lapse sequence of a shadow lengthening. And then it coiled like a whip and lashed towards her.

Evie dived. She threw herself hard to the left, out of the boy's grip and out of the way of whatever was coming towards her. She heard a crack as it smashed into the tarmac and another frustrated shriek from the boy.

She staggered backwards, her eyes on the space that had opened up between her and the guy in the coat. The whip or rope or

313

whatever it was was lashing rapidly back and forth between them. Evie's brain refused to process the possibility that what her eyes were actually looking at was neither a rope nor a whip but a tail. There were scales on it and it moved like a rattlesnake. Ropes didn't look like that.

The boy dropped to the floor now, and started scrabbling around on the ground for something. His glasses, Evie thought, spying them lying cracked in half on the asphalt by her car.

'Need some help, Caleb?' A girl's voice called out from the edge of the darkness.

The boy with blood-red eyes swore at her in reply.

'If you want help you need to put your tail away and ask nicely,' the girl added.

The word punctured Evie's brain like a poison dart. *Tail.* She tripped backwards, trying to feel for the door behind her. She stumbled on the step, and felt herself bump up against something solid. It wasn't the door.

She spun around and found herself stepping on the toes of a white-faced boy. A girl in a neon pink mini-dress stood next to him, smiling *surrrrprise*.

Evie skittered backwards, letting out a yelp. How many of these freaks *were* there?

These two weren't wearing sunglasses and their eyes weren't red. The boy was dressed in scruffy jeans, bashed-up Converse and a Nix cap. The girl was tall with long black hair and the bright pink of her dress clashed with the green tinge of her skin.

'We've got this, Caleb,' the girl in the pink dress called out to the one with the tail, not taking her eyes off Evie.

'Well, hurry up, would you, I don't want to be here all night,' another boy's voice answered from the darkness.

So there were more of them over there, Evie thought, panic starting to weave its tentacles around her limbs. How many did that make? Four or five at least. What the hell were they all doing looking for her?

'What do you want?' Evie asked desperately, spinning around to face the girl and boy blocking the back door.

'We want *you*, Evie Tremain,' the girl in pink said, striding forward. She put her hand on Evie's arm and Evie looked down, as her skin began to burn intensely.

She screamed and, with a final injection of adrenaline and anger, swung the tin of coffee grinds she was still holding at the girl's head. It wasn't a powerful swing but the girl let go of her instantly and started yelling.

Evie skittered back out of her way, skidding towards her car, dodging around the boy on the ground with the tail.

With a tail! Her brain screamed at her as though it wanted her to pause and figure it out. But her arm was still burning as though the bone itself had caught alight and the skin was blistering and it was all she could do not to faint right there and then. She started fumbling with her one good hand for her car key, buried in the pocket of her jeans, and felt the sob start to crescendo in her chest.

The boy in the Nix cap was bent double, pointing and laughing at the girl Evie had hit. And the sound of it, the childish hysteria of it, was like a shucking knife opening Evie up. She glanced upwards even as she scrambled for her keys. The girl was holding the side of her head, screaming and trying to scrape wet coffee grinds off her face, she spat a gloop of saliva and glared furiously at Evie.

At last Evie's fingers closed on her keys. She yanked them from her pocket, watching as the girl and boy moved in on her. She was just prey, she realised. She was completely cornered. There was no way out.

315

Acknowledgements

Thank you:

John, for your belief in outrageous potential and the three weeks alone on a beach in Goa to just write. I stole your eyes and a lot more than that and gave them to Alex, I hope you don't mind.

Vic and Nic, for being the best friends and best readers a girl could hope for – I only finished this book because you were both cheering me on.

Tom, for your endless support and for being the kind of big brother Jacks are made of.

Sara, for that first phone call letting me know I could write.

Tara – Goan roomie and American editor – I owe you big time for explaining the difference between a vest and a tank top (and a few million other things like that).

All my blog readers – the kindness of strangers never ceases to amaze and inspire me.

Laurie, my very great friend, with whom I first road-tripped California before this story was even a twinkle in my eye and with whom I hope to do many more road trips in the future.

Amanda, agent extraordinaire, for loving Lila and Alex as much as I do (I was worried for a time that we wouldn't want to share Alex but thank goodness we got over that).

And finally to Venetia and the team at Simon & Schuster, for showing such faith in a debut writer. I can't tell you how much I appreciate it – well, I could, but it would mean writing a whole other book and we need to get on with editing the sequel to this one.

About the Author

Having spent most of her life in London, apart from university in Bristol and a year living in Italy, Sarah quit her job in 2009 and took off on a round-the-world trip with her husband and daughter, on a mission to find a new place to call home. After almost a year of travels that took them through India, Singapore, Australia and the US, they settled in Bali where Sarah now spends her days writing and drinking coconuts. *Hunting Lila* is her first novel and she is currently working on the sequel.